NEW
YORK
SON

NEW YORK SON

STORIES BY
MIKE FEDER

DELTA
FICTION

A Delta Book
Published by
Dell Publishing
a division of
Bantam Doubleday Dell Publishing Group, Inc.
666 Fifth Avenue
New York, New York 10103

The story "Here's Herbie" first appeared in the March 1988 issue of *Harper's* magazine.

ISBN: 0-385-29905-2

Reprinted by arrangement with Crown Publishers, Inc.

Printed in the United States of America

Published simultaneously in Canada

July 1990

10   9   8   7   6   5   4   3   2   1

BVG

to my children
Emily and Sam

CONTENTS

NEW YORK SON

HERE'S
HERBIE

When I was about fifteen, I was possessed of a great many psychosomatic complaints. I'm sure a lot of this had to do with trying to compete, although fruitlessly, with my mother, who was always sick on a grand scale—mentally and physically. Nevertheless, I had, as a loving son, inherited a large number of her ailments and complaints, although I was probably much healthier than I thought I was.

I was very allergic in those days. I was allergic to cats, grass, trees, anything you could imagine. A lot of Jewish boys are familiar with this condition. The allergist I had to go to worked in Manhattan, which for a little wimp boy like myself was a long adventurous trip. It held a lot of terrors for me, one of which was that I had to get on the subway. I lived way out in Laurelton, Queens, near Nassau County—at the edge of the city. I had to take a bus to the subway and then the F train into Manhattan, get off, go to the allergist, and come back.

One morning, I was leaving my house to see the allergist and I was in my constant state of teenage depression because in those days my mother was sick all the time. She was sitting in her room moaning, or calling her mother to complain that she wished she had never had children, which was sort of a cheery way to start my day. Naturally, I did not enjoy going to the allergist, to say the least; it was not just because I had to go through all the dangers and terrors of the trip, but also because the damn guy stuck me with five or six needles every time. Besides all this, he was a turd, a real insensitive jerk. I did this twice a week for a couple of years.

I got the bus, and changed for the subway. I went downstairs and got the F train, somewhere out in Jamaica, Queens. Right away, I was scared. Now there's so much personal violence in the train, you have to watch out for the people. When I was a kid, there wasn't all that much violence. You didn't have teenagers wandering around eating people and throwing them on the tracks. What bothered me then was there were so many powerful machines down there, and it was so dark and so far underground that I always felt that the station would fall in on me, that the train would smash into a wall and kill us all—I had a department store full of fears to play with. I should have just brought a book. I would have been better off.

I got on the front car. Now, this is important. I always got on the front car of the train and to this day I still like to get on the front car. I think it has something to do with (maybe this is just masculine— maybe not) some sort of identification with the surge of power that you feel in the front of a train. When you're a teenager in the city, one of the most powerful things you can have any personal connection with, since there are no horses or bulls or other powerful animals around, is a subway train. When that train comes rumbling and roaring into the station, it just fills your blood with a kind of crazy excitement. So I always got on the front car. Also, without realizing it, I always sat somewhere near the front of the front car and looked toward that little front window with the wires going through it. But one thing I never seemed to have the nerve to do, although I wanted to, it tugged at me, was to go up and look out of the window.

I felt it would be very embarrassing, extremely uncool, to stand up there like some jerkoff and just be staring out the window of the train. I mean, I was fifteen, I didn't want to seem as if I was six. Because I wanted to look out the front of the train and I never would, a kind of terrible tug-of-war took place in my mind. The best I could do in my half-assed way was to sit close to the window and look at it from the corner of my eye.

The train kept rumbling along, and then stopped, and then roared up again through the stations, and I was thinking about my mother at home and how she was sick and how her sickness made me sick, and how I never wanted to go home again, and all I was looking forward to was being stuck in the arm by this allergy creature in Manhattan.

At the third or fourth stop, the doors opened and closed but just before they closed absolutely, a big fat hand thrust through the doors. The doors opened again, because this hand wouldn't move, and in came what we teenagers used to call, with great sensitivity, a retard. This guy, who could have been anywhere from fifteen to thirty-five, entered the train with a nutty lopsided look on his face. Now, on this car there were four or five people—two businessmen, a couple of ladies going shopping—and they were all looking at books or Bibles or reading the *New York Times,* or something like that. I, of course, wasn't doing anything except sitting there starkly worried—the Jewish Hamlet from Queens wondering whether to be or not to be on the F train.

This guy came into the center of the car and said, "Herbie's here. Here's Herbie!" in a very loud voice, looking around with a big wide stupid grin. He was kind of slump-shouldered, with a potbelly, and had big flat black shoes. He wore a very loose jacket that ballooned out in the front, as if he were pregnant. He had these very dim eyes, a big thick jaw, and big hairy ears. To nobody in particular, but in a very loud happy voice, he said again, "Here's Herbie. Herbie is here!"

I was thinking to myself, Oh God, I've got enough troubles, please don't let this retard sit down next to me and drive me nuts the whole way to the city. I want a little privacy in my misery. And, of course, all the other people on the train just kept staring at their newspapers. I wasn't that old and I hadn't had that much experience with the typical subway ride in New York. So everybody kept looking at their papers and books, except once in a while I could see a little smile of condescension and amusement twitching at the corners of their mouths.

I couldn't help watching this guy Herbie with that kind of terrible sick knowledge that people who are a little bit freakish or lonely, or live in a very strange family the way I did, have in common with other people who have problems. I was watching him with a combined feeling of disgust and terrible unwanted identity. He kept yelling, "Here's Herbie, here's Herbie," looked around, saw after a while that nobody really cared that Herbie was here, and then, without further ado, unzipped his jacket and pulled out, of all things, a plastic steering wheel—the kind that you give kids, with a suction cup to stick on the dashboard. He went over to the train's front window, which I had been looking at but didn't have the nerve to go to. He just walked right over to it as if he owned it, and after moistening the suction cup with some spit, stuck the steering wheel right on the window.

So in effect, Herbie, this retard, was now steering the train. And he had absolutely no doubts. This was a guy who knew just what he wanted to do. He's like Albert Schweitzer or Jonas Salk—from the day he was born he knew he was going to conquer the Zambezi or be the greatest ice cream salesman that ever lived. Whereas I, a total nerd, had no idea what I wanted to do, or if I even wanted to be.

The train pulled into Continental Avenue, the train pulled out of Continental Avenue, rumbling along on the tracks, clackety clackety clack. Herbie just kept steering the train, and making noises to go with it. On a hard curve, he just sort of leaned into it. And he was having the time of his life. Since he wasn't looking around, everybody else was gazing at him now with amused, pitying looks.

I was fascinated. Jesus Christ, here's this guy, a retard, a half-wit, and I am so brilliant, I do well in school, I'm a handsome little devil, my mother loves me, I'm athletic, I can run faster than other people, do baseball cards better, and here's this guy who nobody could possibly care about, who looks like a pile of hay, who comes on and does the one thing that I had always wanted to do. He just went right up there and he's driving the train.

We hit a real heavy turn, which Herbie negotiated beautifully. The door swung open and right next to him who did I see but the engineer of the train himself, the real driver. He's got his little railroad hat on. He was an older black guy, hunched over the lever of the train with a totally bored look on his face, half-asleep. As far as he was concerned, he might as well have been watching television. Next to him, about a foot away, although he couldn't see him, was Herbie, standing up, riding for his life, driving what might as well have been the U.S.S. *Enterprise* on its five-year mission through space.

We went into the tunnel to Manhattan, really roaring along, with more and more people getting on the train, and they all saw Herbie, and looked away—you know how in New York you have to create a vacuum between yourself and whomever happens to be the nut du jour. Herbie noticed not a bit. "Here's Herbie, here's Herbie," he screamed at the top of his lungs. He was driving that train wherever it had to go.

Well, all strange things come to an end. We got to the stop in midtown where I had to get off. As I left, Herbie was waiting at the window, sort of drumming his foot, impatient to drive his train to the next stop.

I went upstairs, and here I was in Manhattan, which I detested. I mean, Queens was hard enough for me with the occasional person I ran into, but with my kind of shyness and neurosis, Manhattan was like a terrible carnival that somebody dropped me into without warning or protection. So I walked along the streets, I got to the allergist, and here was this schmegege waiting for me. He was World War II vintage, about fifty, tough, bluff, and hearty, and he made his living by sticking needles in young people. Now, although this guy was an allergist, he had some dim understanding of the psychological causes of diseases. "How's Mother?" he asked. Of course he wouldn't say, "How's your mother?" but, "How's Mother?" thereby immediately making her a principal of existence, the basic fact of life, rather than just my mother, an ordinary human being, whom I was having trouble enough understanding to begin with.

What could I say? "She's okay, she's all right." He stuck a couple of needles in my arm and I got out of there real fast. The nurse said good-bye to me—I thought she was going to ask, "How's Mother?" too. As far as I was concerned, at that point, all women looked like spies working for my mother.

So I got back on the train and sat down, headed toward Queens. It was about three in the afternoon, and I was very depressed. Seeing Herbie driving the train and me not being able to do it really got to me. I knew when I got home my mother would be in her room, and she was going to be sitting there tired, and she was going to be upset, and the rabbi or the doctor was going to be there, probably. Somebody was going to be there, kowtowing to her, and I'd walk in and have to be quiet. It was my old half-life again. Back hiding in my room. What a miserable way to live. I was smarting from the injections in my arm, thinking about Herbie.

I'd gotten on the first car again. I looked sideways at the front window, and this feeling came over me: what the hell? My life was a cesspool anyhow. I didn't want to go home to that woman, and here I was—life was passing me by, there were millions of things I wanted to do and never did. I was just gonna do it.

So I got up and I walked over, even though in the front car of the train there were several people who could have been my mother or spies working for my mother. I walked over, and I just put my face right up against the window of the train, and I looked out. The train began to pick up some speed and it was going through the stations— Forty-second Street, Lexington Avenue—and I became fascinated. I started not caring that anybody might be looking at me. I looked out and it was as beautiful as I ever imagined it to be. Here I was in the front part of this great train which had no thought for anybody else at all. It just surged through the tunnel. It was like the feeling the first sperm has. When the gun goes off and those millions and billions of sperms just get out there and start to race for that egg, the first, strongest, biggest sperm just would go whammo—he knows just where he's going. Well that's what that train was doing. It was charging through that tunnel and rushing along, passing people by on the opposite platform as if they were ants.

Have you ever had enough guts or child in you to get up there—it doesn't matter how old you are—and look out the front of a train? It's a terrific sight. You have this long, beautiful, dark tunnel, and the train charges through it with the walls only half a foot away. It seems like you're moving at one hundred miles an hour. At the far end you can see the lights of another station, but in between when it's really dark, you can see all kinds of red and green traffic signals. You have no idea what they mean, nor do you care, but they look like beautiful stars or jewels in the distance.

All of a sudden everything just disappeared, and it was just me and this train. I was this train, zooming along in this tunnel, going a million miles an hour, and the stops were coming. I could feel my fingers twitching and I wished I had had the same kind of steering wheel that Herbie had, because right now I was in charge of this train. I had a great feeling of responsibility.

Once we were in Queens, I passed by one of those spots where you can see a train coming in the other direction because there's not a wall in between, just some steel girders. The train slowed down a little bit, but it was still going at a pretty good speed, and I saw coming in the distance another train. I looked in the front window and who did I see but Herbie driving the train the other way! I couldn't believe it. There he was, getting closer and closer, and then I knew he saw me. I saw him with his steering wheel, driving the train, he saw me, driving this train, and it was a moment of identification I cannot describe to you. It was a moment that only a few people have in common. We were both driving these powerful machines, responsible to many people, lives dependent on us, the destiny perhaps of the universe in our hands, and we were coming closer and closer. He lifted his hand and smiled and waved at me. I forgot everything. I forgot my self-consciousness. I forgot I wasn't a retard. I forgot he was a retard. I forgot I was a wimp. I raised my hand and we just gave each other a salute, kind of a grim but professional understanding that two great men, responsible for the destinies of millions of people, were at the helm.

Herbie's train zoomed past and I kept driving. I drove all the way into Queens. And finally, I had this kind of sinking feeling because I knew, I knew that we were coming to the end and that I'd have to go back home. I got off the train and got on the bus, and I could feel my shoulders start to droop. I start picking at my fingernails, scratching my allergy injections. I got off the bus and walked the few blocks to my house, and sure enough, God damn it, there was the rabbi's car and the doctor's car in front of my mother's house. I was thinking to myself, oh God, I hope her bedroom door is closed and she doesn't bother me, because I had felt so exhilarated before. I sneaked in the house. Fortunately her door was closed. She was being ministered to in there, and being given all kinds of pills. I walked quietly upstairs to my room so she wouldn't hear me. I closed the door and I looked out the window. The vision came back to me of this charging subway train and driving down this tunnel at a hundred miles an hour, the power of the universe in my capable hands. And I saw Herbie driving the other way and I felt a comradeship with some of the greatest men that have ever lived. For a moment there, I had been in total command of my life.

MOTHER

I have a recurring dream, really a nightmare. I'm alone in a dark room; against one wall, and attached to my solar plexus, is a steel cable. This cable is connected to me from some dark presence on the other side of the room, something I can't see and can't understand. But I know it's something I don't want to be connected to. I pull really hard, but the more I pull, the more it stretches, like taffy. It gets thinner and longer but it never snaps. All of a sudden—dream time—I'm in the middle of the room, still attached to it, but now I'm trying to chop the cable with an ax. Whack, whack, whack—as hard as I've ever done anything. Every time I hit it with the ax, the ax bounces back. It won't even cut a little bit. It's a terrible feeling of impotence. I wake sick to my stomach and in a terrible sweat.

It scares me to talk about my mother. When I talk about her or even think about her I begin to get symptoms—symptoms like hers. She was full of fear and dread, envy and deep hatreds. She had endless nervous tics, psychosomatic aches and pains. I become like her. That's natural enough—I'm the one in the family who was closer to her than anyone else.

Talking about my childhood is like deliberately walking into a pit of alligators. Under the best of circumstances I'm not very stable or mature, but as I think about growing up in my mother's house, I start once again to feel the dread and fury of being there and I have some trouble breathing again. My nose starts to itch and run, I have a coldness in the bottom of my stomach. I reach for the tranquilizers.

My poor wife. She's getting ready for a full, hard day of work and getting the kids ready for their day and I sit like a catatonic on the couch, depressed and sullen just the way I was as a child. I look at myself in the mirror. People always said I had my mother's eyes. My daughter says to my wife, "What's the matter with Dad? He's more frowny than usual." My wife tells her I'm thinking about my mother and feeling sad. Well, that's the truth.

Of course my daughter starts to go to extremes to cheer me up, doing handstands, making faces, telling silly seven-year-old jokes. When none of this works she gets angry; she tells me I hate her and runs into her room, slamming the door behind her. This rouses me from my stupor. I worry about these outbursts from my daughter. These spurts of melodrama naturally make me think that she has inherited the family curse. I've been loony all my life, indulging in almost hourly ups and downs of temperament. The slightest word or incident can set me off into a boil of anguish or self-pity.

Since my mother was like this and worse most of her life, I associate my daughter's behavior with hers. Two years ago Easter, I bought her a chocolate bunny. She nibbled the tail a little and got a stomachache from the chocolate, so we wrapped the bunny in aluminum foil and put it in the refrigerator. The next night, at two in the morning, I awoke feeling lonely and upset. I went to the fridge, hungry for *something*. I saw the chocolate bunny and I bit its head off. This seemed to satisfy my craving, but right away I felt guilty so I wrapped it up again and hid it way behind the vegetables on the bottom shelf. She forgot about it the next day and the day after. Six months passed. One day she was looking in the fridge for something to nibble and what did she find but the decapitated bunny. I was in the next room and all of a sudden I heard this awful heart-rending sobbing. She was on the floor, tears gushing. "What's the problem?" I asked.

"Somebody ate my bunny's head." Right. And she'll never play the violin again. Her entire life is ruined. This scares me. I figure it's my mother's ghost.

After my sister was born, when I was four years old, my mother went into what used to be called postpartum depression. She descended straight from that into serious mental illness. In a few weeks she was in a mental hospital. After that time in her life she was never really stable or sane. If she was not actually in a hospital or trying to kill herself, she stayed for days in her room, taking heavy medication. She came out only to be driven all over the city to see a succession of psychiatrists. A couple of times, ambulances and doctors came in the middle of the night to take her away.

I never understood what was happening. One time she almost killed herself. I was about six years old. I woke and she was gone. There was dried blood on the walls downstairs. A couple of weeks later I was taken to visit her at the hospital which was somewhere in Westchester. When they brought me into a room to see her, I was terrified. They had given her electroshock treatments and her hair had turned white. It had been black; beautiful long black hair. Now it was a sick gray-white. She had lines all over her face and she was wearing a faded old housecoat. She reached out to me.

"Give Mommy a hug."

I couldn't even speak. I hid behind my grandfather. She was a stranger to me, an old witch; she was not my mother.

My father left the house when I was about four and a half. It was a small house we lived in, my mother, my sister, and I, but those five and a half rooms seemed endless, cavernous; every corner was haunted and strange. It didn't help that my room was in the attic and the window overlooked the largest Jewish cemetery in Queens. I saw hundreds of funerals during the time I lived there. I watched the cars pull up, listened to the rabbis' eulogies, and saw thousands of grief-stricken relatives and not-so-grief-stricken relatives. At night the big trees swayed over the tombstones in the moonlight. Rabbits and birds jumped between the graves. This view follows me everywhere. Eight years ago, we needed to find an apartment quickly because my daughter was due in a couple of months. There was a half percent vacancy rate in New York but finally, by bribing a real estate broker, I found a two-bedroom apartment. She brought me around to look at it. It seemed all right. There was enough room for the three of us. It seemed a safe building and it had a lot of sunlight. The neighborhood was noisy but there was really very little choice because the baby was due soon and we had to have the place. I gave her the money for rent and security (and her bribe), and we moved in. On the first day we were there, I went over to the kitchen window. Right across the street was the largest Jewish funeral home in Manhattan. I hadn't even realized it. This is where I live now.

All the time I lived in my mother's house, I could hear her crying or moaning or throwing up in the middle of the night. She used to spend most of her life in her room, reading, watching TV, just sitting and worrying. She rarely came out and almost never left the house. She had a phobia about going out of the house. She stayed in there almost thirty years. Once she went shopping on the main street of town, three blocks away, and she fainted. She had to be brought home in a police car. She always communicated this dread to me: IF YOU GO OUTSIDE SOMETHING AWFUL WILL HAPPEN TO YOU. As if we were cave dwellers, the outside became our great fear.

I had a habit, when I was a kid, of playing outside in our back yard for many hours at a stretch—usually by myself. This was safe enough; it was behind the house and there were fences. I played in the dirt; there *was* actual dirt in Queens, not like in Manhattan. I had something called a punk, which was, I think, just a plain stick of incense. For hours I would kill ants with it. I lit it and held it over one ant at a time until it curled up and died from the heat. I killed hundreds, thousands of ants. That no one ever noticed this or stopped me from doing it was strange. I think the reason was that my mother hardly ever left her room and was probably glad not to have me bothering her. My other relatives, like my aunt and uncle next door and my grandparents two blocks away, were too busy concentrating on my mother to notice a little mass murderer in the back yard. Maybe, to be charitable, they figured: "Let's just leave him alone . . . he's outside in the fresh air playing. He's away from her for a while."

When I came home from school or playing, no matter how old I was, I always knew she'd be there. Now, to most people, this might sound sort of comforting, to know there was always a grown-up waiting for you at home. But, of course, it depends on who was waiting. Since it was my mother, I always tried to postpone going home or even entering the house. I'd dawdle on the street, or lie on the grass and stare at clouds or cars passing. Sometimes I hung out in the neighbors' kitchens. Frequently my mother had to call for me out the front door or search around by phone to locate me. I got more depressed as I neared the front door. A hollow feeling grew in my chest. All my life, right up to the present, I feel that same panic and emptiness when I come home at the end of my day outside. It doesn't matter where I live or who is waiting for me inside. I still don't want to go home.

*   *   *

When I did finally go in the house, I tried immediately to jump to the stairs to scurry up to my room and close the door. But a lot of times I got caught. My mother might be lying on a sofa in the living room watching television soap operas. It could be midsummer, a bright day, but she had all the shades drawn so it was dark—no lamp on. She was tearing at her cuticles or picking her lips or obsessively twisting something in her hands. The poor woman, I've inherited all her tics; picking and poking at myself until I draw blood. I've even added a couple of my own, like cracking my knuckles. Sometimes, in the lunchroom of the office where I used to work, someone would smack my hand and say, "You're doing that again!" "Sorry," I'd say, "I didn't realize it. Sorry."

I entered the dark house and there was my mother, lying on the sofa in the gloom. The flickering light from the TV made changing shadows on her sharp face. She turned around to look at me. I froze. She got up, came close to me, and gripped me by the shoulders. She put her big scary eyes in front of me and said, "How was school today, darling?"

For a moment I was dead, then I'd vomit out a torrent of words. I went on for what seemed like hours. Everything that happened and a lot that didn't. "You know, they put a new curb in at the corner of 222nd Street and today a whole line of ants followed me a whole block on the way to school, and when I got to school, Mrs. Steinberg had her hair dyed red and she broke her glasses and a bee came in the window and . . ."

I couldn't stop. I felt I *had* to do this. And it was true, the more I entertained and excited her, made her laugh with my descriptions and exaggerations, the more cheerful and normal she appeared. I was the probe she sent out into the deep space of Laurelton, Queens, and I was programmed to tell her everything I saw and heard upon my retrieval. After a while, she'd let go of me and say, "Well, sweetheart, do you want some milk and cookies?" Just like a normal mother. When my daughter comes home from school, I go over to say hello and she says, with seven-year-old world-weariness, "Please don't ask me how school was today. I'm going in my room now."

But sometimes I'd come home and in front of the house there was a flotilla of official-looking cars. Sometimes there would be an ambulance, but usually it was the rabbi, the doctor, my grandfather, and even an occasional police car. When I came into the house, my aunt or my grandmother would be there. "Shhh," they'd say. "You have to be very quiet, your mother's not feeling well."

"What's wrong?"

"She's very nervous."

As I got older it was actually a relief to see all this activity. At least I wasn't trapped alone with her in that gloomy house. The rabbi would come out of my mother's bedroom, shutting the door against the whispering inside. He'd shake my hand and say, "Hello there, young man" very solemnly, as if he were at a funeral. "You know, Michael, you have to be very good to your mother. You don't want to upset her. She's very nervous."

She was never *crazy*, she was never *insane*, she was just "nervous." Ruthie is very high-strung, people would say. She has a lot of worries.

Then the doctor came out, old, tired, with his black bag. He'd given her an injection of something. He put his hand on my shoulder. "How are you, young fellow? Now make sure you don't upset your mother. She needs peace and quiet."

"Yeah, sure."

A lot of people thought my attitude was too casual, even rude. My grandmother and my aunt would lecture me. "Don't give me any smart talk, Michael. You know your mother needs rest." I went up to my room, pulled a chair over to my window, and watched the cemetery for a while. Downstairs, the women kept watch and made supper. Everybody in my mother's family—all her sisters, their husbands, my grandmother and her husband—spent great portions of their lives hovering over my mother, trying to make sure she wasn't too nervous. It was the family raison d'être. As my grandmother was dying, when I was fifteen, virtually her last words to my aunts, uncles, and me were "Take care of Ruthie." It was a sacred mission.

Being young in that house was to have my emotions stolen from me. It was the oddest sensation, as if someone had mugged me and run away with my feelings. I came home from the second grade, just like my daughter does now, and I'd say to my mother, "I got a ninety-five on my math test!" I was very excited. But as excited as I'd be, my mother would get *twice* as excited. She'd say, "A ninety-five!" She'd squeeze me too long and too hard. "A ninety-five!" She grabbed the phone and called people up to tell them. "Michael got a ninety-five on his test!" As I stood there with the test (which she hadn't noticed at all) in my hand, it seemed that *I* didn't get the ninety-five, *she* got the ninety-five. I had nothing.

If I came in with a cut or a scraped knee from playing, she'd grab me and yell, "Oh God, you're bleeding!" She'd run to the phone and call the local hospital. "Give me the emergency room! What do I do about a cut?" She ran to the medicine chest, grabbing bottles and packages, smashing things on the floor. She put five Band-Aids on me, and took my temperature. She'd tell me to lie down. All of a sudden I felt as if I wasn't bleeding at all. I wasn't hurt, she was. It induced a strange numbness in me. It's funny, I'm still like that. I don't react at all to pain or cuts. If I cut myself shaving, it seems like it might be happening to someone else.

When I was eleven or twelve I started to grow, and as soon as I got big enough I pushed my mother away from me if she got too near. I wouldn't let her touch me—a rule that lasted the rest of my life. I closed down entirely. And she stayed away from me; she was afraid that I might hurt her. That was okay with me. I thought of her as some kind of devil or vampire.

Right around this time was when she first took me to see a shrink. I was thirteen years old, in the ninth grade. Actually the junior high school recommended she take me since I was failing all my tests and paying no attention in school. This was the first of the great parade of shrinks I've seen. And, naturally, who did she take me to see but her own doctor. He was the most recent of the several she had already seen, and not the last by a long shot. When I got older, I realized that as soon as she was about to make some progress with one of these guys, she'd drop him and switch to a new one. She claimed they were stupid or really didn't understand her. The man she took me to see—her man—was a guy she had grown up with in the city. He had known me since I was born. My grandfather drove us, once a week, on Saturday afternoon, all the way up to the Bronx, where the doctor had his office. My grandfather would drop us off and then stay outside to wait in the car for two hours. The loyal retainer.

I remember our first session. She went into the doctor's office ahead of me. I sat in the waiting room, scared and bored. I read the AMA journals and horrified myself with illustrated diseases. I sneaked up and put my ear to the door. I heard ominous silences, then crying, shouting, urgent crazy whisperings, but never actual sentences that I could understand. The door was thick. Crying, a curse, then, "My uncle took his hand and . . ." I went back to the medical magazines. After a while she came out crying. The doctor had his arm around her. My grandfather appeared and helped her into the car. It was my turn.

I sat on the side of his desk, staring at him. He was not really a psychiatrist, but an internist. During World War II he was a beachmaster on D-day. On June 6, 1944, thousands of guys landed on the beach at Normandy, met by hundreds of thousands of rifle and machine gun bullets, mortar, and artillery shells. Men were getting killed right and left. The rest of them, scared to death, hugged the dirt. The army had appointed some men, captains and majors, to get the GIs off the beach and over the defenses. These guys walked around the beach, straight up, with sticks or weapons in their hands, in the midst of this death storm, and whacked these poor guys on the back, yelling at each one, "Get up, you son of a bitch." This is what this shrink did in the war. He then became an internist. And so, on the walls of his office were his degree from medical school, his various certificates from hospitals and the State of New York, and a large picture of him standing on Omaha Beach with a rifle. A man in the Helping Professions. Maybe this picture was there to provoke the emotions of his patients. Maybe I'm being too generous.

He sat, ramrod straight behind his desk, still with his army crew cut. I slumped in the patient's chair. I was a big slumper. In school, I always sat in the back row of every class, pushed way down in my seat. From the teachers' perspective I must have looked like an alligator. All they could see over my little desktop were a pair of sullen, scowling eyes. Most of my teachers were women about my mother's age. I hoped they would all burst into flames.

He said, "How are you, son?" I said nothing. In those days, nothing was coming in and nothing was going out. Emotionally I was closed for business. He saw me slumping there and a look of contempt came over him. He said, "Do you think you can sit up straight, Mike?"

"Nope," I said.

"Well," he said, "in my office you *will* sit up straight." Right. Get up, you coward, storm that neurosis! This was the beginning of a fruitless year of emotional arm-wrestling. Unsurprisingly, he then made a short speech about how nervous my poor mother was and how it was our job to see that we all got along and didn't upset her any more. This was how I got my start in therapy.

About a year ago I was talking to a psychologist (the fifth I've seen) and I realized that every time I've walked into a shrink's office (and by now it's been a couple of thousand times), I felt as if my mother was with me, actually in my shoes, sitting in the chair with me. I was carrying on a family tradition. Her taking me with her to see her doctor was an initiation rite, like a father in the Midwest taking his son duck hunting or a potter passing down to his child the secrets of the wheel. Of course, all my initiations had to be from my mother. Who else was there?

When I was twelve years old and I had my first girlfriend (we held hands, I carried her books), I told my mother, "I'm going over to see Florence Kohlberg."

My mother says, "A girl?"

"Yeah, a girl."

"That's nice, darling." She was without a man; but she tried hard to be as normal as she could be for us. But when she heard I was going two blocks to visit a girl, I could see a look in her eyes, as if she'd just gotten a telegram with terrible news.

At age thirteen, I was sitting at the kitchen table with her and I said, very embarrassed, "You know Mom, I feel kind of funny when I see Barbara." (Barbara was the hot number of 223rd Street.) My mother turned pale, absolutely paper white. Holding hands was bad enough, but anything really sexual terrified her. "I get this strange feeling . . ." I trailed off.

But she did her best. "Well," she said, gripping the table, her hands shaking. "Sometimes, darling, you'll get a funny kind of feeling when you're with girls and your penis will get hard." I could hear her screaming inside. But just like a soldier she got off that beach and charged those cliffs. A crazy mother, raising a teenaged boy.

During my freshman year in college, I saw a psychologist who told me, "If you don't move out of that house, you'll go crazy. You'll either wind up in a hospital or be dead before you're twenty-five." He never let up on me and said the whole treatment would be useless unless I got out: "You have got to find an apartment," he said. But the idea was too scary. I couldn't even picture myself living alone, not in my mother's house. I stayed where I was.

My first job out of college, with my one-size-fits-all BA in political science, was as a caseworker in the New York City Welfare Department. Naturally, I would get a job where my main assignment was to help depressed single mothers with children. I actually did try to get other sorts of jobs. I put on a tie and jacket and went on interviews, mostly, I remember, at insurance companies. They were always looking for fresh new salesmen. I was always very personable. I could get any job I tried for. The interviewer would say, "Well, Mike, you scored 96 percent on the aptitude test. That's pretty impressive. Mike, I won't beat around the bush. We'd really like to have you on the team here at Mutual Guarantee."

On the team. Good, and I'm only six months from burning ants in my back yard. "Well," I'd say, "I'm glad you want me." I was a psychopathic pleaser.

"When can you start?" he'd ask.

"When do you want me to start?"

"Monday?"

"I'll be here."

We stood up and shook hands and that was the last he ever saw of me.

In the welfare department, I spent most of my time walking the streets of Williamsburg or the Lower East Side, helping women who were miserable, angry, and overwhelmed by life. They had missing husbands and kids who were hanging all over them or else in trouble with school or the cops; they had mental troubles, physical troubles, everything.

I was cheating and stealing from the welfare department to get them as much money as I could. I tried every way I knew to help them. After six months on the job, I realized I wanted to move out of my mother's house.

From the start of that winter I looked for an apartment in Queens; God forbid I should move too far away from my mother. I made sure to tell all the real estate agents and landlords that under no circumstances were they ever to call the house. I found a place with my aunt's help. Although she seemed doomed to serve lifetime sentry duty over my mother she felt that I, at least, deserved a chance. It was a two-room apartment in Kew Gardens, about ten miles from Laurelton, closer to Manhattan, clean, quiet, sunny, and cost $97 a month. I was scared but excited. My aunt was happy for me and she went out with me to buy towels, pots and pans, silverware, and other essentials. All this had to be done secretly without my mother catching on. We were sitting in the kitchen of the new place after shopping for paper towels and such and my aunt was telling me with great fondness about the first apartment she had. It was in Brooklyn, when she first married my uncle. "Michael, it was such a beautiful little place, lots of sun coming in." A picture of her hopeful youth.

We drove through the snow back in Laurelton, talking about my new life and her old one. I was happy to have some support for this move; it seemed so dangerous. We got out of the car, and my aunt went into her house next door. I walked up to the door of my house, soon not to be my house anymore. As I reached the steps, my mother flung open the door. She was barefoot, dressed only in a nightgown. She had the habit, since I was a little kid, of walking around the house wearing practically nothing. My grandmother would yell at her, "Ruthie, put some clothes on, the children!" She didn't pay any attention. I think I was about fifteen when it dawned on me that maybe it didn't matter to her how she dressed or looked (her hair and teeth were always a mess) because there was no man around to impress, to look good for. If there were other reasons for her semi-nakedness I wasn't aware of them. Actually, there was one man, a guy she met during one of her longer periods of stability. I was fourteen then. She joined a group called Parents Without Partners, and went to weekly events—card parties, lectures, dinners. One time she came home and told me she was going to go to dinner with a guy named Lou who owned his own printing business somewhere in Queens. When the poor guy came to the house to pick her up, I was surly. When she came back I told her I thought he was stupid and ugly and I didn't want her to go out with him anymore. I think she saw him one or two more times, but I was nasty and angry. He stopped coming after that. "Don't worry, Lou won't be coming here anymore," she told me. Maybe she didn't like him for her own reasons?

She stood in the doorway in her nightgown, staring at me with her mad, accusing eyes. I realized instantly that some fool of a broker had called the house. "So you're moving out, hah? You're getting your own place," she said very slowly.

Oh shit, I thought, the jig is really up. She blocked the doorway, shivering and staring at me standing there in the snow.

"Get out of the way."

"No," she said. So I just shoved her aside and ran upstairs to my room. I had to push her; she didn't see the boundaries between people. I threw a lot of stuff into a big suitcase, rushed downstairs and out the door. It was dark now and very cold. My mother followed me outside, followed me out in her nightgown and bare feet in the snow. I was nearly to the car, almost to the curb, when I turned around. She was standing two feet away from me, pointing her bony finger at me, her eyes blazing and her hair flying in the wind. "You're leaving me again," she said.

I stood and looked at her with utter loathing. I hated her more at that moment than any other time in my life. She stepped closer, practically touching me, and looked hard into my face. Then her eyelids started to flutter and she fainted, full length in the snow. Just the way it happens in a Victorian novel—she swooned. I can't think of any better word for it.

I didn't catch her. I just stood there looking at her lying on the sidewalk. I had a winter coat on. The truth is I was content to stand there and stare at her on the ground until she froze to death. Then the lights came on next door, and my aunt and uncle ran out the door. They picked her up and then magically, she awoke. She was moaning. "Ohhh, he's leaving me again, he's leaving me again."

I couldn't even talk, I just spit in the snow. "You better go, Michael," my aunt said. I got in the car and drove off. Congratulations on your first apartment.

In my new place, I paced around like a political prisoner who never even knew what he was guilty of. I jumped at noises and thought I saw bugs all the time. The first couple of months I had a recurring nightmare. A gigantic roaring dragon was coming to eat me up. Every time I woke sweating and shaking from this dream, it was almost exactly 3:00 A.M. One morning, I awoke at 2:30, maybe trying to postpone the nightmare. I sat on the side of the bed looking at the clock, and at 3:01, a Long Island Railroad train went roaring underneath my window. I hadn't even realized that I lived right over the tracks. The train woke me up for a couple of weeks after that, but I didn't have the dream anymore.

Still I couldn't sleep and had to get tranquilizers from a doctor. I was scared all the time. A typical dinner: I would stand over the stove eating Heinz pork and beans right out of the can, which I had heated over the burner. I didn't even stir it, so naturally the top beans were cold and the bottom ones were burned. I used only paper plates and plastic utensils though I had a cabinet full of dishes, knives, forks, and cups. I was always looking at the front door, making sure it was locked. I felt, almost constantly, that someone was coming to get me. I still feel that way. I rest better, even now, when there's a bolt on the door, and I know my family and I are safe.

In the beginning, my mother would call, sometimes five or six times a day. As soon as I heard her voice I hung up. The calls diminished and after about a month they stopped altogether. Everybody thought I was heartless. How can you just hang up on your mother like that? What could I tell them?

I lived my life but it was very difficult. I carried around with me a constant, undefined dread, at work, at home, on the street.

It was hard to leave the place to actually go out the door; to work, to visit friends, even to shop. I was afraid something might happen to me, but I didn't know what. I was terribly lonely.

After a couple of months, I got to be friends with a girl in my training unit in the welfare department. We went out for coffee, then for lunch. She liked me! Her name was Mary-Ann. She was from Paramus, New Jersey, and Irish Catholic. She was short and round with dark hair and dark eyes, very efficient, very serious. I thought she was sexy. We started going back to my place after work. She told me she loved me and wanted us to get married. On the way back to my apartment we bought steak or something for dinner. Whatever we bought inevitably burned in the kitchen while we made out feverishly in the other room. We were both shy and even prudish about sex but we worked hard to get over it. Still, she didn't want me to go all the way because she wasn't sure if I really loved her and I never seemed to want to discuss marriage and children (whom she wanted to raise as Catholics). I just wanted the comfort, the company, and the sex. Marriage and children? I was barely surviving, mentally and physically.

Naturally, I decided to bring Mary-Ann out to meet my mother. I was twenty-two then. We sat in my mother's kitchen. She was smiling and chatting, putting on a brave front for Mary-Ann, but I knew there was something bad coming. And what else should I have expected? You know I was not going to bring a girl to meet my mother who was in *any* way acceptable to her.

"So, dear," asked my mother, "what religion are you?"

"Roman Catholic." She was cheery, calm, honestly blunt.

My mother didn't react too much to Mary-Ann's casual revelation, but I could feel the hatred boiling just below the surface. We had been there only twenty minutes when she tripped and spilled hot black coffee all over my girlfriend's new dress. My mother immediately apologized hysterically and grabbed towels to dry off the dress. It was a disaster. We left right after that. In the car my girlfriend asked me, "Why did you bring me out here?"

"Well, you're talking about getting married, so you should meet my mother, right?" Mary-Ann just looked at me.

Well, I survived. I moved from center to center in the welfare department and when I was twenty-five and living in Brooklyn Heights, I met a woman who was very efficient and very serious and very sexy and this time I moved in with her.

Exactly one year to the day after we moved in together, I went crazy and was committed to Kings County Hospital in Brooklyn. My relationship to her had been degenerating almost since the day it started but that really had very little to do with me losing my sanity. It would have happened no matter whom I lived with or even if I had lived alone. I was due for it.

I believe there is a kind of emotional physics in life. The first principle is: What goes in, must come out. So, three months past my twenty-sixth birthday, Saturday night, September 26, I was locked up in a mental hospital. I had horrible hallucinations. I was listed as suicidal and homicidal. They put me on a twenty-four-hour watch and pumped me full of Thorazine and sleeping pills. Everybody in the family knew about it—everybody except my mother. Since I only spoke to her four or five times a year, and then only when *I* called her, she wasn't likely to wonder too much that I didn't contact her for a while. And, of course, more important than any other consideration, the family decided that for her to hear about it would make her too nervous. The Feder first commandment: Don't do anything that will upset Ruthie. Don't tell her that Michael's sick, don't tell her that her friends are getting old and dying, don't let her know that life is actually continuing, that right outside the door that she's afraid to touch there are flowers blooming.

I was released from the hospital after a couple of months but I had to start my life at zero again. My job was gone, I had no real friends, and my home life was in ruins. I managed to get reinstated in the probation department. I had to take the test over again and lie about my hospitalization. I lived with my father for a while out on Long Island but then I moved back to Brooklyn and found a studio apartment. I made new friends and discovered that there was a sex life to be had, even for me. In January 1975 I was living with another woman and selling used and rare books to collectors by mail. It was a craft I picked up from my lifelong addiction to reading and my fascination with the physical beauty and mystery of books.

My mother called one Sunday morning, January 31, 1975, and told me that my father had just been killed in a plane crash outside of Istanbul. The company he was working for had just called her with the news.

After a couple of months of depression—moping around my apartment—I set up a used book store on the main street of the neighborhood. I laid the carpet, put up the bookshelves, plastered, painted, and drove all over Brooklyn, buying thousands of books from thrift stores and people's houses. I was able to do this because my father's accident left me a good chunk of money. I bought books on collecting and pricing books and studied them obsessively. I was proud of what I had created. About a week after I opened, there were some customers quietly browsing in the store. It was a Saturday afternoon. My mother called me. She had brightened considerably in the months after my father died. At first I was angry with that; I figured it was her usual coldness and sadism, but then I realized it was something more. She had been freed from a kind of spell. His death seemed to release her from one of the chains that bound her to the past. She was better, but she still went in and out. I stayed away from Laurelton, as usual, just to preserve my sanity. It still enraged me to see her.

"Hello, darling. I hear you have a new bookstore." She heard everything from my relatives. It was the only way she knew what I was doing or even if I was still alive.

"Yeah," I said.

"I guess you're not going to invite me to see it," she said, keeping the bright tone in her voice. My stomach was turning cold. This was my mother at her most sarcastic, with her most vicious twist of the knife. Her outright tantrums were shattering enough, but her polite indictments of felonious mother abuse were the worst for me.

On the phone I'm stumbling: "Well, no, you see, I didn't want to have anybody the first week because I, uh, wanted to make sure it was a success first and . . ."

What I really meant was I didn't want her to come to my store and poison it with her presence. After all I had lived through, she was still like a witch to me, capable of supernatural curses.

"All right, sweetheart, if that's how you feel. Maybe you'll change your mind later." And I did, out of guilt, out of the eternal child's eternal hope for a mother's love. She came out and looked around. She was on her best behavior, no doubt warned by my aunt not to cause a scene. She left after about twenty minutes.

After that, she took to calling me at the store every couple of weeks, and even though she was generally better, I still wished she'd leave me alone. Even a simple conversation with her could turn strange very quickly.

"Hello, darling, isn't the weather lovely?"

"Yeah?"

"I went shopping at A & S today."

"Good."

"By the way, sweetheart, I just want you to know, I've been going over my will again and I've decided to leave your sister all the jewelry."

"Great, Ma." Customers were coming up and asking questions about the books.

"By the way, darling, you haven't called me in a few weeks."

"Well, I've been busy, Ma."

Without realizing it, my voice had gotten a violent edge to it. I could see customers looking at me. I swiveled in my chair and looked out the window.

"Are you going to invite me to your store again, Michael?"

That did it. It never took much between us, maybe it was her calling me by my name. I hated to hear my name coming out of her mouth. "No," I said. "I'm not inviting you, now or ever!"

"Well," she screamed, "then I'm cutting you out of my will!"

"Go ahead," I yelled. "Cut me out of your fucking will!" I slammed the phone down and smashed my fist on the desk. Everybody in the store was staring at me. A couple of them put books back on the shelves and walked out.

About a year had gone by, with only a few more of these awful exchanges between my mother and me, when my sister called me with astounding news. My mother had found a new place to live! After thirty years of being a self-condemned prisoner in her bedroom, she had gone out on her own and gotten a new place. Over the last several years, Laurelton had been what was called in those days "changing." This meant black people were finally moving in. White people reacted by moving out, some to Long Island, some farther away. The more white people moved out, the more black people moved in. This was not something my family could handle.

Finally the last blow fell. My aunt, my mother's older sister and her lifelong caretaker and nurse, was fed up with living in New York. My uncle was in his late sixties and the daily commute into Manhattan was too wearing for him. He had been mugged twice and the winters were getting hard for him and my aunt to bear. And, of course, almost every one of their old friends lived in Florida. They took a trip down and bought a condominium. That my aunt had the nerve to do this, to abandon her charge and defy my grandmother's deathbed pronouncement, was amazing. But now she was going. She wanted to live her last years in some comfort, among her old friends.

My mother was now faced with utter isolation, no friends, no family. No one.

So without even announcing it, she went to a broker and found a condominium of her own at the tip of northwestern Queens, just at the Nassau County border. She called me and told me. She actually sounded happy! I was stunned. She asked me if I would drive her out to the new place to see it and help her figure out what she needed to bring from Laurelton. I can't tell you how good I felt, how full. Would I drive her out? Of course I would.

It was a well-maintained garden apartment complex, with grass and courtyards. She gave me the keys and I opened the door. She drifted around the sunny rooms, chattering away about this and that. She was very enthusiastic. I opened the window in the living room. It was mid-September and there was a slight cool breeze. My mother looked at me and said, "I'm going to move next week."

At that moment I felt something I had never felt before, a sense of tremendous pride in her. But it wasn't just her, you see. It was also the possibilities for me. If she, so filled with fear, could do this, move out of that old haunted house, then what wasn't there that I couldn't do in my life? And if she had finally found the guts to change, this scared rabbit, then I could do anything. Absolutely anything. I could fly.

Standing there in the sunshine my mother said, "I might get a new washing machine. Do you think I should, Michael?"

A *new* washing machine. Everything new! I was filled with love. "Absolutely," I said. "A brand new washing machine." I saw a screwdriver lying on the windowsill and I picked it up and began fixing the blinds which weren't working just right. I don't know how to fix blinds. I can hardly fix blinds now. But then, all of a sudden, I was fixing things. "Here," I said, "let me move that refrigerator back a little . . . there." I was so happy I actually let her hug me. It was the first time in twenty years.

A couple of days later I was driving two of my friends back to New Brunswick when I felt a great chill come over me. I pulled over to the side of the road. It came to me with complete certainty that my mother would be dead within a week. I can't explain it. I just knew. I sat there for a couple of minutes, then I got back on the highway.

Two days later, Monday, a phone call woke me up at six thirty in the morning. It was my aunt. "You better get out here," she said. "Your mother has killed herself." I could say I was surprised or shocked but I wasn't. It was not just the premonition I'd had two days before, but the whole life before it.

I did what I usually do when there's serious trouble. I took charge, issued orders. "Hold a mirror over her mouth," I told my aunt.

"I already did that," she said. "There's no mist. Michael, she's dead. You better get out here."

I drove out to Laurelton. There was a police car and another official-looking black car parked in front of the house. Familiar. I walked in to see a fat old sergeant sitting on the couch. As I stood there looking at him and my aunt and uncle, a bored little man in a creased gray suit walked past and out the door. He was the medical examiner, off to visit another corpse. In my mother's bedroom there was a young cop standing at attention in the middle of the room. "What the hell are you doing here?" I asked.

"Guarding the evidence," he said.

The evidence was, as I looked around, about a dozen pill bottles. She had emptied them all: Thorazine, Lithium, Valium, codeine . . . "Get out," I said. He looked at me for a second and then left. At a time like that you don't have to worry about proprieties.

My mother lay on her bed, a small single bed, neatly made up with a quilt. She was lying very straight and had folded her hands together across her stomach. She was waxy looking. Dead. I opened the window to let some air in. I looked at the pill bottles, the dates and the labels. Obviously she had saved up all these pills, going back more than a year. She was not fooling. As I looked at her I felt there was something, an essential part of this scene that was missing. My aunt poked her head in the room. I said, "Did she leave a note?"

My aunt shook her head."Uh, no, no . . ."

"Get it," I said. She went out. I knew there had to be a note. My mother would not leave this world without a final word.

I pulled up the one chair in the room and sat next to her with my knees touching the bed. I talked to her. "You couldn't do it, could you? You couldn't finally move out." My first feeling was one of sadness, then betrayal. "Why couldn't you do it for us?" I said, thinking of my aunt and uncle and all our relatives who were close to her as well as myself. I sat there for a long time looking at her. I touched her cheek. Then I noticed she was wearing a necklace. I didn't want to give it to the city of New York as a gift so I picked up her head and took off the chain and put it in my pocket. Evidence. Two men came in from the coroner's office. They had to take her, they explained, to do an autopsy. They put her in a thick rubber bag and zipped a zipper over her head, put "the body," as they called it, on a stretcher, and left.

My aunt came back in from next door and handed me a note printed in pencil: "I can no longer live without the respect of my children."

Well, that was no surprise to me. The strain that runs from my mother through me to my daughter, the sense of drama, is never absent, up to and including the last moment.

I was alone in the room with the pill bottles, the note, and the empty bed. I had the oddest feeling then. My sadness and anger had passed and was taken by the bravery of what she had done. Strange as it may sound, I felt very proud of her. She actually had the guts to kill herself. I don't know, maybe I had to manufacture something to prop myself up, to lift from this horror, but I really did feel a genuine sense of pride in my mother. All her life she had hidden, been afraid to take the slightest positive action. The new place was too much for her. She had been scared all her life, but finally she had done the one thing that terrifies all of us, and she did it to the hilt. She deliberately stepped into the next world. Over the years, when I have thought about her suicide, I have had many feelings—shame, anger, sadness—but this perverse pride has never gone away.

A few days later, I had to go out to sell the condominium. At the door, I met the couple who wanted to look at it. As I searched around for the keys, I started to cry. My hands were shaking so much that the man had to take the keys from me and open the door himself. I couldn't go on. The man told his wife to stay with me while he looked around. Then he stood next to me in the hall while she went in. They said they liked it. They wanted to buy it. He had to lock the door for me.

About two months later I drove out to Long Island to visit my Aunt Frances, my father's older sister. I liked her. My father's side of the family were all tough and generally cheerful, not like my mother's side, screaming, "Oh God, a cut, call the Mayo Clinic!" I sat down with my aunt in her living room. I wanted her to tell me about my mother and father. They were both gone—what harm could there be now? My aunt was hesitant. She wasn't the type to gossip.

"Ah, Mike," she said, "you don't want to hear about those things."

"C'mon, Frances, tell me."

"All right," she said at last. "I'll tell you. Your father comes home from a date one night, this is 1943, and he says, 'I met the most wonderful, beautiful girl in the world!' He's carrying on about her, how terrific she is. He wants to marry her. Your father was very—"

"I know," I said. "Yeah, so he wants to marry her."

The family sent Frances out to Brooklyn, a scout in enemy territory, to check out this "terrific girl," Ruthie. Frances called up and made an appointment. Comes the day, she walked up to the door of Ruthie's mother's house in East New York. It was a dark, heavy-feeling house. She knocked and knocked but there was no answer. She was about to give up and go away when the front door swung open slowly, like a bad horror movie. My grandmother was standing there telling her to come in. It was the middle of the day but all the curtains were drawn. My grandmother closed the door behind her.

My aunt said, "Hello, I'm Fran—"

"Shhh!" said my grandmother and put her finger to her lips. Frances was about to say something else when my grandmother turned her back on her and rushed into the kitchen. My aunt was left standing for a long time in the vestibule. Suddenly, like clowns pouring out of a circus car, people rushed from the kitchen and up the stairs carrying pots of hot water, towels, and bottles of medicine, running up and down the stairs. "More hot water." "More towels."

Finally, my aunt got irritated. She grabbed my grandmother. "What's going on? Is something wrong?"

My grandmother said, "Shhhh . . . Ruthie's having her period!"

She rushed back upstairs. Frances waited in the gloom for a couple of minutes and then left. My poor mother.

I remember the day my son, Sam, was born. I was right there of course, just as I was when my daughter, Emily, had been born. In my enlightened eighties circle, you had to be there to help your mate. No more Van Johnson waiting around in the waiting room for June Allyson to give birth and the nurse comes and says, "It's a boy!" You don't get off the hook that easy anymore. So I birthed and parented twice. Both kids were delivered at Columbia Presbyterian Hospital by the same doctor. This doctor is very different from me. He's tall, handsome, blond, bouncy, cheerful. He has some high position at the hospital, but despite all that I actually like him. When my daughter was being delivered he watched me anxiously because a lot of new fathers faint or get so sick they have to be sent out of the room; they can't take it. The worst part is watching your wife in such pain for so long with nothing you can do about it. That *was* awful, but blood and guts never fazed me. Murders on the street, epileptic seizures, throwing up—any kind of physical emergency I'm very good at. What I have trouble with is getting up in the morning, sitting at the table and eating with my family, going to work . . . things like that.

Finally the baby came out—truly a miracle to see. It was still attached to its mother by the umbilical cord. Have you ever seen an umbilical cord? It looks just like a coiled telephone cord but it's much thicker and slimier of course. It glistens. You can't take your eyes off it.

My son had entered the world. The doctor, bouncy and cheerful as ever, picked up a pair of very sharp surgical scissors and said to me, "Want to cut the cord?"

I was chilled to the bone. I said, "What? Cut the cord?"

You understand, he thought he was giving me a gift here. I took the scissors in my hand. After all, I couldn't let him think I was a sissy. I could cut any cord he could. I was very worried though. I didn't want to hurt anybody. I cut the cord right smack in the middle, right between baby and mother. Snip. And at that moment I was seized with a horrible, twisting revulsion, a sense of utter despair and loneliness. I suddenly remembered that scene in *2001* where the mad computer snaps the cable that connected the astronaut to the ship. He tumbled silently over and over away from the ship, over and over till he got smaller and smaller and was just a tiny speck out in cold, dead space.

Poor little baby, I thought. He's already been born into New York City. He could have been born in Iowa or Ohio—someplace pleasant. Well, the cord was cut. For better or worse he was in it now.

THE FISHING TRIP

At the end of the summer of 1968, right after the Chicago Convention, the assassinations of Martin Luther King, Jr., and Robert Kennedy, with the Vietnam War still blazing, I was a twenty-three-year-old who spent nearly all of his time lying in bed, looking at the walls, feeling like a creep. I was then in the midst, the very depth I should say, of a monumental neurosis, not to mention psychosomatic diseases, hallucinations, and, last but not least, my poor, pitiful attempts at associating with the opposite sex. This was certainly the Siberia of the soul for me—the summer of 1968.

My father was off in Louisiana building a fertilizer plant. From the time I was four years old, he had traveled all over the world as an engineer and, when I was growing up, he was just as likely to be in Paraguay, Brazil, Germany, India, or Japan as home in New York City. He built steel plants, chemical plants, and incidentally did a little side work for the U.S. government—something he only once hinted at but never really confessed. In any case, by the time 1968 had arrived, his wandering was limited to the continental USA.

One very warm evening late in August I was sitting at the window of my apartment in Brooklyn Heights, looking out on the street, watching what appeared to be hundreds of happy couples walking past. I was not sharing in their happiness. The telephone rang, proving it actually worked. It was my father, calling from Baton Rouge. "Hey, wanna take a trip?" he said.

I was always glad to hear my father's voice. Here's a guy who had been going away for two, three, sometimes six months at a stretch. He sent me postcards, and I'd occasionally get a letter or a phone call. So naturally when he called and invited me down, I jumped at the chance to see him.

You should understand that my father had always been larger than life to me precisely because I had never spent much time with him. Besides his world wandering, he was divorced from my mother since I was four years old. Over the years he became a kind of mythical figure to me. He enriched this myth by looking and acting like Ernest Hemingway—he was a big guy, over six feet, maybe 220 pounds, very rough, coarse, with a bad, almost violent temper. He was a tough guy from the Depression, and he was also a boss. Wherever he went he was in charge. He was (whenever I got a photograph or a postcard with a photograph on it) the biggest guy in the picture and the others looked like they were his employees, which they usually were.

I got on the phone (he paid for the ticket of course—I didn't have much money) and flew down to New Orleans.

Now, only people who come from New Orleans, or who have been to the Texas gulf in the summer, can understand what it's like down there at the end of August. This is a place where you go if you've been bad all your life. When I got off the plane it must have been over one hundred degrees, and the humidity was about 95 percent. Nobody does anything down there in August except stay in the car or the house, with the air conditioner on—or at least just lie in the shade.

He met me at the airport. I was not disappointed. Here he was again, my old man, just the way I remembered him, very big guy, joking, young-looking though he was fifty-one, a cigar stuck in his face (I love the smell of cigars because they remind me of him). His face was red because he had a tendency to eat and drink a little bit too much, and his blood pressure was too high. Also, he was one of those guys who when he shaved, either used an ax or no shaving cream, or a six-year-old blade, and the result was a face that looked like red sandpaper. His hair was just beginning to turn a little gray. Rough and tough—Ernest Hemingway.

He took my suitcase and threw it in the back seat as if it were a matchbox. This was a suitcase I thought I was going to have a serious heart attack just dragging from the plane to the terminal. He always does this for effect. It's as if to say, "You're with a real man now, son. I'll take that suitcase!" But also he had a good heart and he simply didn't want me lugging around this big suitcase. We went off to the Holiday Inn.

When we got to the motel, I discovered that we were staying in the same room. I was not happy to hear this. I'll tell you why. All my life I had been fortunate enough to have my own room in our small house in Queens—a room tucked away in the attic, with a door that closed. My room. After that, I lived in studio apartments, always pathologically alone, like Dostoevski's underground man. I had developed a terrible fear, a horror, of living in the same room with anybody. When I did have my rare sexual contact, I always made sure that I was sufficiently cold, abstract, or nasty so that the girl would leave quickly and I could have my cherished cave back to myself.

I was with my father so rarely that I never really saw him with his clothes off. He didn't like to go swimming because he didn't like to walk around with just his swim trunks on. I don't know why exactly, but when it came to the subject of sex or nudity, he was an extraordinary conservative. Considering this, I was surprised to discover that I was supposed to stay in the same room with him.

I slipped into a teeth-chattering kind of fear. He wouldn't understand my problem, because he grew up in a generation where people were much more chummy and comradely, and financial reasons alone forced people to buddy up and to share the same room.

Well, I'll just ask him to get me another room, I thought. I was sure I couldn't even sleep if he was in the same room. But what's *that* gonna sound like? Is he gonna think I'm some kind of sissy or what? At the very least, if I dashed for another room, he'd be insulted. He's generous and he's offering me his room. I kept quiet. After all, it's not as if I had to stay in the same bed with him. My bed was all the way at the other end. What I really dreaded, though, was the idea of (*a*) him seeing me naked, and (*b*) me seeing him. I had a couple of drinks and I figured well, it'll be all right.

Then he decided he wanted to show me his fertilizer plant. Naturally I expected this, but it had an added dimension to it. My father had always competed with me in a way that made him seem more like a teenager than my father. He always had to show me who the tougher guy was. He was always way ahead of me. So if we were playing pool or pitching horseshoes or the like, he made it clear that he was the better man. One thing that always certified this, and it was the easiest way for him, was to take me to his plants, his constructions. He would always point out to me the tallest building, the largest *erection* in the place, and ask me what I thought of it. Once when I was seventeen or eighteen, he took me out to Long Island where he was foreman in the construction of a huge tower in the center of the Brookhaven

Laboratories—where they did nuclear fission experiments. We drove up to this *gigantic* tower. It must have been three hundred or four hundred feet high. "There it is," he said. "That's my tower!"

We drove to the plant way out in the backwoods, somewhere outside of Baton Rouge. It was very humid, to say the least, and extremely hot. Most people were just sort of lying on the side of the road.

This whole place was one big soup of red mud. There was a lot of iron in the dirt which turns it red, a fact I picked up from my father. It was very close to the bayou. Mist, a thick, almost yellow-colored mist, hung over us just about the level of a low tree branch.

Everywhere, men were toiling away like ants. There were guys without their shirts on carrying steel girders around. There was the sound of machinery—a slap, you know, that you hear at construction sites: *hoomp-bamp! hoomp-bamp!*—and hundreds of pipes since it was a chemical plant, with various kinds of steam coming from them to join the mist hanging in the trees.

We went into a trailer. There's always a trailer on big construction sites, an office where all the noise stops. Three air conditioners were turned on high.

In construction sites up north, there are always a few men you'll notice with flannel shirts or steel hats lounging around telling all the others what to do. Well, when you combined that standard construction site ritual with the southern way of life in the midst of August in the Louisiana backwoods, you got a *lot* of hanging around. So the good ol' boys were in there drinking very strong black coffee and yakking with the "girls," all of whom, of course, were in their forties. "Shee, you don't mean that. Why, I was over to Charley McBride's last Thursday . . ."

When we came in, all the talking stopped temporarily because my father was the big boss from up North. After a brief silence one of the "girls" said, "That your son, Phil? He sure is good-lookin', just like you," and she dug him in the ribs.

Well, I couldn't believe it. What was this? A reference to sexuality! My father's face turned even redder. He hardly ever referred to sex, and between us, it was especially touchy because I was obviously scared of sex, and he had been gone the whole time I was growing up. I remember once, he was driving me back to my mother's house—we had just seen a Knicks game—and we were stopped at a light on Queens Boulevard. You understand, this was maybe the second time I'd seen him in about five months. Out of the blue he says, "Well, um, uh, what about girls?" I did a triple take.

"Girls?" So much for sex education.

And now in the trailer this woman said, "Phil, you gotta bring your boy over to my house. You *know* how good my cookin' is." She dug him again in the ribs.

I was amazed! I was forced to entertain the thought that my father was messing around down here. My father didn't do *that;* he just worked. Well, he laughed, and then we went into another office in the back which was the *real* office, where the boss worked. Immediately he was explaining things, showing me blueprints of this and that, telling how he's gonna make fertilizer and Louisiana will turn green and sprout six-foot ears of corn, and I really couldn't have cared less. All I wanted to do was just sit and be where my father was, smell his cigar smoke, and look at him.

I was loving it. Whenever I visited him in the locations of his grandeur, I was never disappointed. If you've lived any, you know that such a continuing idealization of somebody can be extremely dangerous. But here I was twenty-three years old and not once did he ever appear to have any faults.

I was soaking up his "bossism." In other words, if he was my father and he was the boss, then *I* must be someone of importance too. It was like having my identity recharged. I reveled in him. I could run for months on just ten minutes of exposure to my father's self-confidence.

Suddenly, the whole trailer tilted. It felt like an earthquake. I heard a terrible commotion outside, and then the door banged open, and I saw the biggest man I have ever seen outside of a basketball game or a circus. He looked around for a second or two, grinned and said, "Well, hi, e'rbody!"

This guy's name was Fred Bowman, and he actually ran the plant for my father day to day. He came from Texas and he was a good ol' boy himself. Fred Bowman was easily 6 foot 6, 6 foot 7 and he was huge! I don't mean he was stocky or heavily built. I mean this guy had to weigh at least 350 pounds. But he had a tiny little head, and when he spoke he didn't sound like a bullfrog or a moose. He had, rather, a little sweet voice, and a quick boyish grin.

He was so massive that he must have known that people's initial reaction to him was terror. So what he did was develop a very calm, behavior-modification type voice. He was gentle. He never made any sudden moves.

But despite Fred's smile and his gentleness, I disliked him initially. Why? Because he was intruding on my father's turf, stealing away his importance and command of the situation. To take away my father's power was to take mine too. So, after shaking hands, I just glared at him. It turned out my father and Fred had some problems to discuss. My father tossed me the car keys. "Take a ride around," he said. "We'll be done in an hour or so." So I drove around Baton Rouge—mud, shacks, fields, mansions, a foreign world. I picked him up about five o'clock and drove back to the Holiday Inn.

In the room, my father said, "We've gotta eat some supper now, because we're going to sleep real early."

I said, "What for?"

"We're going fishing at dawn."

Fishing? Well, all right, we've gone fishing before. Besides, anything my father wanted to do was okay with me.

"We're going fishing in the bayou. An overnight trip. It's a little rough, but you'll like it."

Now I got my second big anxiety attack. I was already trying to get used to the idea that I would have to sleep in the same room with him, but to go on a fishing trip, overnight? Do you know what that meant? That meant that I would have to sleep with my father. In a little, tiny tent. And who knew, maybe with strangers too. Sure enough, my father said, "Fred's coming with us." Oh, God!

I'm a city boy, a 100 percent bookworm, concrete-playground kid. I was going to have to go out there and sleep on the ground, for Christ's sake. And this was not the Adirondack State Park, you understand. This was the bayou—a swamp—a fucking jungle! Hot, nasty. This was a place where there are bugs so big you need a butterfly net just to remove them from the immediate environment. This was a place where alligators are not in little glass cages and a keeper throws in meat twice a day. This is real. And on top of all this I would live in very close quarters with strangers. This was too much for me. I was an immediate nervous wreck when I heard this.

It *was* exciting too, you see, because I'd get a chance to go out and be Ernest Hemingway, Jr., with my father. I had to have *some* courage of my convictions. If I had gone down there to soak up his juice, and to get from him what he had to give me as a man, then what better test could there be than to go out and confront the Big Fish?

Next morning, about 5 A.M., before the sun even came up, he shook me awake. No matter what time I ever got up, even if it was two in the morning, my father would have been up a half-hour before me. He was a guy from the Depression, a guy who woke up every morning at six whether he needed to or not, banged on the door, flipped on the lights and said, "Get up, already! I don't know what you're doing sleeping so late. I just built the Hoover Dam and made breakfast for eighty people and you're sleeping. Jesus!"

Anyhow, it was reveille at dawn. By the time my eyes opened, he was headed outside. "Hafta check the car!" Right. So I jumped up and took advantage of his absence—so that he shouldn't see me naked. I ran into the bathroom to get dressed. He must have felt the same way, I guess, because now that I think about it, I never saw *him* naked either. So there we were, both decently dressed before seeing each other. We had coffee at the motel dining room and then it was off into the woods.

After half an hour on a few rough roads that got rougher as we went along, we arrived at Fred Bowman's trailer. Fred had planted his trailer as far as possible from anywhere—right near the beginnings of the bayou. Outside was parked an old army jeep.

We went into the trailer. "Good morning, good morning. How y'all doin'," said Fred, handing us two mugs of coffee. I was already buzzing from the two cups I had before. Fred's trailer was a total mess. This guy had never been married, never lived with anybody, he was the original wild American boy, and he was out there doing it. His trailer was full of guns: shotguns, handguns, ammunition, gun cleaning oil, gun rags, gun magazines, and about ten cats and three dogs, all covered with fleas. Inside and out, the trailer was dented all over like a tube of toothpaste. It looked like it had been over Niagara Falls. The only picture in the place was dangling over a sinkful of dishes. It was a small photograph of him looking young and uncreased in an army uniform in front of what looked like a medieval church. There he was, as huge as ever, with his arm around a big beautiful blond girl. He looked like he was in his early twenties. When I met him he was probably in his mid-thirties.

"Fred, who's that in the picture?" I asked.

"It's not important, it's nothing," he said, taking out a can of beer. This was the first of maybe sixty cans of beer that this guy drank in the course of the day. I have never before or since seen anybody drink so much beer. In his refrigerator were about three quarts of coffee he had made for the trip, a couple of bags full of coffee beans, and maybe four or five cases of beer. He had several more cases piled up against the sink. He chain-drank beer. As soon as he finished one can he would crush it in his hand, throw it in the garbage or just on the floor, and take another can. He drank a full can of beer the same way you'd drink maybe a small juice glass of water. He just sucked it right up. He drank, and drank, and he never seemed to show the effects of it. Beer at six in the morning.

After packing provisions and equipment, we got into the jeep and we drove. Fred drove like a maniac. I should have realized right there that I was with a person who was possibly going to cause my death. He was going fast around turns about thirty feet above a river that was getting wilder as we went on. He was doing 50 mph on the straights, drinking beer with one hand and driving with the other. He threw the empty cans back over his shoulder onto the road. I thought to myself, well, I haven't lived a bad life, and although I hadn't done many things I wanted to, at least I've done a couple, and if I was going to die I was in the company of some nice guys, *and* I was with my father. I had no doubts he could take care of me in heaven.

We got to a beat-up, rattling dock after about twelve miles of this. Now the sun was fully up, except that you could hardly see it, because it was both hazy and obscured by the giant trees hanging over everything like prehistoric monsters. The flowers growing all over the banks looked indecent. They were gigantic, red, blue, all different colors. They looked hungry. Birds were sitting on stumps, staring at us, making unfriendly noises. Noises I never heard. I looked at my father. He was loving it.

We got into the boat, and the river took us away into another world entirely, completely silent except for the sound of the small outboard motor. Not another human being appeared on the shore. The sun shone through the trees. Occasionally I heard the sound of a bird or the splash of an animal jumping into the river. The bayou snaked around. The Mississippi down here was not a river that ran straight and massively like the Hudson, which is a very busy, very time-is-money sort of river. This river was a small, casual, old river. Sometimes it hardly seemed to move. Time slowed down and slowed down until it almost stopped. I was truly relaxed for a change. This isn't so bad, I thought.

"Wouldn't do that 'f I was you," Fred said.

"Do what?" I asked.

"Trail my hand in the water there."

"Why not?"

"Gators."

Sure enough, I looked over and saw two huge eyes staring at me not four feet from the boat. I whipped my hand back in. This brought back my old fears—but still the water was soothing.

We went on and on and it got wilder and wilder. We passed an overgrown field, the only evidence that people had once been here.

After a time, we floated up to another old crumbly dock. Fred went up and into a cabin, and came back with a young boy, about fifteen or sixteen, wearing only a pair of red shorts, barefoot. He had several broken fingers which had been set wrong. His nose was a little mashed, and he had almost colorless light blue eyes, like a wolf. Dozens of healed and unhealed scars covered his body. I could see that he seldom wore any clothes but these faded red shorts. He carried an old, moldy duffel bag, and a Winchester Model 94, a lever-action .30 caliber rifle. The gun looked like it had been well used but also well cared for. He got into the boat and Fred explained to us that he was our guide. His name was Jean (pronounced Zhan), and he was a Cajun.

Now, I don't know exactly what a Cajun is, but it's some combination of Indian, French, British, and black. Jean was to me a very exotic character. His skin was reddish tan, like the clay and mud. I never saw him smile one time. And for a long time, he never said a word.

Jean got into the boat and sat across from me. We stared at each other. For me it was like looking at a Martian, and I'm sure he felt the same way. Here I am with US Keds and my jeans, and a T-shirt that said Dump Humphrey. I had the feeling he was storing me up, so he could tell people about me later.

We're already out in God-knows-where, I thought—where could be worse than this that we need a guide? But there was worse, because as we went on, the river got narrower and narrower, and the trees grew even closer to the boat. The noise of the animals and the birds was louder. Finally, we pushed through some thick foliage, which we had to part right in the middle of the river, and we emerged onto a small bay in the middle of the river. Jutting into the bay was a small promontory—just bare, red dirt with a huge oak tree presiding over it, giving a lot of shade. That was to be our campsite for the night. We pulled up to it and tied the boat.

We climbed up the bank and put up the tent. My worst fears came true. It was a small pup tent. I thought, we're all going to sleep in this? Oh, shit. I resigned myself to not getting any sleep. The sun was going behind some silvery gray clouds. We had been going for several hours and it was late afternoon. We figured we'd better get out on the water and get some fishing done. It was a whole different experience from being out on a northern lake. There's a kind of cold, clear, crisp feeling to the water and the woods in the north. On a lake, let's say in upstate New York, if the moon is out, everything's sharp and bright, all toned up and fitted correctly. But down in the bayou there is instead a flattening effect; everything is fuzzy and large and soft, muddy and lazy. But the silence is the same, the same beautiful silence out on the water.

We threw the lines in and waited. We stayed out there about three hours. Nobody caught anything, but of course that's hardly ever the object of casual fishing. The air was clear. It was truly beautiful, with just the sound of line and sinker hitting the water—plop—and a slight breeze in the trees. In the east, the sky was deep violet and in the west it was turning orange-crimson-red.

Then, in what seemed like an instant, the sun set, and the sky turned black and filled with stars. It got very humid. The wind died down completely. Jean said this happened every day around the same time—no wind and high humidity. This combination was the signal for mosquitoes, the size of B-52s, to come out and attack us like kamikaze pilots. We pulled in the lines and made it back to shore *real* fast, and rubbed insect repellent all over ourselves—except for Jean the Cajun. He was beyond all that. He didn't care. He had so many scars that probably the mosquitoes couldn't get through anyhow.

We sat around the fire eating beans and fried strips of beef from a big black skillet. Delicious! And we passed around a bottle of bourbon, which must have been 100 proof.

The mosquitoes and other bugs were amazing. They had no fear whatsoever. At one point I felt a bug on my shoulder. I grabbed it off, then opened my hand to take a look at it. It looked like a prehistoric animal, armored and horned. I was disgusted, but my father thought it was pretty funny. "Whatsamatter, never saw a locust before?"

A *locust?* "These things belong in the Old Testament," I said and threw it out into the bay.

There was a noise not twenty feet away in the bushes. I jumped. "Hey, calm down," my father said. "It's not even their feeding time yet!" Ha ha.

Supper went on. We were drinking and getting pretty loose. Cajun Jean and Fred were talking about guns.

"I saw a lot of guns at the Chicago Convention," I said, sounding authoritative, looking for a conversation.

Jean said to me, "What's that?" It turned out, of course, that he had no idea what the Chicago Convention was. In fact, he didn't even know what a convention was at all. He had the most rudimentary idea of the political system. He had no idea that the parties got together every few years and had a convention. He had no idea that they elected candidates. He just knew that someone was President and he was doing a bad job or a good job, whatever the guys told him in the local tavern. I was amazed. This guy's entire background and culture were completely alien to me.

I developed a very unfortunate attitude toward him. I was extremely condescending. I thought he was stupid and ignorant. Is this what this country's all about? Jesus, I thought to myself, we'll never be able to save or educate these people. I didn't say all this, but it's what I was thinking. There I am in all my city glory, you know? All my Queens College political science courses, all my books, all the media I consumed, the TV, all the candidates I knew, and all the demonstrations I'd gone to. This guy didn't know or care one shit about any of it; his idea of life was fishing, shooting "varmints," and going to the tavern and getting in a knife fight on a Saturday night. He seemed like a caveman to me.

After this turn in the conversation the atmosphere got very cool, although the air was even more stifling than before. It was time to turn in because we had to get up early to fish. Jean went to lie down on a blanket beneath a tree, holding his rifle in his arms. I had to get into the tent. Fred moved over to one side, then my father settled in the middle, and then came me. Thank God, I thought—at least I didn't have to sleep between these two guys. If that was the case I probably would have just blown my brains out with Jean's gun and not even bothered to go through the night. But it was bad enough anyway. I was lying right next to my father—two inches away from him. He fell right to sleep and started snoring like a bear.

My father was one of those guys who had either no conscience at all or a very clear one, because he could sleep as soon as he put his head down—even on a rock or in the middle of a crowded subway. You know these people? How do they do that? Of course, I was the opposite. I could down an entire bottle of Thorazine, get smashed in the head by a sledge hammer, and still wake at the slightest noise.

So put these things together—there I was in the tent with my father, and next to him, snoring even louder, like some kind of giant wart hog, was Fred, on a night so humid you could wring the pillow out and get a full cup of water. Water seeped through the tent even though it wasn't raining. I figured any second my father would roll over and crush me like a bug. I was sweating, and it was hot, and then I had this terrible urge . . .

I had been so scared all day long that despite the fact I'd been drinking beer and coffee nonstop, I had not once urinated the entire day. So here I was, nine o'clock at night, in the middle of the jungle, with werewolves and Cajuns in the underbrush a foot away from me, things that probably could eat me if they wanted to, lying next to my father and another monster, with the humidity at almost 100 percent, and all of a sudden I started to feel this tremendous pressure in my bladder. I have *got* to go take a piss, I told myself, but if I get up, who knows what these guys are going to do to me? And then if I made it out of the tent, Jean would probably put a bullet through my head with his Winchester. On top of that, there was no way I could get out of there without bumping into and sliding along some portion of my father's anatomy, a thought that caused me unbearable anguish.

So I lay there, completely rigid, covered with sweat. The two guys were snoring and I was tense as a wire, and there was a growing expansion in my bladder. I felt like any moment it was going to blow up. In fact, I started to have visions, clear awful visions of an exploding bladder. I'm going to be poisoned. Human waste will course through my body. My brain will fill up and I will explode in a shower of rancid urine. I'll embarrass everybody. And I was lying there absolutely still because if I moved even a little bit I was going to touch my father.

Finally it got so bad, and I was so certain I would explode, that I made small, careful motions to get up and go out and relieve myself. And then, as I moved just slightly, the snoring stopped as if they had both been listening to me, and Fred chuckled. I said, "I gotta go, I gotta go."

"You go out there this time of the night, son, something's gonna eat you."

Oh man, I couldn't believe it. I wasn't scared enough, right? I said, "Are you kidding me? I gotta go."

My father started to laugh. Big joke, right? These creeps, they think it's hilarious. What do they do with it? Do they swallow it? Fuck it. I started to get up.

"I'm serious," Fred said. "You go out there, there's bobcats, there's snakes."

Of course, that was it for me. As bad as I needed to go, and it was as bad as I ever needed to go, I wasn't going to go out there and have my Queens College genitals ripped off. I had horrible visions of squatting out there in the grass and losing all those parts that make life even slightly worthwhile. So I stayed in the tent. And, of course, my bladder was so large now that it felt like it was actually bumping up against my Adam's apple. I knew I was gonna die. I pictured what heaven might be like. I went into a kind of yoga-like trance. I could have been sleeping on nails and I wouldn't have known it. By this time, of course, there was a rash all over my body, my nose had started to run, and my eyes were twitching uncontrollably. Then, just about the time when I thought I was going to blow up and die and my father would be disgusted that he had some kind of a freak for a son, the sun started to break through the canvas of the tent. It was dawn.

Both my father and this other guy—these two bears—stopped snoring and immediately got up and went outside. I heard them getting breakfast ready. Jean, who had slept beside the fire like an animal, was talking. Now that I'd realized it was safe, I got off my sleeping bag, which was soaking wet, and, slowly making my way outside like a zombie, I walked over to the bushes and peed. I have never been so physically relieved as I was at that moment.

I walked back to the campsite, but now it was too late for me. I had been through such a night of torment that I had broken into a virtual symphony of psychosomatic diseases. My nose ran, my head throbbed, my teeth ached, my bones cracked, I felt like there were little mice running up and down my insides, my feet itched, my vision started to go, I was dizzy, I saw lights in the sky. I was gone—completely over the edge.

I stumbled over to the fire. They were all sitting around, all these guys, John Wayne, Ernest Hemingway, Injun Joe—and me, entering stage right, the Urban Cowboy. They were all staring at me but I could only see them through a haze.

At that moment I felt a tremendous hatred, a grinding red hatred, for my father, that he could take me out—me, a sensitive youth, his own son—into the middle of a jungle and subject me to this kind of torment. I wanted to kill him. I hated all men. I was certainly at that point, as far as I was concerned, not among their species. I was either a woman, some kind of strange visitor from another planet, or a freak, but I certainly wasn't a man, because a man goes right to sleep in the middle of wildcats, snakes, mosquitoes, a hundred-degree temperature, sleeps, gets up and has bacon, yawns, and says, "Whooie! I feel *good* this morning!"

After two or three minutes of attempting to kid me out of it, they realized that the fishing trip was going to have to be cut short, because they had a certified hospital case on their hands.

Jean was looking at me with intense fascination. He knew that not only had he never seen a human being act like this, but he probably never would again. He was storing it up for conversation at the tavern that night. "Shee, I saw a city boy, you won't believe . . ."

Fred was watching me with kind of a condescending amused look. My father? He looked at me with what I knew was great hatred and disgust that I, his own son, was embarrassing him in front of "the guys." But at that point I didn't care. In fact, even in the midst of my anguish, I felt a pang of malicious glee—that he was suffering with terrible embarrassment was revenge.

They packed up the tent and the other gear. I was a stretcher case. They sort of loaded me into the boat, and I stayed apart from the rest of them, just staring, keeping myself in a trance so the bones in my body wouldn't actually slip out.

We got back to Fred's trailer sometime in the afternoon and miraculously enough he had a Contac, which was just exactly what I needed. It looked beautiful to me, like a religious object. I swallowed it. He turned on the air conditioner. He had clean sheets, strangely enough. I got into bed, and drifted off. It was beautiful. I felt as if I had been rescued from death.

I woke up a few hours later—it was nighttime. I stumbled into the kitchen. My father was sitting at the table drinking coffee. "How are you, son?" he asked. He poured me a cup of coffee and handed it to me.

It was clear he forgave me for doing what I did. I practically started to cry. I sipped my coffee quietly, thinking of all kinds of important things to say to my father. I wanted to confess and admit every intimate personal disappointment and feeling that I had about him. But he must have seen the anticipatory, pleading look on my face because instantly he clammed up. He pushed back his chair and stood. "Got to be getting back."

Outside Fred was tinkering with the jeep. We said good-bye, got in the car, and drove back to the hotel.

It was about eight o'clock. I lay on my bed and must have dozed off for a bit. I opened my eyes and stared across the room, where my father was reading the paper. There was a tremendous silence between us. After about a whole half-hour of silence he threw down the paper and said, "Let's go to New Orleans. We'll hear some Dixieland."

Everything'll be okay now, I thought. So we got in the car, hit the highway, and burned some rubber, a great feeling. You know, when everything's gone bad, you can jump in the car and start to move and it's all right again?

We got to New Orleans and went to the French Quarter. We went to an old French restaurant and had their specialty, a delicious shrimp with a special wine sauce. We had cold white wine. It was a very mellow night, not too hot, not even too humid. We left the restaurant,

walking and talking, quiet and calm. The French Quarter was beautiful. With its old iron grillwork, it was magically out of time, just like
the bayou.

When you walk the streets of the French Quarter there's music
pouring out of the doors. You are surrounded by warm lights glowing
through stained-glass windows, you hear wailing trumpets and clari-
nets, people are friendly, you emerge onto beautiful plazas, fountains
with goldfish swimming in them. Everybody you meet is intoxicated—
with alcohol, all feeling the magic of the music and the summer night.
It is sheer, easy benevolence. And the music follows you everywhere,
triumphant, eternal music. Do you know Dixieland? It's got suffering
and sadness and human misery in it, yet it's triumphant, always
triumphant. Dixieland says: "This is life and that's all there is, but
we're gonna go on because it's beautiful; and if it isn't beautiful, well,
the only thing left to do is to go on anyway!"

Everywhere this music filled the streets. We wound up at Preserva-
tion Hall—an old wooden building where the original Dixieland guys
played, all of them about eighty years old. For a dollar they'd playing
any song you want. They just played and played on into the night as
we sat on benches, absorbed and together.

But like all magic, it had to end. About one in the morning, we got
back in the car and headed back to the motel. I sat back in the seat
with my eyes closed. I didn't want this night to end. There I was next
to my father. I felt closer to him than ever before. I had this beer and
wine in me, and the beautiful music was still singing in my head. I
loved it. It was surely one of the best nights of my life. We got back to
the motel, got ready for bed. It was very sad then; I had to leave the
next morning. I was flying back to New York, and slowly but surely
the night ebbed away from me. The wine and the music wore off.
Outside, cars whizzed past on the highway. Here it was again, another
good-bye.

The moon was shining in through the window. I looked over at his
bed and felt like I was floating away from him, carried away from the
shore, away from the warm lights and houses. His bed got smaller and
smaller, until I could hardly see it. I fell asleep.

The next morning it was business as usual. "Morning, Mike. How
ya doing? Let's get going." We had a cup of coffee and drove to the
airport. I got on the plane and found a window seat. I looked out and

saw him standing on the observation deck, not thirty feet away from me. The plane was in shadow; I don't think he could see me. My father. I had never truly thought of him as my father.

As I stared at him I realized that he was just like everybody else. He was sad. He didn't want to see me go. I felt the same way. His face was heavy and full of lines; his eyes were searching. But though his face was sad it did something for me. It made me understand that I *really was* connected to him. The very fact that we were saying good-bye, that we were separating, meant that we had been *together*—at least for a time. And I felt, for the first time in my life, a tremendous love for my father. He wasn't like a God. He hurt like everybody else. As the plane went down the runway I remembered the magic of the night before. I closed my eyes as the plane lifted off and heard that wonderful music again—felt him swaying next to me on the bench, chomping on his cigar, clapping his hands. My father and me. Didn't we ramble.

SANFORD
BRODSKY

The Probation Department of Brooklyn Family Court was the graduate school for survivors of the welfare department, like me. In the sixties there were a lot of us liberal arts graduates who did not absolutely *know* that we had a vocation to become doctors or lawyers; with no specific desires or goals to fulfill, we half-educated vagrants tumbled and drifted into the world of work. Some of us hit the employment agencies, got disgusted, and just dropped out. We became what *Life* magazine called "flower children," or hippies. We packed knapsacks and hit the road to Morocco or Katmandu. However, the remaining middle-class children, unfit for IBM or Metropolitan Life, joined the welfare department. I think now it's called the Department of Social Services.

I ended up working for the Brooklyn Family Court. I was only there from January of 1970 through the beginning of June, just a few months, because I was planning a cross-country excursion, a drive across the Midwest to the Pacific and back through the South. It was something I'd dreamed about for years. It seemed like all of my friends had made this trip—the great escape. You know, leave home with nothing but a rusty old car and a knapsack, head out on the highway. Break away. I used to spend whole days planning the route.

My job at family court was to prepare pre-sentencing reports. In family court the judge renders the decision—there's no jury. The killings and muggings made the headlines but mostly the cases were kids in need of supervision; they were called "persons in need of supervision," PINS. Some just had to be watched or sent to some agency or maybe returned to their mother's custody. Before the judge makes such a decision, he wants to have an investigation, naturally, into the family's background—to find out more about the child. The probation department exists to do this for him. Generally each investigation was very superficial because, again, there were so many cases. If I had had only five or six cases to work with every month, I could have done quite a job. Unfortunately, I always had more than I could adequately handle. However, I had the ability to work very fast, and could turn out a couple of decent investigations. I wrapped up the routine cases in a couple of days and concentrated on the more serious and complicated ones.

I shared my office with two other guys, Dave and Sheldon. Dave, who was my age, twenty-four, was just treading water. It seemed to me that he really didn't care what happened to his cases. To him the probation department was just a nine-to-five job with good benefits. Sheldon, who was older than us and an Orthodox Jew, was truly dedicated—he lived to help other people. Then there was me.

I worked hard enough, but something was missing. One of the reasons I wasn't effective, despite my sincerity and intelligence, was simply that I didn't know myself very well. I was going to leave and go cross-country that summer to find myself, you know, by traveling to California. I would read *Steppenwolf* along the route and toast marshmallows on the banks of the Colorado River. So you see, I suspected there was a hidden inner me that had yet to be charted. But in work matters, at the age of twenty-four I considered myself tested and wise.

A veteran, I had four years at the welfare department under my belt; that was fighting war in the trenches. I knew what it was like, right? I was at the point in life *before* you have those repeated revelations or shocks of circumstance that finally open your eyes. Nevertheless at that time I was convinced I was a combination of Dashiell Hammett and Margaret Mead. There I was, tough and smart. *I* knew what I was doing.

Our boss, Mr. Charles Johnson, was small and thin, about fifty-five, and very tough. He is, I imagine, still thriving someplace. At least, I hope he is. Johnson was an extremely sharp, hardnosed individual and was universally regarded in the Brooklyn Probation Department as a hard, go-by-the-book supervisor. Now, since my father left when I was a kid, I was always auditioning fathers—a kind of permanent open casting call. I took to Johnson immediately. And of course, I imagined he was either disappointed in his own son or maybe even without one. He returned my affection; we were instant buddies. He recognized the fact that I had at least some brains and wanted to do a good job. So, while all the other trainees in my department were scared to death of him, I reveled in his attention. We spent hours talking in his office, me and my new old man, Charles Johnson.

About three or four weeks into the job, Johnson handed me an interesting case. A young boy had been dragged into court by his parents. According to them, he was incorrigible.

The family lived in Brooklyn in a predominantly Jewish neighborhood. The father, Mr. Brodsky, was an assistant manager in a shoe store. This gave me a bit of a clue to his problems. Here was a guy who was already almost forty and still an *assistant* manager. Obviously, the man did not have a lot of drive. Mrs. Brodsky was not working; she was a housewife. There were two children: a boy named Sanford, about twelve years old, and a girl, about seven or eight.

Mr. and Mrs. Brodsky had brought Sanford to Brooklyn Family Court because he was running away from home; they couldn't control him. Nothing they did could make him stay at home. And the amazing thing was that he was running away to stay at an Orthodox synagogue and yeshiva.

His parents were what is called in the Jewish community "Conservative Jews." And, if they were at all like my family, they were "high holiday Jews," which meant they dressed up and observed a few of the less painful rituals at home and three or four of the major holidays, very much like Christians who just go to church around Easter or Christmas, put up the tree, and call it a year.

I'm sure that not all Conservative Jews are like that, but what's important here is that a serious kid is apt to see such behavior as hypocritical. I did with my family. Sanford seemed to want the pure product. Repeatedly he ran off to stay at an Orthodox yeshiva, which was two train stops away—about half a mile from his house. Each time the parents dragged him back. But each time he ran away again. Finally they called the police to come and get him out of the place, because the people at the yeshiva didn't seem to want to let Sanford go.

Three days later, the family sat around my desk for an interview. On my left, slumped in his chair, was Mr. Milton Brodsky, who looked like a giant mouse with a suit on. Next to him was Mrs. Brodsky. She was overweight, had quite a few rings and bracelets and dyed, bright-blond hair. Even before she sat down, she was taking charge of the scene. "It's drafty in here, you can catch pneumonia.

And the sun's too bright. Pull down the shade!'' When I seemed too slow getting up, she strode over to the window, slammed it down, and pulled the blinds hard. She was outrageous. I felt as if she were instantly trying to reorganize my entire cell structure. And not a word from Mr. B. I think he was traded from his mother for two thousand dollars and a first draft pick. He just sat there listening to this storm of ego burst over his head and was in his own private bomb shelter.

Next to her sat Sanford, thin and intense, with a big Jewish beak. As soon as I looked at him sitting there next to his mother, I could see what this war was all about. He was only twelve years old but he projected the energy and intellect of a grown man. He sat forward in his seat, his eyes burning like those of a mad Russian saint. I could see why this case was so unusual. It's not that often that kids in the jet age—television babies—go running off to join Orthodox Jewish sects. It just doesn't happen. And this was going on at a time when the older Orthodox Jews were disappearing rapidly, and not enough young Jews remained loyal to their rituals and beliefs. So naturally, this synagogue was happy to have Sanford. They had a dynamic and brilliant kid who wanted to live with them, and even study to be a rabbi! Sanford stared furiously at his mother, and his mother stared furiously back. You could almost see the electricity crackle between them. Next to Sanford, barely visible, was the younger sister, whose name was . . . naturally, how could I remember what her name was? She was in the silent league with her father.

As an arbitrator, I was supposed to hear everybody's story. Naturally I had to practically put a muzzle on Mrs. Brodsky to allow anyone else a chance. "So," I said, "Mr. Brodsky, what's your feeling about this situation?"

"I'll tell you what it is—I'll tell you!" Mrs. Brodsky yelled and pointed at Sanford. "It's him, he's no good, he's trying to drive me crazy, running away to those filthy rabbis!"

"She's the one who's crazy," Sanford spat back. "I don't care what she says, she can kill me! But I'm never staying with her!"

I tried to calm them down—I had no training as a family therapist and in this case Sanford and his mother were using me like a Ping-Pong ball.

"He doesn't know how much I love him." Mrs. Brodsky was in tears now.

"Oh, what bullshit!" Sanford said with disgust.

"Look how he talks to me—he's killing me. I'll put him in jail before I'll let him go to those vicious dirty Hasidim!"

Great. She loves him so much she'd have him locked up in Spofford Juvenile Detention Center in the Bronx, a real zoo. But her threats didn't matter. Sanford was in total revolution. The two of them were fighting to the death.

After almost an hour, I finally managed to get Sanford to agree to stay at home for a while, so I could investigate things further—check out the facts, talk to his teachers, all that. I even managed to get Mrs. Brodsky to agree to have the family see the court psychiatrist for an evaluation. She actually liked that idea. "Then," she said, "then we'll have it all down in black and white, how he's a juvenile delinquent."

"Oh, what crap," Sanford muttered. "I don't care what any doctor says, I'm going to stay at the yeshiva!"

Their hearing date was about three months off, in May. The judge in the case was named Selma Green. She was the first woman judge in the Brooklyn Family Court. She was the most sympathetic and intelligent judge in the system. She always tried to learn the facts of each case; she was good-hearted; she was perceptive. She was actually interested in justice, not like most of the hacks who were her colleagues. The Brodskys were lucky to have her on their case.

Judge Green had given them until May, three months, to get their house in order, to try to compromise. And, in the meantime, supervision was given to the probation department. Judge Green gave it to my boss, Mr. Johnson, and Johnson handed it to me. "Feder," he grinned, "this is a very interesting case and I think *you* should take it on."

There was a strange glint in his eye that disturbed me a little. But since he was my substitute father, I naturally said, "Sure, I'll take this case and I'll do a good job. I'll solve it for you."

Sometimes, these cases were put off—adjourned, occasionally for a year—and I wanted to resolve this one before I quit in June to take off across country to discover myself. I was determined that nothing was going to stand in the way of this journey of mine, but I also really wanted to dig into this case—to solve it.

About four or five days later Sanford came in and spoke to the psychiatrist, Dr. Klein. Dr. Klein was a tall man, obviously very smart, who had terrible nicotine stains on his fingers from smoking endless cigarettes. I think he was the worst chain-smoker I ever saw. When he wasn't smoking, his hands shook terribly. In spite of his nerves, he was the court psychiatrist and he was very smart. Sanford had a long talk with him and I even managed to persuade Mr. Mouseky and his wife, Attila the Hun, to come in and see him, too. I got the reports back about a week later. Dr. Klein verified what I had figured out myself—that Mr. and Mrs. Brodsky composed a certain family "constellation" that could probably be guaranteed to drive Sanford completely out of his mind.

I was going to get this kid out of this family. Now, I didn't tell anybody this because I was determined, like every twenty-four-year-old rookie, to appear utterly professional, in control, you see. Also, I was supposed to be objective. However, I did mention to Johnson that I was "considering" the possibility of getting Sanford out of their house and into a saner environment, maybe a foster home or something. There was something about all this that seemed to amuse him. "Spend more time on this case, Feder," he said, fiddling with his elephant paperweight and looking at me with a sly smile. "Why don't you go and talk to the rabbi? I wouldn't be so quick to judge this." I'm sure he could see immediately that I was burning in my heart to save this kid.

I knew very deep in my heart that I had already completely identified with Sanford emotionally, that I *was* this kid. He was thin, like I was, and tense. He was a revolutionary, just like I had been, too. He had a crazy mother like I did. The only difference was that whereas my father had just entirely disappeared from the house, his father had accomplished that feat emotionally. There was one more important difference between Sanford and me, but I didn't realize that till later.

After two weeks, I got a frantic call from Mrs. Brodsky. She actually had the operator interrupt a call I was already on. I always admired people who had the nerve to have an operator interrupt a call. Mrs. Brodsky jumped on the line. She was yelling hysterically that Sanford had been kidnapped by the Orthodox Jews. "You better do something about it!" she screamed. Or what? Or she's going to call the cops, she's going to burn the synagogue down, she's going to hang Sanford, or all three.

I finally managed to get her calmed down and I said, "Look, take it easy, Mrs. Brodsky. I'll get out there right now."

So I got on the train and I went out to the depths of Brooklyn. It was a part of the borough I'd never been to before—somewhere way out in Coney Island, near an elevated train. When I climbed out of the subway station, I felt as if I had been transported to old Warsaw. The signs on the stores were in Hebrew script: kosher chickens, gefilte fish, religious articles. This was the real deal. Hundreds of Orthodox Jews were walking around with various kinds of exotic hats and coats, sweating in black wool in the warm weather. And there I was with my ski boots and Levi's and my "cool" mustache—Serpico visits Jerusalem.

I should say too that I was, at the age of twenty-four, filled with contempt for people who were religious—especially Jews, since I was Jewish. You know how that works. If you were once Catholic, and you leave the church, you hate religious Catholics more than anybody else possibly could. And, if you were Jewish and decided it was hypocritical, then in the brilliant perception of your twenty-four-year-old eyes, you burned with contempt.

To me, these old fools with their long beards and their coats seemed filthy and stupid, altogether disgusting. Looking at them, I was embarrassed to be Jewish. I could actually understand, for a moment, why Mrs. Brodsky was so hysterical and resolute about the situation.

Finally I got to this place, Congregation Whateveritwas, a huge old house converted into a synagogue many years ago. Next to it was a modern three-story brick building that was the yeshiva, the live-in school for kids who studied the Orthodox religion. I knocked on the door and I was admitted. Even in the vestibule I was in another world. It was close, stuffy and cluttered, not so much dirty and messy as it was very old-fashioned, permeated with the smells of people, old books, and frying food. A woman came out, and said, with great reverence and awe in her voice, "The rabbi will see you now." I walked down two steps into the rabbi's office, a tiny room with practically no light coming in. It was in the basement of the house, so at the top of the single, small window I saw only a bit of grass and sky. Otherwise, except for an old desk lamp, it was very dark—a real scholar's den.

The place was littered with papers and books. It looked like an old junk shop, the classic old absent-minded professor's study. Stuff was piled all over the place. As I got accustomed to the dim light, I looked a little more closely and I saw many framed degrees on the wall.

Probably from the Polish Institute of Science or the Warsaw Yeshiva or something like that, I thought, not a *real* school, like NYU or Harvard.

The rabbi came in behind me and introduced himself. He was no more than about 5 foot 1 or 5 foot 2. He had a short, frizzy beard and grubby cuffs sticking out of his black coat. He smelled a little ripe. My suspicions were immediately confirmed. Aha! I told myself, I'm dealing with an old Jewish fanatic here—savages, heathens. Well, have no fear, the marines have landed—I'm getting Sanford out of here. The poor kid is obviously more deranged than I thought.

He shook my hand and we sat down across the desk from each other. He studied me. I studied him. He was a very old man, close to eighty, and somewhat crumpled. Who knows the things he'd been through in his life? He was extremely sharp-looking and bright-eyed, like a sparrow, with wrinkles around the sides of his eyes, the kind people get from being permanently amused by life. Finally I blurted out, "Where's Sanford? I've got to talk to him. He doesn't belong in a place like this. He's got to be home and you should know better than to keep him." The rabbi smiled slightly.

"Listen," I said, "the court says he's not supposed to stay here—I'm a representative of the city of New York, and I demand that you let me see him!"

He listened to me very patiently, looking me in the face, smiling, fingering his beard. Then he said, "Ah, Mr. Feder, you're Jewish?"

Instantly I got red. "Yes, I'm Jewish, but what does that have to do with anything? That means nothing. I'm here on a case, I'm an official of the city of New York! Here's my badge." I actually flashed my badge at this old rabbi. "Where's Sanford? I want to see him immediately."

There was a long pause—he just looked at me with a little smile. "Your father is Jewish?"

"Of course he's Jewish! If I'm Jewish my father is Jewish."

He says, "Mmm. You go to synagogue regularly?" By this time, he had more than a little gleam in his eye.

His questions were making me nervous, and I made a conscious effort to calm down. As he contemplated me I took a sharper look at the degrees on the wall and I saw, through the gloom of the study, that these certificates were from *American* universities. In fact, the man had a PhD in psychology from NYU and a couple of other degrees in language and philosophy from Columbia, apart from his various rabbinical degrees. Now I was more uncomfortable than ever.

"You know Mr. Feder, this is an Orthodox yeshiva," the rabbi said. "Students live here . . . and you know Sanford is a very intelligent boy. Very special." He looked at me intensely once again. "You've met Mr. Brodsky?"

"Yes."

"You've met Mrs. Brodsky?"

"Yes."

"You know, Mr. Feder, I don't know what kind of family you have. I don't know your father and mother. But since you've met Mr. and Mrs. Brodsky . . ." He leaned forward and folded his hands and said very reasonably, "They are extremely disturbed people." He used a few clinical words to describe them. "You know Mr. Brodsky—and I'm not going to put this in terms of Judaism, I'm going to put this in terms you can more clearly understand." (I caught that little personal dig.) "Mr. Brodsky is not much of a father. He doesn't really provide any leadership or male identity to Sanford, and Sanford needs this desperately. Mrs. Brodsky has already emasculated Mr. Brodsky. He is virtually useless to Sanford. The reason Sanford comes here is to be in a place where there is authority, where there is a male figure and rituals he can understand—where there are principles and faith. He needs to believe in God."

The rabbi looked at me bluntly. "There is no God, there is no man, and there is no discipline in his family, Mr. Feder. *You* must understand this. You're a man who, ah . . ." (He grinned a little.) "You're a man who has a father and knows the value of doing what his father does. You know, the son imitates the father." (This last with a very amused gleam in his eyes.)

Well, I flushed and realized this guy had really gotten my number. I was really embarrassed now. I said, "Well, you know something, I agree with you that Sanford probably does need to have more structure." I proceeded with more humility. "Tell me about the school."

He explained to me that Sanford was studying at the school and did intend to be a rabbi, that there was certainly nothing wrong with that, and naturally they weren't holding him against his will. "Not holding him against his will!"—with that phrase he gave me to understand he knew the penal code of the state of New York. "Of course, if you want to take Sanford home right now I am perfectly willing to help you." Did I want to talk to him?

I said, "Fine, let's talk to him."

By this time the old man had taken all the steam out of me. We went out and found Sanford, who was sitting at a lunch table, angry and ready to bite. He was twelve years old and in trouble, so naturally he had to maintain an attitude of total belligerence to survive.

I said, "Sanford . . ."

Nothing. He glared at me.

"Sanford, talk to the man," the rabbi said. He put his arm around him. "Sanford," he said, "Mr. Feder is a good man and he wants to help you." He looked at me meaningfully, as if to say, You'd better. I pulled up a chair. The rabbi gave me another look: Do the right thing here, or else. And with that silent command he left me alone with Sanford.

There we were, sitting at the cafeteria table in this gloomy yeshiva basement. "Sanford," I said, "you can't do this. Your mother . . ." (I thought to myself, God, I hope this kid doesn't repeat what I say.) "Sanford, I know your mother's really nuts. And I know it's awful living at home, *and* I know your father doesn't do any good for you. But you've got to go back home until I can get this done legally."

I as much as promised him right there that I would see to it in my capacity as probation officer that he would be legally removed from his family and allowed to live at this school. Now, I had no right to promise him something like this. But the rabbi and my own sense of justice in this situation got the better of me.

I could see him struggling to trust me. Finally he said, "Okay, I'll go home, but don't forget—you promised." He fixed those burning eyes on me. "I want to stay here with the rabbi."

I could see that he was completely in love with the old man and determined. "Okay," I said. "Let's go." I got him his jacket, and I said good-bye to the rabbi. He shook my hand and sent me another message: I hope you know what you're doing. Jewish telepathy. You realize that you're dealing with somebody who's just like yourself, so be generous and be just.

I took Sanford back to his house on the bus. His crazy mother answered the door and practically pulled his arm off yanking him inside. As she slammed the door I saw his face holding me to my promise. Seeing this, I was more resolved than ever that I would get him out of this house.

Just as I arrived back at my office, Mrs. Brodsky called me to say I should arrest the rabbi. I said, "Sure, sure, let me look into it."

I got out the psychological study. I read all the previous history. I worked way overtime and prepared a really beautiful written report. I showed it to Johnson and he said, "Good, but keep working on it."

Well, three or four weeks went by and I was sniffing summer in the air. It was late April and I was mentally preparing for my cross-country trip. The closer it came to the trip, the more I burned with images of me on the road, leaving all the oppression of New York behind. The date for Sanford's hearing was only a few weeks or so away and I hadn't heard a word from the family. This was unusual. Then one day Mrs. Brodsky called. She said, with definite triumph in her voice, "We've sold the house and we're moving." I was really angry. She was pulling a fast one here, moving all the way out to Long Island so that Sanford would physically not be able to get back to Brooklyn. They had gotten a house in Farmingdale—all the way out on the island. They didn't trust him and they didn't trust anybody else either. She had this move planned the whole time they were dealing with me.

Mrs. Brodsky must have suspected that I was the enemy. She had probably detected the passion of rescue in my eyes. So, bang! Sanford was gone and enrolled in a public school on Long Island. But despite her move, the Brooklyn court still had jurisdiction.

I constructed a perfect case. Like Clarence Darrow in the Monkey Trial, I was going to present irrefutable evidence to Judge Green. First, I had to present the evidence to Johnson. If there was one redeeming thing I could do before I left this job, I told him, I could save Sanford from the kind of fate I had—a crazy mother and a useless father. After my confession to Johnson, he grinned his usual grin and said, "Don't you think you're getting a little personally involved in this case, Feder?"

I said, "Well, I may be personally involved, but still it's the right thing to do. You saw the psychiatric report and you have the history." I had laid out very lucidly in great detail and very persuasively, I hoped, how this kid *had* to be rescued from his family, and the rabbi given custody. As far as I was concerned, it was open and shut.

Johnson listened very carefully and told me to check a few more details and type the report.

At the beginning of May, only one week before court, I got a frantic call from Mrs. Brodsky. "He's run away again!" She was screaming and cursing at me, at the rabbi, and at Sanford.

What happened was that Sanford had stolen money from his mother's pocketbook, gotten on the Long Island Railroad, and made it all the way back to Brooklyn to the rabbi—and there he was.

I said to Mrs. Brodsky, "Well, that's just terrible. I'm going to have to look into this."

All the time I was thinking, "All right! Way to go, kid!" I felt a tremendous sense of vicarious triumph. He actually did it, I thought. Here I had lived with a terrible mother just like his, but I always gave in. I stayed at home, I stayed in my room, I got sick, I complained. But Sanford was having none of it. This kid, twelve years old, refused to take it. He was going to assert himself—to get what he needed.

I called the yeshiva and spoke to the rabbi. He said Sanford refused to leave. He was not going home. He said he'd rather go to jail. The rabbi thought Sanford would probably do something violent if anybody tried to get him out of there.

I called up Mrs. Brodsky and told her: "Listen, if we go in there and try to drag this kid out he's going to hurt himself or hurt somebody else and he will go to jail." I described in detail what the jail was like.

Amazingly enough, she calmed down and said, "Okay, he can stay there, but I am going to obtain a court order with my lawyer in about a week or so and he's going to come back and live here and that's that. I'll have this rabbi arrested, locked up for kidnapping."

She was deadly serious. "Give him a week," I said. "The case is coming up, and then we'll see what we can do." Of course I didn't tell her what my recommendation would be.

Just one day before Sanford was supposed to appear in court, I arranged a special appointment with Judge Green to discuss the case. I was in a courtroom paneled in blond wood. High above me sat the judge in her back robes. Next to her was her assistant, a beautiful dark-haired law clerk with sad eyes.

The courtroom was completely empty, and I stood in front of the bench, arguing as if I were in front of the Supreme Court, with more passion than I'd ever done anything before. I had the report in my hand and I walked back and forth illustrating the case, inflamed with righteousness.

I read all the reports to her. If she needed any clarification she'd hold up her hand. I spoke for about an hour and a half, taking up her precious time, trying to persuade her that this kid *had* to be taken out of his house: "You can see," I said, "the psychiatrist states these people will drive him crazy. I'm not religious myself, Your Honor, but I believe that this rabbi provides the male figure he desperately needs. You have to give the rabbi and the yeshiva custody." I finished and stood there vibrating.

The judge held up her hand and said in her calm, deliberate way that she wanted to think about it for a while. Feverishly I waited as she pondered silently for a few minutes. Then she called me forward: "You know, Mr. Feder, you're absolutely right. I can see that you're dedicated, that you really believe in what you're saying, and I have the psychiatrist's report here, telling me that this child is probably in serious emotional difficulty if he stays in that home, but, Mr. Feder, I hate to say this to you—the law is on the mother's side. The law leaves no doubt that he's got to remain in the house. I'll tell you now that I'm going to have to decide for the mother. I will continue custody of Sanford to his parents."

I was staggered. For a moment I was speechless, then I exploded. "Judge Green, you don't understand! They're going to drive this kid nuts!" I felt like saying, "They drove *me* nuts." I said, "You don't understand, Judge. They're going to kill this kid. He's a valuable kid. He's intelligent. He's smart. You can't do this!" I lost all restraint. Any distinction between myself and Sanford was obliterated.

After a moment she held up her hands and said, "I'm sorry, Mr. Feder, but that's the way the law is. It's tragic to know that this boy's life will probably be damaged even more in the next few years, but there's nothing I can do about it."

I was really angry now. "Jesus Christ," I said, "that's ridiculous!" I was holding the report, and shaking with disgust. "Okay, that's it." And I walked out of the courtroom without saying another word.

I was very depressed.

Johnson asked, "What's wrong with you?"

"They're going to leave this kid in the house!" I practically screamed. "Can you believe it? They're going to leave Sanford with his parents! They'll drive him out of mind."

"I know," he said.

And then I poured it out, my whole life story, to Johnson, my substitute father. How *my* father left, how my mother had spent her life in and out of mental hospitals. Everything.

Then for the first time he got serious—no more grin. "Well, you know," he said, "I put you on this case because I knew you could do a good job on it. I knew that the kid probably should be taken out, and to tell you the truth I hoped maybe if you, being very much like Sanford, presented it to the judge, she might do the right thing. But I also knew . . ." Johnson shook his head. "I also knew from the beginning that the law was all on her side."

"You shouldn't have given me the goddamned case in the first place!" I yelled, pacing the office, looking for some inanimate, or animate, object to punch. Johnson just smiled a little. "Maybe you learned something," he said. He patted me on the shoulder but I was too miserable for comfort and understanding.

I went home and sat in my apartment with shades drawn.

The next day I called up the yeshiva and told the rabbi what the decision would be. He didn't agree with it, but he said he understood. He said, "Well, all right, Mr. Feder, I'll tell Sanford." He didn't react the way I thought he would. With the rabbi's influence, Sanford went home. The final hearing was postponed until the third week of May. I was disgusted with the whole system. I felt there was no justice and I could feel Sanford's eyes on me. Broken promises.

In the next several days, I wrapped up all my other cases. At the appointed time I appeared in court. It was all over very quickly—the judge gave absolute custody to the parents. Although the judge read my recommendations, I wasn't allowed to say anything. Sanford refused to speak to me—he just glared straight ahead with tears in his eyes. After the gavel went down, Mrs. Brodsky looked at me in triumph. I wanted to kill her. She took Sanford's arm and pulled him out of court, her foolish husband bringing up the rear. Shit.

I went upstairs and sat at my desk staring at the wall. I felt like my entire tenure at the place had been a waste. I had failed Sanford. I had betrayed him.

Well, about a week went by and on my next-to-last day on the job, my co-workers bought me a cake and threw me a party. No party could change my mood. About three in the afternoon, while we were "celebrating," a call came in. I picked up the phone and I heard somebody say, "Just a minute," and who got on the phone but Sanford Brodsky. He said, "I'm back here in Brooklyn with the rabbi and nobody is ever getting me out of here." Then he hung up.

I got off the phone with tears in my eyes, and I turned to Johnson, sitting there eating my farewell cake. "The kid did it! He did it! Nobody is ever going to keep him away from that place." I was overjoyed. Johnson just smiled.

On the way home from the office I was elated. There are people in this world whose desire to get what they need, I thought, just to get out there and go toward it, no matter what, is overwhelming. Nothing will stop it. They are like grass cracking through concrete. I could see Sanford riding the train back from Long Island, the ticket clutched in his hand, see him sitting in the yeshiva, the rabbi's arm around his shoulders. I wished then that I had a lot more Sanford Brodsky in me.

The next day was my last. I packed the stuff in my desk and said good-bye to everybody. Johnson shook my hand a little too hard. He told me I was wasting my life running off cross-country "like a hippie." I know he wanted me to stay on. I don't know why I didn't. I had lived twice as long as Sanford Brodsky, but during those extra twelve years I couldn't ever seem to discover *my* rabbi, or feel that strong arm around *my* shoulders.

THE HOSPITAL

The summer of 1971, the summer that Attica blew up, I went crazy. I wasn't working. My home life was a complete disaster. The whole summer was the slow, inevitable process of going crazy. At the end of August I was sufficiently over the edge to make even looking for work impossible. I couldn't function at all and I was having frequent and increasingly frightening hallucinations. I started to lose track of time. At night I would lie in my bed and I couldn't remember where my hands and feet were. I woke up every morning around five and was immediately very anxious.

Now, when you're in the process of losing your mind, time expands so that every minute seems like an eternity. Imagine the usual twenty-four hours in which you dress, make breakfast, go to work, have dinner, make love, construct a model sailboat, whatever—it flies by. But when you're sliding into insanity and you're out of work because you can't work, you experience every second ticking by. Time is an endless desert in which you wander searching for a plant or a drop of water. Along with this is a sort of agoraphobia—fear of open places. The future stretches before you, an expanse of white haze.

I was committed to Kings County Hospital the night of September 16, a Saturday night and, coincidentally, exactly one year to the day that I had moved in with my girlfriend.

That morning I woke up in a cold sweat, terrified; I felt like my voice was separate from my body. I got on the bus to visit my girlfriend at work. I desperately needed to hold on to someone. I was having hallucinations.

Now, you may imagine you've had hallucinations but if you've ever really had them it's something you don't mistake, or ever forget. Material objects bend and change into other shapes, usually into threatening things. I was walking down the street, keeping close to the walls of buildings, and all of a sudden a light pole would bend in half and turn all the colors of the rainbow. Maybe under other circumstances such a sight could have been ecstatic but then it was just further proof that I was being attacked from all sides. Everybody and everything was after me. Do you remember Walt Disney's *Alice in Wonderland*—when she first enters the other world? She's out in this forest in the dark of night and all the trees have frightening faces— their branches become arms and try to grab her. That's just how I felt then.

On the bus, I looked up from a book I was trying to read and was convinced that every eye on the bus was boring into me. The eyes were all red like the eyes of wolves or the eyes of people caught in flashbulb pictures—demon eyes. Then their teeth started to grow out of their mouths, sharp and white. Everybody on that midtown bus looked like a wolf ready to tear my throat out. Naturally, I wanted to avoid that. The real danger of course was not from them but from me. If I was threatened by predators it occurred to me it might be a good idea to get them first. When your nightmares start to play in broad daylight you are in serious trouble. However, I still had enough reason left to get up and tell the bus driver to let me off. He took one look at me and stopped the bus between stops and opened the door. I jumped out.

My poor girlfriend couldn't figure out what was going on. She left her office and talked with me on the street. She came from a family where no one had this experience, let alone even visited a therapist. For her, it happened to other people and wasn't it a shame. ". . . the Smith family, yes, it's a pity, they had to put her away. . . ."

I told her I felt like I was going to die—I was losing my mind. She said, "You have to get a grip on yourself!"

"How?"

"Just calm down and do one thing at a time; go to the bathroom and shave, go to the kitchen and make a cup of coffee."

I held on to her. Finally she said, "You'd better go home. I'll try to leave work early."

At home, in bed, I couldn't calm down. I was getting worse. After what seemed like years she came back from work. I was crying, "It's useless. First my mother, now me!"

She said, "That doesn't mean you have to imitate her."

"I can't help it," I said. "You don't understand, my whole family is crazy!"

She was getting angry now. "Just control yourself!"

I yelled back at her: "You fucking Christian Scientist!"

I smashed my hand down on the kitchen table. She went into the bathroom.

"Here, you'd better take these," she said. She handed me a couple of mild tranquilizers that had been lying around for a few months. I took them and lay down. The minutes stretched out like days.

She came into the bedroom and sat next to me. I held her hand. She had tears in her eyes. "What can I do?" she asked.

"I don't know."

"If you could only find something to do, even a simple job."

"I can't, don't you see what's going on? I can hardly leave the house!"

The truth was, being out of work couldn't be blamed for pulling me under. My caving in was really the culmination of the whole pattern of my life: fear and passivity. My relationship with my girlfriend was a mess; she was very sure of herself, very confident, and I gave in to her 100 percent of the time. All I ever wanted to do was avoid trouble—avoid life, really.

"What do you want for dinner?"

"I don't know, whatever you want." If she had said "broiled shoe" I'd have said "okay." I did everything she wanted and at this point I didn't care anymore. She sighed and went out again. I could hear her making noise in the kitchen.

I hadn't slept for two or three days—I didn't even bother to look in the mirror because I probably would have scared myself to death. I got up and went into the kitchen. My girlfriend was standing at the sink washing vegetables and I looked over her head at the rack of carving knives. I walked over and started to put my hand out to one of the knives. I thought it would be a very good idea—it seemed perfectly reasonable to me at the time—to kill her and then kill myself. This would solve all my problems.

When you're suffering so badly, it occurs to you that if you kill yourself or kill somebody else, naturally that will stop time. It's the only way you can stop the clock and the calendar from moving because only death stops time, at least the time that you're living in.

She turned around from the sink and she knew something was wrong—wrong beyond repair. "What is it?" she asked.

"I need to go away someplace. I cannot stay here anymore."

That was it. She had had enough. She'd been trying as hard as she could to handle me—to try to help me get over my madness. She tried to be friendly, kind, nasty, angry—anything she could figure out to get me through it—but it wasn't working.

She called up my psychiatrist and my father as well, my father not just for moral support but perhaps for some physical restraint—she sensed I was dangerous.

We got on the phone with the psychiatrist. He kept asking me questions, but I could hardly understand him. I had no sense of responsibility. No judgment.

He said to me, "Do you think you need to go to the hospital?"

"Sure," I said, "yes."

But really I had a vague wish that he would offer me some other way to save myself. I wanted him to say, "Why don't you go out to live with your father?" or "Here are some stronger pills, I'll come visit you"—you know, some putting himself out, some personal extending of himself. Well, it didn't happen.

"I'll call Kings County and tell them you're coming in," he said.

"Okay," said my girlfriend, "I'll call his father."

My father drove in from Long Island and they took me over to Kings County Hospital.

So there I was on a Saturday night in September in the admitting room downstairs. The paint was green and peeling, the benches broken and scarred. I was almost incoherent and yet I had the sensation that somebody was finally going to take care of me. All I wanted then was a massive dose of drugs. I got to the point—this must be what a junkie feels—when all I wanted with every cell in my body was to be at peace. I hadn't slept more than a few hours that past week. The muscles and tendons and ligaments all over my body were stretched like bowstrings and I felt that if something wasn't done for me soon I would literally explode. I needed to be unconscious.

They walked me into a tiny office, and behind a scratched old metal desk there was this poor pitiful doctor, a psychiatrist-in-training, a very young guy, and I'm sure to this day his name was Dr. Jerkoff. This poor mama's boy was handling rapists, and ax-murderers, and people who thought they were God, and he looked like he was still eating buttered bread and chicken soup in his mother's kitchen.

So Dr. Jerkoff, no older than I was, asked me a lot of textbook questions. Psychiatrists are always so detached and intellectual. This guy was discussing my insanity with me as if I were perfectly sane. He'd ask me very reasonable, intelligent questions about my condition, which I attempted to answer when all I wanted was to lay my head in somebody's lap and have them feed me cookies. Dr. Jerkoff finally realized I needed to be admitted to Kings County Hospital. And while I was talking to him, the cops were bringing people in—they were screaming and throwing up on the floor, some of them were covered with blood. Saturday night *and* it was a full moon!

Right away I see that I am entering a different world. I'm going into a place where most of the people were *poor*. I was lower middle class, and my girlfriend grew up rich. Men and women were screaming and yelling, some in Spanish, and the cops were shouting and throwing them against the walls. My girlfriend had never seen anything like this—never. I felt so sorry for her. She was bewildered but trying to do her best for me.

Just before they took me upstairs to do who knows what to me, she came in to see me one last time. I lay alone in a room on one of those rolling metal tables. She came over to me, and touched me on the shoulder. I could see that, down-to-earth person that she was, she had the idea that just her touch, that one last touch of her love, could save me. She touched my face and kissed me. I looked at her and I wanted to say, "Yes, let's try, you can save me, you can do it." But immediately following this urge I had a more powerful feeling—I just didn't care anymore. I didn't care about her. I didn't care what happened to anybody as long as I got my dope, a massive injection of something to put me out. I needed to be unconscious more than I needed her—more than I needed life itself. To this day I'll always remember that look on her face . . . she was trying in some magic, mute way to rescue me, to pull me back, but it didn't work.

They took me upstairs and wheeled me through at least twelve locked doors that banged shut behind me. It was like being in prison. A couple of years before I had worked in the probation department. I had been in prisons before, been locked in cells behind massive metal doors. Now, here I was on the other end of it—locked in.

They put me in a hospital gown that didn't really cover me. You know those things. I felt embarrassed, reduced to a kind of generic blot. I was in a huge overcrowded dayroom. They got me off the table and I stood against a wall. Off the hallways were rooms with several beds crowded together. For some reason the beds were very high off the floor—even more, it seemed, than regular hospital beds. A lot of them had heavy leather straps on them. The whole ward was very crowded, with people pacing back and forth. Every description of humanity was in there, and they were *nuts*. These people were really crazy—and so was *I!*

A lot were talking to themselves. One guy kept grabbing the fire extinguisher off the wall and the attendants began to beat him up. They finally put him in a straitjacket. That was horrible! He couldn't move and he had *no* power over it whatsoever. Awful—I watched that and consciously decided not to cause any disturbance.

In Kings County Hospital, on the ward, you learned very fast—a speeded-up process of education—that if you did something wrong, if you broke the rules, you were in *a lot of trouble*. And it was going to hurt. I did not scream or yell or break anything. What I did was withdraw.

Still against the wall, I sat down on my knees, like an Asian peasant—war exploding all around me. I stayed in the hallway and I watched everybody. I became The Watcher.

A kid came over to me, maybe eighteen or nineteen years old, very pale, with long blond hair, very tall. He looked to me like those pictures you see of Jesus Christ in old illustrated Bibles.

Sure enough, he bent down and said, "I see that you're troubled."

I had nothing to say. I felt like a tiny animal looking out of the darkness from the underbrush.

He said, "Don't worry, for I am Jesus Christ, and I can help you. I can take away your problems."

I just stared at him and after a while he wandered off. I wasn't going to give *him* my problems—after all I was Jewish. If I'm going to go crazy I'd rather have Moses come help me. Jesus went down the hall to tend his flock.

Some guys still had blood on them. A few of them were strapped to their beds, one or two in straitjackets. Other people were pounding on the walls, screaming, "I didn't mean to do it" or "I'll kill you, I'll kill you."

The ward attendants were *vicious*—it was clear that they were recruited to restrain lunatics and if I got out of line they would hit me fast with their hands or a drug or maybe with a straitjacket. They were taking no shit from anybody. I'll tell you, I had seen a lot of cops and correction guards who were renowned for their violence, but ward attendants in public mental hospitals had to head the list of vicious evil bastards. They were treating people like dogs, not one trace of kindness in them.

Some time around nine o'clock—after what seemed like days— there was an announcement of medication. This was what I had been waiting for. I was keeping my cool. I was not speaking too extensively to Jesus. I was not interrupting anybody with blood on them. I was staying in my own little corner, like a good little squirrel. They herded us into a room. After a long wait, I got a huge shot of Thorazine. They shot me in the ass and put me into a room, right next to the guy with the most blood on him.

For some reason they did not wash the blood off this guy. Maybe it was inadvisable to touch him because he was pretty wild. He had an extra strap over his ankles. He was yelling in Spanish—which I knew a little of from working in the welfare department—screaming, "I'm sorry I killed her." He screamed all night long until they gave him I don't know how many shots of Thorazine. "I didn't kill her, I didn't kill her"—and I'm thinking, "Oh Jesus, what has happened to me?" I didn't mean the Jesus in the next room, I meant the real Jesus.

Maybe an hour after I had gotten to sleep, I had the urge to urinate. I was so full of Thorazine that I had to guide myself along the walls. I stumbled a few times. The place was very brightly lit. I walked down the hall to the bathroom, a huge room, with rows of urinals. I remember standing in front of the urinal. Then I was on the floor. I felt a slight aching throb in my foot.

Next I was being carried, picked up off the ground by the attendants. They put me back in my bed next to the man who didn't kill her, who was still mumbling his confession in his sleep. By now, he's got the sheets all covered with blood. As they threw me down on the bed they told me, "Don't get up again!"

But I needed to get up. After all, I may have been crazy but I wasn't going to embarrass myself. So I made my way to the bathroom again and before I even got past the door once again I fell over— unconscious.

They picked me up off the floor and screamed, "We told you not to
get up again—shit!" I was thrown onto a rolling metal trolley which
they put under the brightest light in the place for the rest of the night.

After a while, the drug started to wear off and as I lay under this
light, unable to go to sleep, unable to put my arms anywhere, with the
guards playing cards with the nurses in the back, I felt there was
something wrong with my foot. I looked down and sure enough, two
of my toes were turning purple. One at least was certainly broken. I
spent the rest of the night fixed under that glaring light.

In the morning we got plastic spoons and plastic forks and were told
to line up. We got some cereal which I couldn't even look at. I had no
use for food whatsoever. All through breakfast time, everybody was
walking around, cursing, mumbling, throwing food. Jesus Christ was
preaching, but nobody was listening to him.

There is nothing that will make you crazier than being in a mental
hospital. Life can make you crazy, your girlfriend can make you crazy,
your job can make you crazy, your husband or wife, your mother,
violence or rape can—but nothing will ever make you crazier than
being locked in a mental hospital ward. I knew I had to get out of
there.

Now, I had been told by my doctor—who was a member of the
faculty of Downstate Medical Center right across the street, and a
much saner place than Kings County—that he could get a bed for me
there *sometime*, he wasn't sure when. About three that afternoon, a
doctor showed up and decided that they could find a bed for me over
there.

I tried to act very normal—you know, like in the movies, "I'm not
crazy, I'm just fine . . . everything's okay, sure, ha ha, look, the
weather, very nice, eh?" I was trying to be extremely polite so they
would let me out of this place.

Finally, my father showed up to sign me out. They had to have a
relative to do this. In a few minutes I was out and my father was
walking me across the street to Downstate Medical Center.

It was strange; I had left Kings County, a Gothic horror dungeon,
and I went out past these huge smokestacks—something I imagined
from Nazi Germany—past all these vicious guards and locked doors,
vomit and blood. I got outside, and suddenly I was in a courtyard, a
beautiful garden—trees, plants, flowers—straight from a nightmare to

an oasis. My father and I walked through this place to get across the street to the other hospital. As I was walking through the garden with my father, I looked at him and felt a tremendous feeling of love. I looked up at him and thought, although I never said anything, Why doesn't he take me home with him? His wife (his second wife) had left him, about a year before. He was living alone. I felt so strongly that no matter how far I had gone, I would not go any further, that I could heal from that day forward if he would drive me out to his house on Long Island and take care of me. "The hell with all these hospitals, kid, let's just get in the car." But he didn't say it.

So the moment passed. He asked me, "How are you?" I thought to myself, not so bad, but why didn't I say it? Why? Because that was part of my illness—never saying what I wanted. We walked over to Downstate and we went in.

As I was checked in he said, "Don't tell them that I'm your father. Don't mention my name." Why? Because this poor guy, for the last twenty or thirty years of his life, had been paying heavily for people who went crazy. First my mother, then his second wife, and then his stepdaughter. He was thirty thousand dollars in debt already, borrowing money to keep people in psychiatrists and institutions. Naturally, the first thing I did at the reception desk was mention his name. He never said anything about it later, but I knew he was sad I had done it. He took it as a betrayal. In the end, though, he was lucky because it turned out that I had medical insurance from a previous job which paid 80 percent of everything. I paid the rest. Nevertheless I put his name down on every form—a kind of unconscious last-ditch revenge for his abandoning me to this hospital.

I was admitted to Downstate—a very different place from Kings County. It was a private hospital with private rooms, and very few patients—no more than twenty-four, sometimes as few as sixteen. There were a lot of nurses and attendants. Everything was more "pleasant," all neat and clean. In fact, it was a little bit like staying in a hotel except the rooms were too small. However, it wasn't really the Holiday Inn because, of course, you know you're crazy.

When they checked me in, they asked me if I felt like killing myself, and I told them, "Yes." So for about forty-eight hours after that they watched me every minute. Have you had an experience like that as an adult, where somebody is detailed to watch every single move you make? Where they look in when you're sleeping, maybe every fifteen or twenty minutes, just to make sure you're not killing yourself? It was very strange, but necessary at the time.

The first night, they put me on some medication which was much lighter than I got across the street in the snake pit. That wasn't too good for me because I was left alone with my mind still ticking.

After the shock wore off, the first feeling I had was an overwhelming sense of shame. I come from a certain cultural level, and everybody in my old neighborhood (with the exception of my mother) was very straight and sober. Any of these people would have considered it a failure to go crazy—to give up like that. My father, who worked his way up from nothing, was very poor during the Depression, went to school at night, worked like a horse, and would never have given in this way. But *I* did give in and I was filled with shame.

Also I thought constantly about my girlfriend. If there was one thing that was going to drive me to do myself in, it was thinking of that look in her eyes, those sad tears coming down when she kissed me that last time. I thought to myself: There she is, home alone without me, wondering what on earth she had done or not done to let me go crazy. I wondered what she would do now.

Also, I had always sworn that I would not be like my mother, who had been in and out of institutions her whole life. You know how it is if you have a parent who was a drunk, a lunatic, or a mean son of a bitch, whatever it was, how you resolve you're not going to be like that? Right? Well, it did happen to me. I had become just like her—to my great shame. It later (much later) occurred to me that going crazy was, maybe, a declaration of love for her: "See Mom, I'm just like you." Imitation is truly the sincerest form of flattery.

It is a constant necessity for nurses and doctors in the hospital to reassure you. They have this "shame" problem with almost everybody: severe cultural shame at being "in a place," an institution, the nut house—giving in, failing, the work ethic finally hitting a stone wall. So they are always reassuring you, but it doesn't do much good. You know in your gut the only thing that's going to make you feel *not* ashamed, *not* guilty, is to get out of there. To get out on the street and take the bus like other people do, to walk in and out of your house, to brush your teeth—the common chores of life. There is something about being twenty-five years old and practically having your diapers changed by a nurse that is not compatible with any notion of adult self-respect.

After a couple of days, when they had taken me off the suicide watch, I noticed, after the curtain of fear and drugs lifted, that I had a roommate. He was an extraordinary-looking man named Sheldon. I say man because he was twenty-four and masculine, but that's as far as that goes. He was a giant baby. He was bald, smooth, weighed about 270 pounds, and he was in a crib! He had abandoned the grown-up world long ago. Sheldon stayed in that crib the whole time and never really got up. He constantly smiled and nodded. The nurses came in to feed him and clean up after him.

The first couple of days I spent looking at my shoes and then looking at Sheldon, looking out the window and then looking over at Sheldon again. His mother visited regularly twice a day. A tiny little old lady; she'd go over to his bed and say, "How's my little Sheldon?" Then she would kiss him on the mouth! The strangest thing I ever saw—a big long kiss on the mouth.

About seven nights after I was admitted they woke me up about two in the morning by making a lot of noise. They were moving Sheldon and his crib out of the room. The next day I heard that he died. He just died in his sleep. I heard a nurse say he was receiving medical treatment for some terminal illness. His death had been expected.

His mother came in to clean up after him. She looked around the room, picked up some of his belongings, and said to me, "Don't worry, darling, everything will be all right."

I didn't know what she was talking about—everything was *not* all right. And yet as she stood where Sheldon's crib had been, smiling at me, I had a quick, tiny sensation that everything *would* be all right. I tried to say something: "I hope . . ."

"Don't worry, darling," she told me again. "Shh . . . everything will be all right." And she hobbled out.

Sheldon's death had really jolted me. To be in a room with somebody who dies in the middle of the night is very sobering. And I assumed, in the midst of my craziness, that he had died from being *insane*. I believed that your mind could just shut off if it was too diseased; and then your body would die too. This shock knocked me back slightly in the direction of sanity.

But I had a long way to go. I had constant hallucinations. People's teeth grew out of their mouths, their eyes turned red—the nurses' teeth especially were like fangs. But, no matter how frightening these visions were, I never ran. I always had a sense of propriety in my insanity. I didn't panic. I just walked very quickly to my room and shut the door to make sure they didn't bite me.

So, there I was, hallucinating, tight as a clenched fist, drowning in shame, but I did achieve something positive. After twenty-five years of saying, "Yes, whatever you say, sure" to everybody, I decided to say, "No thank you, I prefer not to." I decided I didn't want to see my girlfriend or my father. I wanted nothing to do with them, I told the doctor. They called up the hospital and tried to visit but (I still feel bad about this) they were told I couldn't have any visitors. And that negation was the first recognizable step that I *was somebody*—a some-body who had the right to say, "No I don't want to."

I had regular sessions every day with a psychologist. That was supposed to help you get straight. Of course it rarely ever did. As an adjunct to this they would have group therapy, which was actually much more helpful. Six or seven people in a room would discuss how they felt about being in the hospital. How ashamed they were, how angry, who they hated on the outside, and why. But most important, we talked of what we would do when we got out. The rest of the treatment was based on reminding you what it was like on the outside—as a citizen of the "normal" world.

They had a regular activity called community meeting; the whole ward had to attend. Every day they'd drag us out of our rooms; no matter if we were standing there talking to the devil or painting pictures of flying penises, it was an absolute rule, we had to go to these meetings.

The community meeting was interesting. It was patterned after the old-fashioned American town meeting. You talked about conditions on the ward. Everybody voted and committees were formed. There was even a president elected. It was actually very much the way you'd treat kids—everybody got a chance to be the boss, everybody got to play with the blocks. So, every once in a while someone new would be elected president of the community board of the "mental" ward of Downstate Medical Center.

I was elected president once. I think I got 70 percent of the vote, although I didn't spend much money on my campaign—just about two dollars for chewing gum.

The idea of course was to guide you back into the American version of middle-class sanity. Democracy as normal. We even had field trips, on the *Outside!*

The nurses and the missing links (male attendants) took us to the Coney Island Aquarium. There we were, people who actually thought *they* were fish going to visit fish. Of course I was scared to go, but then, I was scared of everything and everybody.

We all had buddies like school kids; we had to hold hands. I was holding Sharon's hand. Sharon was tall and gangly with dark brown hair. Her mind had been burned out by LSD. She had the habit of wearing at least three different sets of clothes in the course of the day—hippie-type long dresses with frills, and endless amounts of jewelry. She had earrings, nose rings, rings on every single finger and toe, and several bracelets on each wrist. She looked like a gypsy trapped in a costume jewelry store. She had that special 1960s vacant, love-drug smile.

We got out of the train on Coney Island Avenue, a big boulevard. Everybody in the group crossed; Sharon crossed; but they couldn't get *me* to cross. The light turned green and red and green again, but I wouldn't go. The nurses were pushing me and pulling me. "It's okay," they told me. "See, there's no cars coming." No use. I wouldn't move. A male attendant grabbed my arm. "C'mon, kid." I shook my head. I looked in both directions a hundred times. It's true, I didn't see any cars coming either, but I did see other things. The street seemed very dangerous to me, like a raging stream of water with sharks in it. I could feel them out there snapping and biting and I was *not* going to step out in it. Finally, though, they managed to convince me that it was okay. "We'll protect you," they said. So I let two nurses help me across the street.

We went into the aquarium, and lo and behold, there were *regular people* there! Grown-ups, children. People not in hospitals. It was like returning to Earth after being shut up in a spaceship for years.

Sharon and I walked into a room where there were penguins swimming in a huge tank, behind a big clear piece of glass. I was holding Sharon's hand and she was smiling. "Oh what a beautiful place, look at the tiles—far out." She was talking too loud, I could tell.

"Shh," I told her.

She tugged on my hand. "C'mon Mike, I wanna see the penguins up close." She was like my little sister.

And there standing in front of the plate glass was this family—a man, a woman, and a child. The father's saying to his little daughter, "Look dear, that's a penguin. They live at the South Pole."

It was heartbreaking to see this. I knew *they* were going to go home afterwards. I knew that the father and mother kissed each other at night. They'd maybe have sex. They'd eat together, go out to the movies, and I was going back to a room to get an injection, to talk to other people who thought they were animals and wanted to kill themselves. I felt cursed, like Moses unable to enter the Promised Land.

Sharon let go of my hand, walked over, and elbowed the mother and the father aside. They looked at her. She put her face up to the glass and a penguin swam up and connected with her immediately. They looked at each other for a moment. "Hello, penguin," she said. "I know you. Where have you been? I've been in the hospital."

I hurried over and grabbed her hand. "Sharon, c'mon."

But this was too much for the father and mother. "Hm-hm," he said. "Let's, let's, uh, go to the next room, honey . . ."

"Yes, let's." And they were gone.

Sharon looked at me with a big smile. "Why did they leave?" she asked. She turned and called after them. "Why did you go?"

You have to understand; she knew why they left and she even knew she was acting crazy. Yet there is a blind spot—a huge blind spot—a blend of immense need and a desire to be taken care of on one hand, and a feeling of great hatred and rage against families on the other. These things combine to make people who are crazy very charming and very scary at the same time. Like dangerous children. So Sharon and I were left in front of the glass, holding hands, alone with the penguins.

A penguin swam up and stared at me. "See," said Sharon, "they know us, they're just like us!" I stared back at the penguin.

At that point I had been in the hospital for several weeks. I was a veteran. In fact, that's why I was Sharon's buddy. I was actually more sane—more responsible—than her. I was there to look after her.

"No we're not," I said.

"What?"

"We're not like them. They're just penguins, we're people."

"I don't feel good," Sharon said after a pause. "I have to find the nurse." She dropped my hand and ran out of the room.

I had the same trouble crossing the street again. "C'mon Mike, it's only a street with cars!" On the bus I sat next to Sharon, who fell asleep with her head on my shoulder, glad to be going back to the ward.

After we'd been there a couple of weeks they let us go down to the lobby of the hospital to get chewing gum and candy from the vending machines. That was always an adventure, especially when you're first committed, because if you think that everybody's trying to kill you and you want to kill yourself, it's no simple matter to take the elevator to the lobby unaccompanied and mix with other people. It was better if you knew you were going to get something for the nurse instead of yourself. Since you'd become a child you actually wanted to do things for your mommy—the nurse.

The head nurse at Downstate was terrific. Her name was Linda—a huge woman, almost six feet, a little hefty, but very sexy. Married (I hated that). She had a tremendous amount of patience and boundless sympathy. Linda was the sort of person who just touched you and you felt better. She knew very well that she was dealing with grown people who were temporarily children; she treated us with patient kindness but with respect as well.

One night, about two in the morning, I was very agitated. I went over to Linda at the nurses' station, and I said, "I feel like killing myself." And I really did.

She looked at me with her calm smile and said, "Go in the kitchen and have some milk and cookies. You'll feel better."

So I did. I went into the ward kitchen and poured myself a glass of milk, telling myself all the while that Linda gave me permission to do this. I took a couple of cookies, and I felt completely at peace.

A woman like that, who could, in the face of a suicide threat, tell you to go have milk and cookies, is worth a hundred psychiatrists. If there is one thing I learned from that stay in the hospital, it's that when you're dealing with people who are out of their minds, an absolutely necessary quality to have is flexibility. If you can't switch back and forth between intuition and intellect with the grace of a ballet dancer, then you're not cut out for the work. Linda was born with this ability. If you wanted to be treated like an adult, she could instantly sense it, and she would talk to you reasonably. If you needed milk and cookies, she realized it immediately—practically telepathically. She always had the right touch, something that is a rarity among most therapists.

Another person who helped me get back into what was hopefully described as the normal world was the janitor, a very old black guy from the South, in his late sixties. He never did tell me his name. After the day of community meetings, three-piece doctor suits, and Thorazine, he would sweep up the ward. He came in around midnight after everyone was asleep, tucked away in their little rooms. He had a kind of a sweet-smelling chemical confetti—disinfectant—that he spread on the floor.

Sometimes I'd wake up in the middle of the night. (I was one of the few patients who could not sleep. They could pump a hundred chemicals into me and throw a pail of Valium down my throat—I just couldn't sleep.) These times I would go into the community room. It was completely dark except for the TV which I'd watch without the sound on. And the old man would be there sweeping up. The nurses were at their station at the other end of the hall, writing up their reports. All the poor souls were in their cocoons asleep. I was sitting there watching some movie. I could hear the sounds of the old man's mop and brush on the floor. He came over to me. "How you doin'?"

"Not good," I said.

"You got troubles?"

"I can't sleep," I told him. "I have bad dreams."

He leaned on his mop. "Well, we all got misery, but it passes, it always passes!" He smiled at me. He had that same thing Linda did, pure unadulterated benevolence.

I got into the habit of getting up after midnight when he came in, just to talk to him. He'd tell me about himself—how he was always poor, but he had come to terms with life. His philosophy was live and let live. Take it easy. After talking to him for about half an hour it was possible for me to go to sleep.

There was one guy on the ward who really wasn't as crazy (out of control) as the rest of us. The guy had gotten married about a year before to his childhood sweetheart. Right after he married this girl she developed some rare heart ailment and died in a matter of weeks.

There he was, married to a girl he had been in love with since he was fourteen, and he had the horrible experience of watching her waste away and die two months after he married her.

The night she died he left the hospital where she was, somewhere in Manhattan, went back to their apartment in Brooklyn, and cut his wrists. He almost succeeded in killing himself, but somebody saw his door open and rescued him. He used to stay in his room all the time, staring at her picture and singing. When you went into his room he was always polite. Actually he was in no way as bad off as the rest of us. He was just very sad. He would sit in front of his dead wife's picture for many hours—sometimes way into the night—singing beautiful haunting melodies.

After about four weeks, he decided he'd better get on with his life, and he signed out of the hospital.

There was a kid named John on the ward, only seventeen. He was very quiet, very sweet. Sharon and he were like Romeo and Juliet; sometimes they spent the nights in each other's rooms.

The nurses hated that. One morning two nurses dragged John out of her room. "You do that again and you go across the street!" That was the ultimate threat—to be sent back to the locked ward at Kings County.

But that didn't stop them. They drank wine, took pills, and had sex all night. They sent John across the street for two weeks; he came back with cuts on his face. The first night he was back, he slipped into Sharon's room. They were so innocent. In the midst of this insane world—holocausts, corrupt politicians, murders, starvation—they were in their small room in the mental hospital, drinking wine and making love. Seventeen and eighteen years old.

After more than two months in the hospital I felt a stirring to get on with my life. I was also feeling guilty about my girlfriend. They had weekend passes for patients deemed almost normal. So after many weeks I went home to visit my girlfriend again. It was pathetic.

The first thing I did was take a shower. Then I lay down next to her on the bed. We'd hardly touched each other in two months but I had no desire. Maybe it was all the drugs but more likely it was fear. It just seemed too "grown-up" to have sex. My mental and emotional age was about nine. I had no interest in falling into that awful adult maze again.

"Do you want me to rub your back?" she asked.

"No, I just want to lie here near you."

We lay for a long time without talking and I fell asleep. The next morning I was a mess. "Can you drive me back to the hospital?"

"But we still have six hours till you're due back there."

She was so sad. I didn't know what to do. I wanted to comfort her but I was too far gone to do anything so unselfish, and I really wanted to return to the safety of the ward. She sighed. "All right, we'll go back then."

She dropped me off at the front entrance. It was almost impossible for me to look at her.

You see, a strange thing had happened. I had come to consider the hospital my real home. No longer was my home in an apartment in Brooklyn with this strange woman, but at the hospital with Linda, the head nurse, and the old janitor, and my little sister, Sharon—they were my family now.

Even Sam, my new roommate on the ward, was part of my family. He was a little Jewish guy from Long Island, about forty-five, who kept saying, "You know I'm not crazy, I'm just confused. I'm very confused!" Sam and I played poker in the day room for hours.

I got to feel more and more in control of myself and the world was no longer slipping away beneath my feet. The next weekend, I told my girlfriend how secure I felt on the ward. "I get up at two in the morning for my milk and cookies, and I feel so good, surrounded by loved ones." She just lay next to me and listened. "I change my bed, clean my room. It's like being seven years old with a lot of parents, uncles, and aunts around to take care of you. You see what I mean?"

She was crying. I put my arm around her and we both cried together. Something *together* for the first time in more than two months. I actually kissed her. But these things came and went in waves. The next morning I again wanted to get back early to the hospital, but when she dropped me off I kissed her and we smiled at each other.

By now it was more than ten weeks since the night I had been locked up in Kings County. On the ward we all had our chores— things to do to get ready for our Thanksgiving dinner. Linda told me, "Your job is place setting, Mike!" And she handed me a bunch of cards with people's names printed on them, patients and guests. At that moment something profound seemed to shift inside me. I looked at her and saw she was staring back at me with a strange, concerned, but amused smile on her face. "What's your family doing for Thanksgiving?" she asked.

My family. Suddenly I knew that I had passed a certain point, I wasn't really a child, I was twenty-five with a real family, a real world to live in, and a real woman waiting for me outside.

I felt sad and happy at the same time. "Here," I said, and I gave her the cards. "I have to make a call." I ran over to the pay phone on the ward and dialed my girlfriend at work. "Hello." She sounded so tentative, so remote.

"Hi," I said. "What are we doing for Thanksgiving?"

"I didn't know what . . . I thought you—"

"If you buy a turkey, we can ask my father over and give it a try."

"Are you sure?" she asked me.

"As sure as I'm going to be . . . please?"

"Okay," and she told me she'd pick me up about 10 A.M. Thanksgiving morning. I hung up scared but excited. At the nurses' station, Linda was smiling at me, more of a smile between adults now than before.

Thanksgiving was very hard. I had small, sharp relapses but still it was an achievement. Within a week I was asking to be checked out of the hospital. There were refusals, cautions, warnings, but now it was inevitable. I felt too much guilt about my girlfriend, too much yearning for the real world; I had to leave.

Two weeks later I was checked out of the ward, but not out of the program entirely. I had to go back every day for occupational therapy. I really didn't think I needed it anymore but the "professional staff" told me I did. I didn't have a job and they didn't want me wandering around loose in Brooklyn (as if I was any crazier than the average person on the street in Brooklyn), job or no job. So I kept going in every day, way into December.

But one dark, rainy afternoon I knew absolutely that I just didn't need that place anymore. I went to the head psychiatrist and told him I wanted to leave. His advice was, You're not ready; stay. They always tell you that. I don't know why. Nevertheless, I was itching to go.

I remember that last day very clearly. Downstate Medical Center was on Clarkson Avenue in Brooklyn. The subway station, during the week, was always deserted, and the trains took a long time in coming. On one side of the platform the train went deep into the farthest reaches of Brooklyn and on the other side it headed for Manhattan. Since I lived in downtown Brooklyn, the train to Manhattan was the one I was supposed to take from the hospital. But very often in those after-hospital days, even though I wasn't crazy anymore and was entering once again the world of adult responsibilities, I would get down on that platform and I wouldn't care which train I took. I was supposed to be going home, you know, home to my girlfriend, to sleep with her, have dinner with her, pay bills, look for a job—but very often I used to play a little game.

I felt so bleak and hopeless, so ashamed of myself, that whenever a train came in, no matter which direction it was going in, I would get on it. I did this many times. So if the first train that came into the station was heading out to Brooklyn, where I knew no one and would be very lonely, I would just get on it anyway, go to the end of the line, get out, and walk around, looking at the trees and houses till it got too cold. I was completely alone.

Now I had signed the papers and that was it for the hospital. I left the place behind, without a good-bye to Linda or Sharon or the old man who kept the night watch with me. I did feel regret because it was a kind of home that I had never had before, where the grown-ups were sober and calm and responsible, and I knew that I was entering a world full of responsibilities that I had no real interest in assuming. But I had to leave.

I got down to the subway platform and I got ready to play my game—you know, "Whichever way the train goes . . ." Naturally, on that very day, at that very moment, two trains came in at the same time—one headed out for Brooklyn and nowhere and the other headed for home, whatever that was. I looked at both of these trains. The doors were open and the conductors were staring at me, as if to say, "Make up your mind." I got on the train for home.

THE PSYCHIC

April 1976. My father had died about fourteen months before, right outside of Istanbul in a plane crash in the Black Sea, and I'd still barely gotten used to the fact of his death. I felt it in my stomach, a kind of throbbing hollow ache. My mother, who was always right on the edge, had gotten worse lately and was calling me all the time. Bizarre, threatening phone calls.

"Hello, darling, the doctor says I'm not doing so well."

"Mom—"

"He says I shouldn't be embarrassed to tell you I had disturbed thoughts. He says if I feel I'm in danger I shouldn't keep it to myself."

"What do you men, in danger?"

"Its okay, Michael, you don't have to be concerned."

She was calling everybody in the family.

In addition to this, I had been living for a year and a half with a woman, and our relationship was deteriorating rapidly. We had frequent fights. She was getting her PhD in psychology—working very hard—and I was moping around the apartment almost all the time, brooding and staring out the window. She accused me of being a useless vegetable. "Why don't you do *something!* At least go to your bookstore." After my father died, I had opened a used book store in the neighborhood, but lately I didn't even bother to visit it for days at a time. I let my friends run it. I was slipping badly. During the first week in May, my girlfriend informed me that she was fed up with living with someone who was wasting his life. "I'm going to find a mature man," she said, "someone who knows his direction in life." She had this notion that she wanted to find a psychiatrist or a psychologist, like herself; they would live together (marry) and share the same offices—work together, like the Leakeys or the Curies. Jesus, can you imagine a life like that?

She informed me she was moving to Manhattan to find Dr. Right.

"Brooklyn," she said, "is for losers anyway." Two weeks later she was gone.

In the midst of all these losses and turbulence, I had been seeing a therapist who was not doing me any good, so I dropped him. I lay alone in my room in the dark and watched color TV. If the phone rang I didn't answer it. I was totally isolated.

You know that feeling when somebody first leaves? Maybe you've been together for a few years. It's like pulling off a Band-Aid you've had on for weeks. That pain has a correspondence in the heart. You feel raw. The other side of the bed seems as big as a football field and the apartment, no matter how small, becomes a vast echoing hall.

One night in June I woke up at about three in the morning; I started up with a sudden sense of terror. About three inches away from my pillow, staring straight at me was the largest black spider I had ever seen in New York City. I am no bug expert but I knew that this spider was up to no good; this was not a benevolent creature. I brushed it off the bed and smashed it a couple of dozen times with my shoe to make sure it was dead. Then I turned on all the lights and watched TV till morning.

But it seemed to me there was a certain message in the appearance of this nasty thing. I finally resolved to *do* something; I went to an astrologer.

Park Slope at that time was loaded with astrologers. They were hanging off the trees like overripe peaches. In fact there were more astrologers than therapists in Park Slope, which is really saying something. People were routinely spending thirty to fifty dollars on charts and readings. The astrologer told me, "Don't worry, in two years the planets will realign and you will meet another woman or get together with the same woman." She made various other cheery predictions, but it was no use. I realized that I wasn't really paying any attention to her because she was younger than I. I've always had the feeling that wisdom is not to be gained from anyone younger than I.

She seemed to sense that I wasn't getting any comfort from her talk so she suggested I might need some heavier medicine. She gave me the name of a psychic who lived in Washington, D.C., a woman named Gwen Miles.

It seemed strange to me that I should have to go all the way to Washington to get straightened out but I understood that it was the journey that was important. It seemed absolutely right that I should go somewhere, to a place or a person. Every country, every place and tribe has its myth of journeying through suffering to gain wisdom and peace. Now although I wasn't going through the valley of fire and over the mountain of dragons, I was going to have to take the Amtrak train through Trenton and Baltimore. That was close enough.

So I called her up—Gwen Miles. She had a beautiful mellifluous voice. "Yes," she said, "I do have an appointment time available." It was in early July, about ten days away.

My best friend thought I was nuts to go to Washington to pay to see a psychic. "Why don't you give me the money," he said, "I'll look in my crystal ball for you." But I didn't care. The summer was groaning on. I was terribly lonely, lying in bed for long stretches watching the color TV with the lights off, which must be like shooting dope straight into your veins. I was having a lot of trouble breathing and it was impossible for me to stop thinking about my father.

And my mother was calling up at least three times a week. The poor woman was really a wreck because her older sister, who had always lived right next door to her, was moving to Florida and wouldn't be able to watch over her anymore. My mother would be completely alone out in Queens. "Michael, I'll have no relatives left. You might as well all be dead. What will happen to me?" She was supposed to be looking for a new place to live after thirty years and that was driving her over the edge.

So, on July 9, an extremely hot day, I left my apartment about eight in the morning to get the Amtrak train to Washington, D.C. Now, in those days, before they modernized the tracks and bought new cars, it could take you five hours to make a three-hour trip. You might go ten miles an hour for a half-hour or sit on a siding for twenty minutes. But none of this mattered to me; I was going on my journey, and besides, I always loved riding on trains. When you're on a train you're going away, you have the feeling that you're leaving all your pain and misery behind you. The terrible IT, whatever IT is, is out of your hands for a while. And I loved that passive rocking motion of a train.

The station was hot, stuffy, and nasty but comfortable compared to the train itself, which left an hour late. The seats were torn, the windows were cracked and filthy, and there were archaeological layers of garbage on the floor. Naturally the air conditioning had broken and the windows couldn't be opened. There were three or four other passengers, lifeless businessmen draped over the seats. Immediately I was sweating all over. This was a perfect start to my journey of suffering.

My appointment with Gwen Miles was for three o'clock but I had given myself a couple of extra hours because I'm like a little old fusspot that way; I have to make sure I'm never late for anything. Also there was Amtrak to consider. And I wanted to take a look at Washington. I wasn't sure exactly why; maybe because it was the capital of the United States and I felt vaguely un-American going to see a psychic. Would John Wayne go to a psychic before a shoot-out?

But of course all those practical considerations were meaningless to me now. I was looking for some sort of promise from Gwen Miles. I was hoping she'd say, "You have a dead father, a mother who lives in outer space, a girlfriend who has decided you're a hopeless lump; your life is a desert. But don't worry, I bring you tidings of peace and joy." That's what I wanted, so this endless train ride and all my doubts were unimportant.

About an hour outside of Washington, a man in his late twenties or early thirties got on the train. This guy was so crippled, probably by cerebral palsy, that it was painful to look at him.

Have you ever walked on the street, especially in New York when it's raining, and seen somebody who, because he's got a birth defect or he's been crippled by some awful disease, must lean very heavily and painfully on a walker or crutches? Since he doesn't have a third arm, there is no way he can hold an umbrella over his head. And, because you're a New Yorker and you're very busy rushing someplace, you wouldn't dream of holding your umbrella over him and walking him where he's going because he's too slow. In Manhattan, to walk slowly is a crime. It shows that you have no ambition. I see these people and I always think how horrible it is, the pain they have to endure.

This man's legs were twisted and his face was permanently marred by pain. His head was slightly bent to the side but he had that kind of transcendent dignity, sheer nobility, that people who suffer like that often achieve. His face looked as if the Ten Commandments had been etched on it.

Immediately I started daydreaming about where he was going. Maybe there was a special clinic where he had to go every day; during the painful walk from his house to the train station, no matter what the weather, he couldn't shelter himself. Every day he visits this clinic, spending hours on tables with pulleys and weights, and all the time some cheerleader nurse urges him on.

As he went to sit down, a very pretty girl, whom I hadn't noticed before, stood up to help him. She took his canes as he lowered himself onto the seat. When he reached up to touch her arm to thank her, she flinched and moved back; that's a reaction a lot of young people have to someone who's sick or old. As she moved away a look of humiliation and sadness passed over his face. You could tell this had happened to him before. I thought to myself, Who would ever love him? What woman would ever give her body or her heart to him?

So this was his journey every day. My journey to the psychic was nothing, kid stuff. I watched him get off the train the stop before Washington—every step painful. I hoped there was a car waiting for him.

The heat in Washington was astonishing. It had to be over a hundred degrees. Inside Union Station, people were speaking in whispers. It was a vast place, shrouded in heat and dust. I found an old map of the city on the wall and located where I had to go. Outside in the blazing sun there were cabs lined up, but even though I had the money I decided to walk; it was about a mile and a half. I had some notion of seeing monuments and famous places and, again, I'm sure I was compelled by the idea that I had to pay dues. There must have been something terribly wrong with me if God or fate or whatever it was took my father away, drove my mother further into insanity, and convinced my girlfriend to leave. I walked down the steps of the station and commenced my march.

Washington is a very empty city, especially in the summer. In July, it's so hot that most people who have the money just abandon the place for Canada, Europe, air-conditioned motels—anyplace. The government is closed; it's a ghost town. On one side of the wide boulevard, there were massive government buildings of pure white marble or whitewashed cement, bright green lawns, polished brass plaques. On the other side, where I was walking, the sidewalks were old and cracked and there was row after row of beaten-up shacks and storefronts. On benches, on broken chairs, on porches sat dozens of miserable poor black people. I walked and walked but there was no end to it: Men and women were lying on the burnt-out grass, staring at me, mean and exhausted people, starving mangy dogs. Cracked doors were hanging off hinges. Every once in a while, past this scene of misery and poverty, a cool black limousine would drift by like a shark gliding through the water. The car would turn into the driveway of a building, and a door would magically open and shut; you could imagine the breath of air conditioning. White and black; this was a city only Melville could have dreamed up.

I was deliberately passing by places where I could get a drink. I was slipping into a trance state because I hadn't eaten or drunk anything since the night before. My feet were burning and my clothes were soaked through with sweat. I was deliberately jamming myself into a state of mystical euphoria. I imagined that one of the men I could dimly see behind the smoked glass of the limousines was my father, who was not dead after all, but watching me on my journey, and my mother was looking at me from behind one of the shanty windows.

I had been walking for what seemed like miles when I looked up and saw the White House right in front of me. What a sad joke. Here I was, walking through a city that looked like living hell, a Dali nightmare, and what do I run into but the White House. I was two hundred yards away from the man who was the King of America and the same distance away from the most depressed people I had ever seen.

The air was shimmering from the heat, the iron fence was freshly painted black, and the lawn was a beautiful dark green. The marine guard just inside the fence wore a perfect dress uniform; the rifle on his shoulder was polished and gleaming. Long limousines were floating up and down the driveway. As I stood up against the fence staring, I realized the guard was talking to me. "You're not allowed to stand on the fence, sir. Please step down." I wanted to tell him off, say something like, "Hey, soldier, I pay your salary," but I was too exhausted and depressed. I stepped down and walked away.

I circled around the White House and started up the street where Gwen Miles lived. It was a broad street with big beautiful old wooden houses, maybe ten- or twelve-room houses built around the turn of the century. Everything was orderly and clean; even the heat seemed less oppressive here.

Another half hour, another mile or so, and I arrived at what had to be the place. Outside on the lawn, instead of statues and flamingos and black jockeys with lanterns, were some very strange constructions made of steel and wood—globes, circles, triangles, ancient Assyrian symbols mixed in with crosses. Ankhs, Jewish stars. Sure enough, there was a plaque over the door with the name on it—Institute for something-or-other.

It was about five minutes to three. I didn't need to look at a watch, because I'm always either right on time or a little early for everything. The door was open so I walked in. It wasn't air-conditioned but as soon as I entered the house I felt cool; not just cool but welcome too.

I stood in the vestibule looking into the living room. There was an air conditioner (not plugged in), a big new television, a clock radio, and a stereo; it was a normal electronic American living room. But there were also several dozen musty old leather volumes on the book-shelves, and many huge jars with what looked like leaves or herbs in them. It was a strange combination of artifacts, and yet the atmosphere of the house seemed so basically good. From somewhere I thought I heard a child's voice.

As I stood there getting a little nervous, Gwen Miles materialized and drifted down from the top of the stairs. You've seen people like her, they're just born noble. She was very tall, quite beautiful, about fifty years old, with smooth skin and a very high forehead. She wore a long gown, not one that flared out, but straight, with brown and gold mystical symbols on it. Her hair was silver and gold and swept back on her head like a lion's mane. To me it seemed as if she had stepped off a cloud. She was coolness itself.

She walked over to me and stopped about a foot away. She stood eye to eye with me. She extended her cool long hand to me and said, "You must be Mike. I'm Gwen." Her voice was a combination of an upper-class hostess's welcome at a cocktail party and something eerie and musical, a special mixture that made you feel as if you had actually stepped into another world. But at the same time you knew it was her world and you were just visiting.

"Shall we go upstairs now?" she asked. I followed her up the steps.

My ever-present anxiety surfaced and I commenced to have very strong fantasies. Why is she taking me upstairs, I wondered. Is some strange sexual ritual going to take place? I've come all the way to Washington, nobody knows I'm here—maybe she'll have a psychic thug up there to beat me and rob me. But if anybody was ever motherly in the most classically benevolent way, it was this woman. I wished she were my mother.

Upstairs in a big sunny room, we sat across from each other at a small table. Her chair was ornate and painted gold. On the table was a small tape recorder. The window was open wide and every once in a while a car would pass by. It was just a lazy, hot, quiet afternoon in Washington, D.C. My mouth was dry from nerves. "Where do we start?" I asked. "How do we begin?"

She smiled and pressed the tape recorder. "We begin with a prayer."

And then followed an experience the like of which I never had before or since. She went into what appeared to be a trance. She closed her eyes, this beautiful woman, and murmured her prayer. To me, it was a very strange prayer, not secular, not sacred, but something in between, a personal ritual she invented. She asked the powers that be to send a guide, someone who had passed into the next world, to explain what was happening to me now and what was to come. After her prayer there was a long moment of silence. I heard a car pass by. I was staring intently at her; after my long journey I felt I had encountered a true oracle and that something significant was going to be revealed to me after all.

She talked for about forty-five minutes in the trance state, speaking very slowly in the voice of an old woman—old but commanding. "I see you passing through a doorway surrounded by red and blue colors. There is a woman there, her face is worn with worry." She spoke mostly in a visual, metaphorical way. It wasn't vague and silly like the daily horoscopes in the paper. It was dramatic and full of pictures, which made it all the more fascinating.

"I see a large square room with a window at one end and a statue at the other."

This was, in fact, a pretty good description of my bedroom in Brooklyn. She quickly mentioned a few more things which were for me proof of her psychic powers. She described my bookstore, what my mother looked like—all in vivid pictures. In about three minutes I was hooked. I was ready to believe. I had made the journey, done my suffering on Amtrak, walking the hot streets, starving myself; I was ready to accept anything. She said the most astonishing things, things that excited my imagination and brought up urgent, desperate questions in my mind, but I was not allowed to say anything because this would interrupt the trance and scare away the guide who was revealing all these things to her.

When she finally came out of her trance, she opened her eyes and looked at me in silence for at least two minutes. To sit and stare at a stranger in a strange town for two solid minutes, after hearing all this overwhelming stuff about myself, was a psychic experience in itself. Then she said, "If you have any questions, you can ask them now."

At one point she had said, "I see you with a huge golden banana." Since sex is never very far away from my mind at any time, no matter what's happening to me, I was thinking, Yeah, right, my huge golden banana, wondering if something sexual was going on here after all. "What's this golden banana?" I asked her.

"Well, I see you holding a large golden yellow banana, peeling it, and sharing it with many others." I suppose one could say that. I had had my attack of satyriasis about two years before. I shared my golden banana as widely and indiscriminately as possible. But that wasn't what she meant at all.

"It represents supply," she said. "Wealth. I see you sharing your good fortune with others." She was absolutely right. My father had left a lot of money and I did give a lot of it to almost anybody who seemed to need it. Where it is now is another story.

Among the dozen or so amazing revelations, there was one that seemed especially strange, perhaps just because it wasn't particularly spectacular; it was in fact somewhat mundane. Near the end of her trance she had said, "You will enter a brown brick building, three or four stories high and square." Now, in Park Slope there was no building like that I was familiar with; I wasn't seeing anybody, either personally or professionally, who lived in such a building. I asked her, "What is this building?"

"It will be three stories high, made of light tan or brownish bricks, and it will have a recessed roof of a green or bronze color," she explained. "When you enter this building something monumental will occur. And when you emerge from it your life will be changed forever." Well, that certainly wasn't mundane. Still, it was a complete mystery to me. I put it in the back of my mind.

She amplified a few more of the prophecies; some have since come true, some haven't. After I asked my questions she gave me my personal symbol. Did you ever get your personal symbol? Mine is a green triangle, equilateral, with a white line running straight up the middle. She told me what it meant. "If you ever attempt to be dishonest in anything, to walk the crooked path, you will lose; your destiny is to walk the straight path." She was right about that. Every time I try to get away with something, try to slide by even in the most minor way, I get caught and punished for it; and the punishment is usually way out of proportion to the crime. So, out of sheer survival, not out of nobility, I usually stick to the truth.

She gave me the cassette tape and as we got up from the table, she closed her eyes again and touched her brow. "I see a large letter *E* being pinned on you. It is a medal for excellence—No, wait; as it comes closer I see it is not a medal but a branding iron. The letter *E* stands for the sorrow of the eons and it is being branded on your forehead."

We walked downstairs to the vestibule. "One last word," she said, and smiled. "I forgot to tell you before because I thought it would seem too silly."

"What?"

"Your guide was saying to me, 'Tell him he's a good boy, a good boy.' "

For some reason this brought tears to my eyes. Sure, it's true, an astrologer in Park Slope or the old lady in the Italian grocery could have told me that, but this was different. Gwen was so regal and motherly and benevolent, and the atmosphere so cool and comforting in her house, that a comment like that was exactly what I had come to hear. I felt as if all the dirt and loneliness, the sense of sin and shame that covered me, had been leeched out of me in a miraculous cleansing motion.

She had done wonders for me. It was everything I could have hoped for; confusing, maybe, a little, but wonderful. I asked her what I owed her. As in all things, you've got to pay. Three thousand years ago, if you went to the oracle at Delphi, you had to bring a bag of gold or a sheep's head or whatever. You see a shrink and it's a hundred dollars for fifty minutes. She asked for a reasonable amount. After all those revelations, it seemed cheap to me.

Just as I was about to step out the door, I thought again about entering that brown brick building. "When's this supposed to happen?" I asked her.

"Sometime in the next three weeks to three months," she said.

I walked all the way back through the heat to the train station, feeling much lighter and purer than when I had come. The train back to New York was another five-hour trip. As I was riding along, I was making notes of things the psychic had said, scribbling on a pad and talking to myself. I was in a state of complete euphoria. Even the railyards and refineries and polluted factories I was passing on my way through Delaware and New Jersey seemed magical and cheerful. I felt like I was surrounded by an invisible, protective wall.

I got home, put the tape on, and listened intently to it, over and over. The next day, I played it for some of my friends, my wise-guy New York friends. "Hey, Mike, your golden banana? Gimme a fuckin' break. How much this woman soak you for?" But what they said made no difference to me because Gwen Miles had created a time of magic in my life. I listened to the tape every day for a week and then I put it away. One thing nagged me though—this brown brick building that was supposed to change my life. The idea that I would walk into a building and come out completely transformed . . . well, that was something I couldn't ignore. I walked all over the Slope searching for the building but nothing turned up.

The summer moved on. I revived somewhat, spent more time in the bookstore, flirted with the women who came in, and had some friends over once in a while. In August I got involved in a prospective commune. I went out to New Jersey with a group who were looking for a farm to live on. They wanted to establish their own self-sustaining community because, like any rational people, they could see the world was falling apart fast, morally and materially, and they wanted to bring up their children in a decent place. They had their eye on a large estate, more than seven hundred acres, with a large farm on it, woods, a stream, and several houses. I pictured myself living alone in one of the smaller houses. In the afternoons, while the women baked bread in their brick ovens and the men were out tilling the land, I'd teach the children how to whittle and sing sea chanteys.

I went out there for several meetings to see if we could afford the place and how the labor would be divided. I was excited but still distracted by the overall malaise still lingering from the spring. It was a bad time. I still missed my father, and I hadn't heard a word from my "ex."

One Saturday afternoon, as some customers were browsing in my bookstore and I was sitting at the front desk reading, my mother called. "Hello, darling?"

"Hello, Ma."

"I just called to find out how the store is doing."

"Fine."

"Well, sweetheart, it's been over a year you've had it—I guess you're not planning to invite me to see it."

"Look, Ma—"

"That's okay, darling. I suppose you have your reasons."

Then she started to cry. "I wouldn't bother you. I would only come for a minute." Silence from me. Then she got angry. "You know, Michael, it wouldn't kill you to be nice to me just once!"

"Look, I don't want you here and don't call me anymore."

"Well then, I'm cutting you out of my will! Your sister will get everything!" She was screaming now.

I screamed back, 'Fine, go ahead, cut me out of your fucking will!" I slammed the phone down. I was shaking with rage. I turned around and everybody in the store was staring at me.

Near the end of September, as I was driving through New Jersey at dusk, I suddenly experienced a physical shock of terror and prophetic doom. I pulled over to the side of the highway, much to the consternation of my passengers—two friends I was driving back to Rutgers.

"What's wrong?"

"I don't know, but I have to stop for a while."

As I sat there in a sweat, it came to me very clearly that within a week my mother would be dead. I usually don't get premonitions but I knew that in a week my mother would not be around anymore. I sat for a minute and the feeling passed. I got back on the road, dropped my friends off, and drove back to Brooklyn to resume my normal life, which was running the bookstore, picking at my emotional scabs, and watching "Kojak" in my dark bedroom.

Three days later, on Monday, the phone woke me at six in the morning. My aunt said, "Michael, you better get out here, your mother has killed herself."

It wasn't really a shock. It seemed so inevitable to me. I knew this was going to happen; I had known it three days before. I got dressed and went out to the car.

I drove out to Queens, met my aunt, and went into the back bedroom. There on her bed against the wall was my mother. She was clearly dead. Her skin was yellowish and her gray hair was lying flat around her head. On the wall above her was her college graduation picture taken in 1940, when she was nineteen. She had long wavy dark hair. She was beautiful.

There is no doubt about it when somebody's dead. Life has gone. And it's strange—it's at that very moment when you see somebody who has just died that you can first believe there is an afterlife, that there is a spark of life that is undefinable but very real. You believe it because it so obviously leaves when death comes. You think to yourself, It must be somewhere.

I looked at her lying there with her hands folded across her stomach. This poor woman had spent her whole life avoiding life and had finally avoided it in the best way possible, which was to leave it entirely. But what could be scarier than deliberately choosing to enter the next world? Even the bravest of us are afraid of that. The fact that she did it seemed like a courageous act. It was of course the most cowardly act imaginable, yet at that moment I thought she was very brave. It was, morbidly speaking, the only thing she had ever really achieved.

Two days later, I was called by the Queens County Coroner's Office. They had done the autopsy and I had to come out to Queens General Hospital to identify the body. I drove out to the hospital, parked in front, and went up to the main desk. "I'm here to see the coroner," I said.

"It's the other building out back," they told me.

I walked outside and drove my car around to the back parking lot. It was a sunny day, late morning, in early October. As I came around the main building of Queens General, what did I see but a three-story tan brick building with a green recessed roof. There was a sign in the front: Coroner's Office. I walked in and sat down on a bench in the waiting room. Someone came over. "Are you Mr. Feder?"

"Yes."

They wanted to see some identification. After they checked my driver's license I was brought over to a window. A curtain was pulled back. They wheeled in "the body." It was my mother and she seemed at peace. I looked at her for a moment and then they pulled the curtain closed. I signed a form absolving them of who knows whatever they had done and affirmed again in writing that yes, that was my mother. I left the building.

I walked about twenty feet back to my car, got in, and sat behind the wheel paralyzed, absolutely paralyzed. Not with fear, and not with shock and not even with grief. I was in a kind of perfect suspension— flooded with the certain knowledge that there was another world. All my life I had watched this poor woman suffer, then finally kill herself. I knew now that this was not the end of things, that there was another place—a place where this spark, this essence of life continues to exist. And the very air around me, the cars, the No Parking signs, the burned stunted grass, even the plastic steering wheel in front of me, all seemed imbued with life. So at the very moment of death, of entering the house of death and coming out of it, I understood for the first time something I had always secretly believed, something that was stronger in me that day than ever before: that there is a soul, an ungraspable essence of life, which invests everything, and which is, in fact, eternal.

ANTIGUA

W elcome aboard, son!"
This wasn't the navy, it was my father-in-law, crushing me
in a bear hug the day of my wedding. May 5, 1979. We were having
the party in my friend's apartment, complete with kisses and hand-
shakes, and slaps on the back. It was something I had to suffer
through. I hate parties, especially if they are attached to some ritual.
And this was the ritual of rituals.

My wife and I had been living together, on and off, for several years,
but we decided to get married because we were planning on having a
kid. And, as generally happens, at least with anybody in our generation, we felt a certain sense of insecurity in the midst of our freedom. I
had seen dozens of marriages, including my parents', explode like
bombs or disintegrate in acid, but my wife hadn't seen so much
wreckage and she wanted the commitment that marriage seemed to
promise.

The next day we were flying to Antigua for our honeymoon. Of
course, we saw through the romantic silliness involved in a honeymoon, yet still there was the mysterious feeling of celebrating a whole
life together. Also, within a year we might very well have a baby to
take care of, and so this seven-day trip was probably the last one we'd
have together for a long time. You can see this honeymoon already
had a little extra weight to it.

I chose Antigua because the travel agent said it was less crowded
than Jamaica and less expensive and gaudy than Paradise Island. It
was off-season and so the price of the airfare and the hotel were
relatively low. Money was a real consideration. I had a pretty small
income and my wife was just completing her doctorate in psychology,
working for low pay at a clinic in Queens. Our budget was tight so
Antigua was our tropical paradise as much by a process of elimination
as anything else.

Later that night after the party, I watched my wife carefully packing the suitcases. She did everything thoughtfully, methodically. I was struck by a sense of newness in our relationship. Even though we'd lived together for years, argued and hurt each other, even though we had made love so many times and shared a thousand routine chores, we were, after all, strangers to each other. Her heart and her mind were still unknown to me. She seemed so mysterious, like a vast continent, and I was an explorer just setting foot on one small stretch of shore.

We were being very tender with each other—not our usual style, which was generally tough and combative. She was having trouble finding room for a homemade cake her mother had brought up from Texas. "Why don't you leave it in the freezer?" I said. "We can have it when we get back."

"No, my mother made this especially for me, for our wedding, and I want to take it."

"Okay, here, let me help you." I pushed the cake into a corner of the suitcase.

Just before bed, we stood at the window looking up at the moon. There was a halo, a double rainbow ring around it. It was very romantic.

"That's good luck," I said, always ready with natural lore, whether I knew it or not.

"Really?"

"Yup. It's one of those things—you just know."

From the air, Antigua looked like a television commercial—blue-green sea, palm trees, sailboats. On the ground it was hot and dusty, with red dirt and scrawny bushes lining the runway. The "arrivals" building was a pile of bare cement blocks and the customs men were depressed and nasty. We were soaked through with sweat by the time we got a cab outside and drove to the other side of the island to where we were staying. The place we were headed for was called The Mansion or The Fortress or some such romance-novel name. It was the British Colonial capitol: an "ivy-covered mansion, replete with eighteenth-century charm," according to the brochure.

We drove through the capital city, Georgetown, which was a mixture of faded pastel shops, run-down old houses, and broken streets. It was incredibly hot. People were lying in the shade staring at us as we drove past. They didn't look happy. But in a couple of minutes we were on the coast road passing white sand beaches and "quaint" little villages. There were mango and papaya trees everywhere and exotic birds high up in the palms. "It's beautiful," said my wife, "so calm and peaceful."

I sighed. "Yeah, it makes Manhattan look like one big pile of garbage."

We drove through the huge wooden gates of The Fortress and parked outside a dignified old stone mansion, the hotel. Out in the harbor there were at least half a dozen huge sailboats, and on the patio where lunch was being served, there was a calypso band playing. We went up to the front desk.

The man behind the desk said, "There's no room in the main house. You'll have to stay in the annex." He didn't even bother to apologize.

"Look," I told him, "we have reservations for the Mansion."

"The whole place is called the Mansion, even the annex." He looked out at the sailboats crowding the harbor. "We have a very large rush of business right now." There was a crowd in the bar. They were tall and blond, with that special air of ownership the rich have. It was obvious we were getting bumped by them.

"We want to speak to the manager," said my wife. She was mad and even under the best of circumstances does not take shit from anyone.

"I am the manager," said the desk man. "It's either the annex or a hotel in town." He obviously didn't give a damn if we stayed at the annex or volunteered to be used as shark bait.

I thought of the hot depressing city we had passed through. "Okay," I said, "let's look at the annex."

We went about fifty yards away from the Mansion, and there, next to a messy, smelly boatyard, was a small group of ugly cement blocks. The annex. My wife and I looked at each other. It was hot and we were trapped. Obviously we stayed here or in town or noplace at all. "Well," I said, "it's more private than the main house and it has its own little veranda." Silence from her. The porter dropped our suitcases in the gravel outside the door and dropped the key in my hand. I gave him a small tip. He walked off muttering.

It was a typical, soulless hotel room; we could have been in Detroit or on Route 22 in New Jersey. This was not a very romantic way to start our new life. I looked out the window at people water-skiing in the harbor while my wife poked around in the bathroom and looked in the closets. She came over to the window and put her arm around me. "Well," she said, "let's make the best of it." That's what I liked about her. If it had been up to me, we would have gotten a cab back to airport right away. We changed into shorts, put on our sunglasses, and went back to the main house.

The bar looked like a Chivas Regal ad—alcohol and money. I was uncomfortable but my wife felt even worse than I did. She was not very well off when she was growing up and had worked hard to get the little she had. These people, so self-assured and smooth as they drifted past the tables, made her feel nervous and awkward. She held my hand, which was unusual. "They're so rich," she said with a little awe, and then, "Look at them, it's disgusting." I felt the same contempt. After eight years working in the probation and welfare departments in New York, it made me angry to look at such bliss-fully ignorant wealth. On the other hand, I envied them their easy lives. Imagine never having to think, even for a split second, about money. Just sign your name or reach for a credit card and you had anything you wanted. It wouldn't be too bad to live like that. "Yeah," I said to my wife, "these people are a living advertisement for communism."

We bought two piña coladas and sat under an umbrella on the patio. The drinks were almost pure rum and it took only about ten minutes before the both of us were high. I watched my wife walk over to the bar for another drink. She had on an old pair of shorts, a plain white T-shirt, and sneakers. She was surrounded by women with stylish skirts and bikinis and gold necklaces, but she stood out. My wife had an inner intelligence and power that was undeniable. She was tall anyway and carried herself with a mixture of command and natural sexiness. Some of those women looked like movie stars but as I watched my wife walk through them I was moved by a feeling of admiration and love for her. I wished I had as much money as some of those guys; I'd buy my wife a sailboat of her own.

"Bitch!" My wife banged the drinks down on the glass table.

"What happened?"

"One of those rich bitches just tried to push past me at the bar. She almost burned me with her cigarette. I told her to fuck off."

She was really angry, practically on the verge of tears. I guess I didn't understand how terrible she felt surrounded by such people. "Look," I said, "don't worry about it. They don't even know what they're doing. They think everybody works for them."

"Well, I don't work for them!" She calmed down after a while and we sat there getting pleasantly drunk, looking at the elegant boats and listening to the sound of the water lapping up against the pier.

About half an hour later we were making love, our first time as officially blessed by the State of New York. But, you know, it felt different from the hundreds of times before, as if something deeper, realer was being exchanged. It was us against those awful people outside, us alone together in a foreign place. Only thirty hours ago, we had sworn to love each other till the day we died.

The next morning we got up early to swim. I could live happily the rest of my days without being anywhere near a beach or going in the water. I even get nervous in the bathtub, and the idea of entering into water teeming with invisible, toothy creatures is out of the question. I picked this place for a honeymoon because there was sailing and swimming for my wife, but also because it had a casino and I love to gamble. I had taken about a hundred dollars to play blackjack. I was a real big spender. My wife detested the whole idea of gambling. But I liked it. As a trade-off, we would spend most of our time in the water.

There was no real beach in the harbor, so we decided to walk to a small bay about a half-mile outside the compound where, according to the advertisements, there was supposed to be a beautiful "deserted beach." The gatekeeper told us to take a cab but since as tourists we already felt we were being milked like cows, we figured we'd save money and walk. "Open the gate, please," I asked him.

"Okay, man, but you going to regret it."

We stepped outside and immediately had to run a gauntlet of angry black people demanding we buy stuff from them: half-rotten fruit, crumbling bead necklaces. "Hey, you buy this!" they shouted. When we kept walking, they glared at us—one woman with a baby on her hip even spat in our direction. We were really shaken. My wife wanted to stop and explain something to them. We kept going. "I guess to them we're rich," I said.

"Well, we're not like those people in their sailboats," said my wife.

"Oh, I know," I said, "but to these people we might as well be the colonial governor."

It was extremely hot and dry. We walked up a long hill and scraped ourselves good in some brambles trying to find a path down to the beach. My wife had brought some food and beer for a picnic. The beach was beautiful—and deserted—a small inlet of blue water, like a jewel, surrounded by palm trees and white sand. I walked a few yards to a shaded wood table and my wife ran right into the water. She swam underwater a ways. I was content to watch her have a good time. She really did love the water. Farther out, in the middle of the bay, there was a boy fishing with a spear gun. He dove and stayed down for what seemed to me an incredibly long time.

Suddenly he burst to the surface holding a huge wriggling creature impaled on his spear. He shouted something, swam in to shore, ran over to us, and threw down a big bloody ray with a long nasty-looking tail. It was flopping all over and staining the sand with blood. "Look, look!" He was really proud of himself, laughing like mad. "Very big!"

He was about fifteen and all muscle; obviously he spent half his life in the water. "Are there more of these out there?" I asked him.

"Oh yes and some barracuda too, ha ha, very big teeth!" He speared the ray and ran off laughing down the beach, waving it around.

"Well that's it for me," I said, "I'm not going in this water."

My wife had come up to shore to look at the ray. She shook her head. "Oh, stop. Those things are way out in the middle, not where we are."

"Yeah, that's twenty yards. Forget it."

"All right, but I'm going back in." She ran over and dove in again. I stood at the shoreline pacing and willing her to get tired and come out. I had terrible pictures in my head of sharks and eels. Finally she came out. We sat in the shade on a beach towel. I opened a couple of aluminum foil packages: hard-boiled eggs, sandwiches, cans of soda. One of the packages smelled bad—it was the cake her mother had brought up from Texas for the wedding party.

"You better not eat this," I said. "I think it's gone bad." I got up to throw it in the trash barrel and she grabbed it out of my hand and sniffed it.

"There's nothing wrong with this. You always think the worst."

"I'm telling you, it's been three days, on airplanes, in the heat, it's not safe."

"Oh, you think everything smells bad." Well, that's true. I'm always inspecting the contents of the refrigerator for possible food poisoning. She took a big bite. "You see," she said, "nothing wrong."

Maybe an hour later, my wife was poking me as I dozed in the sun. "I feel awful," she groaned. She was bent over and holding her stomach. "I feel like I'm going to throw up." She did look awful. I picked up all our stuff and we started to climb the hill to go back to the hotel. Halfway up she threw up and I had to hold her so she could make it the rest of the way up the hill. We ran the gauntlet of islanders again. "Buy this!" Their nasty staring eyes seemed amused that my wife was sick.

In the room she lay on the bed. I felt her forehead. Even in the heat I could tell she had a fever. I was getting nervous. "I told you not to eat that fucking cake. I'm going to find out about a doctor," I told her. "I'll be right back."

At the front desk, they told me the only doctors were in town, way on the other side of the island, and they wouldn't come out unless it was a serious emergency. They told me to go over to the yacht club—there was a woman who worked in the gift store who was a nurse.

When I got there, I had to push my way through a crowd of rich people buying jewelry and clothes. I couldn't stand to look at them. I felt like they were responsible for my wife's getting sick. I could gladly have punched a couple of them. Behind the counter there was a kind-looking woman in her mid-thirties. She agreed it was probably food poisoning but had nothing on her medicine counter that would do any good. I'd have to go to town and get a doctor to prescribe some

real stomach medicine. "I'll call the doctor," she said, and wrote out
the address for me.

I hated it when anybody around me got sick. One of the reasons I
was with my wife was because she never got sick; she didn't whine or
complain like all the hysterical women I had grown up with. If
anybody was supposed to get sick, it was me; I was the one with
allergies and colds and sinus infections. I considered it part of our
unspoken marriage contract that I was the sensitive, weak one, and
she was tough and strong.

In the room, listening to her gasping and being sick in the bathroom, I felt ashamed, and I remembered the countless nights my
mother spent in the bathroom retching and crying. My wife came out
holding her stomach and rolled onto the bed. She was *really* sick, but I
could feel my mouth tighten and hear the coldness in my voice. "I have
to go into town and see a doctor to get a prescription for you."

She looked up at me. "I'm sorry I'm sick. I know how much you
hate it."

"You just rest. I'll be back later." I put my hand on her sweaty
forehead.

I got a cab at the main gate and told the driver I was in a hurry.
Naturally he drove like we were on a sightseeing tour. I leaned
forward in the seat. "Move it," I said. He sped up. I was another
white master giving orders, but I didn't care.

About an hour later I had seen the doctor, filled the prescription,
and was on my way back to the hotel. Beaches gleamed and flowers
bloomed all around me but I was too pissed-off and scared to notice. I
was grumbling to myself about the money I had laid out—more than
sixty dollars counting the cab fares. This was a good chunk of my
gambling budget. Some fucking vacation, I thought. I might as well
have stayed in stinking Manhattan.

"Here's the medicine." I held her head while my wife swallowed
two tablespoons of white syrupy stuff. She lay back on the pillow and
I got some cold wet washcloths to put on her forehead. I sat there next
to her holding her hand. "I'm really sorry," she said. Within a minute
she was asleep. I wiped the sweat off her face with a towel and moved
back some wet strands of hair that were in her eyes. There were clean
sheets in the dresser and I covered her with one. As I watched her
sleeping, my selfishness melted away. I felt suddenly very protective

and loving, the way you feel when someone really needs you and you can give them a little comfort.

It was getting dark now. I sat outside at the table in front of our room watching the lights come on in the sailboats and the houses on the hills around the harbor. Noise and laughter drifted over from the main house, and a slight fragrant breeze came off the water. It was very serene, but I was busy torturing myself with thoughts of rare tropical diseases. "Yes, one minute she was here, vibrant and happy, and the next . . ." What would I tell her mother and father? "I have buried her at sea, as was her last wish. Her last thoughts were of the cake you made especially for our wedding."

I went inside, and to my tremendous relief, she was sitting up in bed. "How are you feeling?"

"Much better. I needed to sleep."

"How's your stomach—you want me to get you something?"

"No, not yet. Why don't you go have dinner?"

Sitting on the terrace, I watched the yacht people eating lobster and drinking champagne. They were as casual as if they had ordered a grilled cheese on rye with a Pepsi. They had natural savoir-faire. I couldn't see one line of worry or doubt on their faces. How I envied them. They were so young and smooth. The world was made just for them. I felt like an alien, Franz Kafka at the health club.

I brought some tea and toast back to my wife. She was feeling better. I sat down next to her on the bed. She must have seen how miserable I felt—I didn't make much of an effort to hide it. She held my hand. "Why don't you go to the casino?"

"What, by myself?"

"Sure. You're just going to feel awful sitting around here—you should go and have some fun. Don't worry about me, I'll read or write in my diary."

Now, this was the wife I married. "Okay," I said. "I'll be back in a couple of hours."

It was cloudy as I rode back across the island to the casino. I felt guilty going off by myself but relieved as well. I wouldn't have liked being cooped up in that room all night reading a book or wandering around the compound by myself watching everybody else act rich. I was getting excited thinking about the casino. What I liked about gambling was the romance of it: the chandeliers, the green blackjack tables, the clicking roulette wheels. I imagined I was James Bond. You know, lethal, lucky at cards, irresistible to women. I had about thirty-five dollars in my wallet.

We cleared some trees at the top of the hill and stopped in front of a big, dark concrete building. There were two policemen or soldiers with rifles guarding the entrance.

"What's this?" I asked the driver.

"Casino, man. Ten dollars." He pulled away as soon as I got out, practically knocked me down. I went over to one of the guards.

"Is this the casino?"

"Yah."

"Well, when does it open?"

"Closed. Government have it closed to further notice."

This was perfect. My wife was back in our honeymoon haven more than likely regurgitating the last of her poisoned wedding cake, and I was standing in front of a closed casino with twenty-five dollars in my pocket, feeling like a total idiot in my permanent-press vacation togs. I walked around the back of the building and found a stairway. It led to a rough cement roof with nothing on it but one rusty old metal lawn chair.

By now it had started to drizzle. I pulled the chair to the edge of the roof and sat looking at the cruise ships all lit up. Out there roulette wheels were spinning and gorgeous women were getting panting drunk on champagne. I heard footsteps behind me. One of the soldiers came over. I noticed he had high black paratrooper's boots. By now I was pretty well soaked and didn't much care what happened to me. He didn't say a word. I sighed and got up. I walked all the way down the hill into the dark town, splashing mud all over my pants. I must have gone ten blocks through the town without seeing anyone, and finally, down near the pier, I found a cab.

When I got back to the hotel, I sat in the bar and drank three piña coladas to warm up. It seemed just too embarrassing to go back and tell my wife what happened, so I sat around for a while watching people drink and dance. When I got back to the room it was fairly late and my wife was asleep. I felt chilled and figured I was probably getting a cold, which served me right for imagining that just once I could actually try to go somewhere and enjoy myself.

Later on, after I had gone to bed, my wife woke me up, whispering to me, "I think there's something in the bathroom."

"What?"

"Something's running around in the bathroom." I put on my sneakers, went into the bathroom, and flipped on the light, expecting lizards, scorpions, snakes. A mouse flashed between my legs and ran into the bedroom. "What is it?" yelled my wife.

"A mouse, a fucking mouse."

I looked under the bed and it ran past me again. I had to chase it for about fifteen minutes before I managed to maneuver it out the door. I turned out the lights and got back into bed. My wife was holding my arm. "How do you think it got in?" she whispered.

"Am I a goddamn mouse? How do I know. Maybe under the door." The door to the room was easily an inch and a half short of the doorstep. Anything could crawl through it.

We lay there in the darkness awhile staring at the band of pale light at the bottom of the door. "Maybe you should put some towels there," my wife said.

"Shit!" I got up and grabbed some towels from the bathroom and stuffed them under the door.

An hour later, I had calmed down enough to start drifting into sleep when an awful noise like a giant mosquito started right outside the window. It was a six-foot-high electric generator whining like it was about to take off. I put on my clothes and ran outside. I was enraged, insane, I could have ripped out somebody's throat. I saw two guys about thirty feet away in the boat shed with welding torches. "What the fuck is going on?"

"Don't worry, man, that thing only on ten minutes every couple hours." They were laughing. I stomped back to the room. As I yanked open the door, the mouse ran past me and into the bathroom.

When I woke up it was late morning and already very hot. I was sweating and miserable. My wife came out whistling and drying her hair. I stared at her. "What are you so happy about?"

"I feel better now. Let's have breakfast." She had her regular cheerful smile back now. I figured, okay, it's our honeymoon, I'll give this place one more chance.

During breakfast she found out from the waiter about a motorboat that made hourly runs to the shell beach on the other side of the harbor. They had snorkeling there—something she loved to do. "Let's go," she said.

I looked across the bay to the beach. "I'll fry to death over there."

"You can stay in the room, but I want to go." I grumbled over to the boat with her and we waited in the hot sun for the noon run.

The beach was mostly rocks and shells; you had to walk carefully not to cut yourself, and the heat was awful. I hadn't brought a hat and I was too afraid of sharks and barracudas to go in the water. There wasn't a shade tree on the entire beach and the hillside was too steep and rocky to find anyplace else to hide. I covered myself with the towel and squinted out to where my wife and some guy were snorkeling. I hated this. I should have stayed in the room and read *Doctor No*. My wife came back onto the beach with a piece of coral. "Great," I said, "that's the most wonderful piece of coral I ever saw." She gave me a black look. One thing she couldn't stand was my sarcasm. I told her I was going back on the next boat.

"Fine," she said, and turned to go back into the water. "I'll see you later."

Back in the room I was stewing so bad I couldn't even read. It was hot and of course I hadn't listened to my wife and put on suntan lotion. Now I was red and burning all over. I was cursing out loud and picturing her with her snorkeling buddy having a great old time, while I writhed on my bed of pain.

She didn't get back for another two hours. When she walked into the room carrying a bag full of shells and coral, I snapped at her, "I thought this was *our* honeymoon."

"Well," she said, "I wanted to snorkel—you don't even want to go in the water."

"I have a terrible sunburn."

"I told you to put on the lotion."

"I hate this place. There's nothing to do but swimming and sailing—all this boring shit."

"Well, you picked this place," she said through clenched teeth. "Why don't you at least try to enjoy it?"

"Fucking stupid island. There's nothing I feel like doing here."

She exploded. "You complain about everything. Tell me where you would be happy—even for five minutes. You're just trying to ruin my vacation!"

"Your vacation? Yours! That's fucking typical. What about me? I took care of you when you were throwing up all over the place. You should at least be grateful!"

Bang. Bam! It was one of the worst fights we had had in a long time. She grabbed her sunglasses and a book and slammed out of the room. I sat there on the bed furious, thinking how you never really know somebody till you have to spend a lot of time alone with her. Inconsiderate selfish bitch. And now we're married! I'm supposed to spend my whole life with her? I picked up *Doctor No*. James Bond never got married, he had brains.

About an hour later, she came back. "I'm going on a sailboat for an evening cruise. Do you want to come?" I didn't say anything, just kept reading my book.

"Look," she said, "you better tell me right now if you want to go because I have to make a reservation."

I put the book down. "How long will it be?"

"I don't know, two hours."

"I don't know if I brought a sweater."

"Jesus!"

"All right," I said, "I'll go."

After a nearly silent dinner, we headed out of the harbor at sunset—straight out to sea. The sailboat was pretty big but besides us there were only two other couples on board. In just a few minutes the sky was purple-black and covered with stars. The sound of the water rushing against the sides of the boat was very soothing. One of the crew came around and gave my wife and me piña coladas. We lay back against some cushions. The cool air felt terrific on my sunburn. "I'm sorry for being so nasty," I said.

"That's all right."

Two hours seemed too short. I lay there with my arm around her and she told me of other trips she'd taken on boats and ships, how the sea was magical to her, the beginning of life. She told me of plans she had for the future, the baby to come, writing books. I was perfectly content to watch the stars and listen. I had never imagined the future

at all and that was something that fascinated me about her—that she
had such optimism. Not for the first time did I wonder why such a
person would choose to spend the rest of her life with a hopeless
malcontent like me. But for the moment I was happy.

Late at night, after we had made love and she was sleeping, I got up
and went outside. The lights on the boats were mostly out and the air
was just a touch cool. I walked over to the terrace outside the main
house. The only sounds were a couple of night birds, crickets, and the
water slapping softly against the boats. There was a man sitting alone
at a table in the moonlight, one of the Yacht People. Without asking I
sat at the table with him. "It's beautiful here," I said. He nodded. He
was maybe twenty-eight, big and very handsome, with gold hair,
dressed in white T-shirt and shorts. On his head, tilted back a bit, was
a white skipper's hat with a blue and gold insignia like a coat of arms.
"What boat you from?" I asked.

"The *Belinda*." He nodded in the direction of the biggest boat in
the harbor. There were people on the deck drinking and laughing. I
could just catch the sounds across the water.

I must have sighed out loud. "I bet it's great, sailing all the time on
one of those."

"Hmn."

"Where you coming from?"

"Jamaica."

"Where you headed?"

"Venezuela, then Rio. . . ."

They had all been in a race starting in Bermuda, going all through
the islands to Montego Bay. Now the race was over and they were
"taking it easy" for a while. Taking it easy. I thought of the 104 bus I
took to work in Manhattan every day. I talked to him for a long time.
It turns out this guy had never worked—not a day in his life except
crewing on various sailboats. Since he left college he had spent his
entire life traveling. From February to May, he sailed all over the
Caribbean and the Atlantic in his yacht. In the summer and fall he was
at home at his house in Newport and in the winter he went skiing in
Europe. I imagined his life, never having to work. "That's incredible," I said.

He nodded and gave me a sleepy smile. "I guess it is." He seemed
not to care.

Looking at him and the people out on the boats who were lounging on the decks drinking, I realized that what I had taken all the time to be arrogance and willful ignorance was actually just boredom, vast inescapable boredom. All of them, young and beautiful, they sailed through these islands like ghosts. It seemed very sad. But I had to catch myself. After all, they were snobby and overbearing, and even more, they were symbols of everything wrong with the world. Maybe I was just trying to rationalize my way out of my envy; yet, now, they seemed less powerful and less threatening to me—they were just like lost children.

The next morning, my wife wanted to escape the compound. We walked over to the gate and found a cab for hire to take us on a tour of the island. The driver said he would also take us to the most beautiful beach on Antigua. I brought the camera and this time I also brought my bathing suit and suntan lotion. I was trying to get into the swing of things, be a regular guy.

The driver looked to be over sixty years old, short and wiry. He had angry eyes and an amused smile. "Where you folks want to go first?"

"Well, it's your country," I said. "Why don't you show us whatever you want?"

He drove inland, on roads that were dryer and dustier than the ones near the beaches. It was very hot and the ground all around was baked and hard-looking. There was nothing much to look at but burned stubble and thorn bushes. We drove slowly through a village. There were little kids playing behind broken fences in yards full of old junk, broken washing machines, rusty car parts. Here and there were a couple of scraggly-looking chickens and goats. The roofs of the little wooden houses were covered in tar paper or tin, and men and women sat on the stoops or chairs staring out at the road. We passed by a restaurant-bar painted bright colors. I was thirsty. "Can we go in and get a beer?" I asked.

"No, man, these people wouldn't be friendly to you."

"Oh."

Everywhere we looked, quiet angry men were sitting, doing nothing, drinking beer; women were yelling at the skinny kids playing in the dirt. We pulled to the top of a rise looking over a beach and the driver stopped the car and started to talk. He used to be a high-school teacher but was fired a couple of years ago along with a quite a few others because the government didn't like their politics. "I'm lucky," he said. "Some of my friends are in jail. Yes, you got to be real careful what you say these days and who you say it to—you get yourself locked up real quick." He looked back at us as if it were vaguely possible that even we were police spies.

We drove down the hill to the beach. He got out and said he was going to have his lunch in the shade and that we should go on down to the water. Down on the sand, under some palms, there was a single picnic table. It was truly a beautiful place, a half-mile of white sand in either direction. I leaned back against a tree and popped open a beer. My wife, as usual, headed straight for the water. I felt the warm breeze on me as I looked out into the empty bay, but behind me I could hear the driver unwrapping the wax paper from his sandwich. If you really think about it, there are no vacations in this world.

My wife swam and dove. God, how she loved the ocean. To me it was just a place to drown or get your leg chewed off. Finally, she came out with her eyes and skin sparkling in the sun, and I thought, This really is her element, the water; anything else was just temporary for her. She was tall and sexy but more than that—she seemed at that moment like a mythical sea goddess. I felt a sudden fear that if I wasn't careful she might disappear back into the waves.

I handed her a towel. She stood, drying her hair and staring out at the bay. "This is surely one of the most beautiful places I've ever seen." We sat on a beach towel eating sandwiches, with no need to talk.

The driver came down and said it was time to go back to the hotel; he had another party he was taking out at two o'clock. When we got back to the room we took showers and dozed off for a bit. I woke up with a strange feeling of urgency, of fear. My wife was lying next to me, eyes open, just staring—something she rarely did. It was a sure sign she was feeling bad. "What's wrong?" I asked.

"I don't know," she said. "What time is it?"

"About four o'clock." She got up and looked out the window.

"It's gray out. We ought to do something—take a walk."

We had some coffee on the terrace and then decided to go up to the old fort, high on a steep hill overlooking the harbor. It was rocky and barren, just a lot of scrubby, mean bushes and cactus. There were a few other vacationers making the climb with us. We scratched our legs a little getting to the top. There wasn't much left, just a few ruined walls of thick black stone, but I could still see the sections where the cannon poked out, and the cannon were still there—old, black, and rusty but still murderous-looking. I jumped down into a deep hole, scaring off a couple of lizards. This was obviously once some underground chamber. There were thick iron rings sunk into the stone blocks. Some guy poked his head over the edge of the hole. I called up to him. "Hey, what was this room, do you know?"

He looked in a pamphlet he was holding, "The dungeon. Says here there was a dungeon for criminals—you know, pirates and escaped slaves." I put my hand through one of the rings. It was cold as ice.

The sky was slate gray with a couple of spots where the sun was streaking through, and there were odd-looking shafts of light covering parts of the hill and harbor. Halfway down, I picked a purple cactus flower and gave it to my wife. "Here," I said, "put it in your hair. It's the same color as your blouse." She put it just above her ear. My wife was not the type to decorate herself; she never used makeup or wore much jewelry. Some pale sunlight streaked her for a moment, and there was a strong breeze blowing her hair around; she smiled at me, a sunny, shy smile, her purple blouse in the wind, purple cactus flower, dark clouds. I still have that picture.

When we got down from the hill, I started on the path to our room, but she stopped. "I want to go over to the house and check on something."

"Right," I said. "I'll see you in a little bit." Just as I got to the room, large warm drops of rain started to fall. I went in and picked up my novel.

My wife came in, fixing me with her special troubled but determined look. "There's a flight tomorrow at eleven A.M." She sat on the bed next to me. Tomorrow at eleven—two days earlier than we were supposed to leave. I sighed but really there was nothing to say. If she hadn't thought of doing it, I probably would have. It was obvious that it was wrong for us to be in this place.

Just across the way in the yacht club, the Yacht People were laughing and dancing. Across the harbor, the lights were coming on in the houses on the hillsides. And outside the compound, the fortress, outside the locked gates of the former colonial governor's mansion, our honeymoon hotel, I could see the last poor woman hefting her baby and gathering up her few pieces of rotten fruit, walking home on that dry miserable road. This island was completely out of balance. Three hundred years of slavery, torture, blood, poverty, and race hatred was baked into the bricks of the buildings, staining the blue-green water, rising up from the twenty yards of ground you walked over to get your piña colada. We had no more business here than the first white soldier or missionary three hundred years before.

The next morning, we packed and then went up to have our last breakfast on the hotel terrace. As soon as we got out the door, I realized something had changed. The boats were gone! There wasn't a yacht left in the harbor. Just like a flock of birds they had disappeared without a trace. It was funny, but I missed them. There were only two other vacationing couples at the tables. Were they honeymooners too? The waiters were considerably cheerier. Maybe they knew we were getting the hell out. It was fine with them.

We cleared the customs after a meticulous and humiliating search of our luggage. Who could blame them? Any fool could see that we were international drug smugglers. Anyway, they were bored and it was a good way to pass the time. One last memory of honeymoon heaven.

Finally we were on the plane ready to take off. "I'm sorry," my wife said. "That was an awful vacation."

"Yeah, it was awful all right. I should have picked another place."

"It wasn't your fault—you couldn't have known."

But I wondered. Was I innocent or stupid? Maybe I should have known. What world did I live in anyway? She held my hand. "Look," she said, "I don't want to come to a place like this again. Is that okay with you?"

"Absolutely."

A couple of days later, I was looking in the refrigerator for some chocolate ice cream to repair the psychic damage of life in New York. In the living room, my wife was looking at the wedding and honeymoon pictures that she had just picked up. The door buzzer buzzed; it was my friend Frank, the best man at the wedding. I got him a beer and we sat down on the couch to look at the pictures: relatives, us cutting the cake, palm trees, my wife coming out of the ocean like Venus, the yachts, and the cannon poking out against the gray sky; my wife again, looking mystical on the hill with her purple cactus flower.

Frank lifted one picture out of the pack. "What's this?"

"Oh, that's the night before we left for our trip. See, there are two rainbow rings around the moon. It's a sign of good luck." My wife and I smiled at each other.

"Good luck?" said Frank, who had been in the navy for three years during Vietnam. "Rings around the moon don't mean good luck."

"What do they mean, then?"

"It's a storm warning." He took a swig of beer. "So," he said, "how was your honeymoon?"

PARALEGAL

I have a dream that I am in a jungle in one of those New Jersey theme parks. I'm standing near the entrance of it, a very wild place where it looks as if the jungle actually got loose. Sometimes, I suppose, even in New Jersey, in the jungle park something gets out and eats somebody from West Orange.

I'm standing near the entrance of this park, and up walks a huge tree, which was actually a camel (remember this *is* a dream). The thing was like one of those *Empire Strikes Back* machines. It's a walking creature that carries people inside it. And it is being driven by a man in his forties. I go over to look at it, and all of a sudden a gigantic python—the longest python anybody has ever seen—drops on top of this thing. Obviously it's going to squeeze all the occupants to death. And I say (just to be helpful), "Wow, that's the largest snake I ever saw."

This driver says, "Don't worry about it, I'm in charge." Just like that, like Captain America. And sure enough, he says to the snake, "Get back!" and drives off. Then the snake turns into a large truck tire, and the man is walking it on a leash. He's wearing a military uniform, he's a colonel. The situation is *completely* under control. And it turns out also that he saved his whole family. His family was in the walking camel-tree, including his aged mother who's very wealthy. He saved them all by sheer manly bravado. Next scene: The jungle has become a law office, and I'm walking down the hall, I'm looking for the guy driving the tree. I know instinctively that the hero is one of the senior partners, because a secretary or a paralegal—even an associate lawyer—couldn't take care of a snake that size. It had to be a senior partner. I go down the hallway, and sure enough in the bathroom, washing up, it *is* one of the senior partners—the one I work with. I say, "I'm amazed that you killed that snake. I'm astonished you're not dead."

And in that perfectly assured manner that only the rich have, he says, "God did not give me six thousand shares of IBM so that he would kill me the next day."

I am awakened by my three-and-a-half-year-old daughter kissing me. She came in from her own room. Now my wife and I had decided that maybe we'd train her, you know, to knock on the door—to say "Can I come in, Mommy and Daddy?" But it's hopeless, she just walks in and slams the door against the bureau. This morning, however, she didn't slam the door the way she usually does. She didn't jump on the bed and hit me with a toy. She just kissed me on the cheek. It was so beautiful.

Outside it's, "Yo! Move it up!" The garbage men are throwing trash cans at six thirty in the morning; they sail the metal tops against the sides of buildings. I open my eyes and say, "Hi."

My daughter says, "Are you ready to play?" Little kids unless they're sick are *always* ready to play. And it makes perfect sense to them that you should be ready to play, too. But this is Monday morning for God's sake! "No, Daddy needs a little time." Boom! Bam! "YO! MOVE IT UP!" You bet your life Daddy needs a little time—about three months in the South of France.

I roll over and see a fine film of ash on the windowsill. I live right across the street from a big funeral parlor. They cremate people there. I have the diesel fuel from all the delivery trucks that come roaring up Amsterdam Avenue; I have all this pollution in my eyes *and* the ash from across the street—probably Beloved Uncle.

"Let's play hide and seek."

I tell her, "I have to get up now. I need to have some coffee because I don't know what I'm doing."

"Why don't you know what you're doing, Daddy?" That's the first of at least four thousand "whys" for the day. She's in a stage where she asks "why" about everything and when you explain something, she just asks "why" again. The only thing you can do to stop it is tickle her or threaten her.

Actually I would like to stay home and play with her right then. Now I don't want to sound like "Father Knows Best" or something—as if my life were centered completely around the kids. No—I don't want to run and jump with her first thing Monday morning but what's *worse* is going downtown to the law office where I'm a paralegal. So she has to get used to the fact that I have to get dressed, put on my tie, and leave.

I'm in the bathroom in my undershirt. I'm shaving and she's sitting on a little stool. It's very sweet. She says, "Why do you have to shave, Daddy?"

"Because men have beards."

"How come women don't grow beards?"

"I don't know." That's the first of the three hundred "I don't knows" of the day. They can make you feel very stupid, kids. The mantra of saying over and over again, all day long, "I don't know, I'm not sure, I can't really tell you," makes you feel like Mortimer Snerd. What *do* I know anyway?

I put my tie on. "Why can't men have babies?"

I say, "Oh, well, you know, they don't have wombs."

"But we all have wombs here. You have a womb," she says.

"No," I tell her, "we have *rooms,* not wombs, like Mommy."

"Why?"

Coffee. I'm in the kitchen now and experiencing the fear, the dread of stepping out into the torrent of the city. I have a tie on, my shirt is buttoned. I have to conform.

I live in one of those sections of the city where several years ago the State of New York emptied its mental hospitals onto the streets. That and the rising crime and increasing poverty all combine to make even a two-block walk to the bus stop an adventure. Anything could happen. So I have to adopt an inhuman hardness, because as soon as you step out into the street it's filth, danger, and lunatics, and after all, I can't go to work with spittle all over me. I can't show up at the office with a stab wound or my shirt ripped open, right? Because it's unseemly and it would violate the prime directive of the law firm: Don't do anything to undermine the Confidence of the Clients. I have pity for people on the street, but you have to get your mind set if you work in an office. You have to become formal and tough.

I'm at the elevator. My daughter says, "Don't go to work, Daddy, you don't have to go to work."

"Why don't I have to go to work?" I ask her.

" 'Cause you don't want to." Now that's the ultimate reasoning of a child and believe me, it surpasses all the reasoning I've ever heard.

"Why do you have to go to work?"

"Because I have to earn money."

"Why do you need money?"

"Well, um, I need money to buy food."

She smiles at me and says, "And to buy presents for your little child."

"Yes," I say, "that's why I have to go to work." The elevator arrives.

I'm on the street at the end of the summer and all the cat piss in New York is steaming and the garbage is reeking.

I sit on the bus with my book. I'm reading Norman Mailer; that's pretty classy. There's a hot book-reading competition on the subways and buses. As soon as I get settled, I look around at other people's books. Well, I think, *he's* stupid, he's reading Sidney Sheldon. Then I look across the aisle, and see a woman reading Jean Genet. And I think, Ah, a soul in my own category.

Of course, the worst thing on the bus is the head-set radios, those Sony Walkmen stuck in people's ears. The sound is worse than an actual radio, because with a radio you can hear the music—you hear the range of notes. But from a Walkman you hear, *chee-ta-chee-chee-chee-ta-chee-chee, chee-ta-chee-chee*. The Fifth Symphony or Light FM, it all sounds exactly the same. It feels as if someone has surgically implanted mosquitoes in your ears. My violent fantasies begin.

The 104 bus goes down Broadway. I look out the window. Every sort of person in the world is out there, bums, businessmen, drunks, killers, ballet dancers—all rushing downtown like mad schools of fish, going to make a big score, become a star. We pass Lincoln Center. Dozens of Japanese tourists are taking snapshots of people shooting a magazine layout.

The bus is lurching and bumping its way downtown. We pass the marquees: *Lick Me Clean . . . Horny Nurses . . . Cats. Cats* has been playing since I started my job. The traffic is jammed up and angry. People waiting to cross the street look vicious or worn-out, and it's only 9 A.M. We make a left turn at Forty-second Street and my terror increases because *I don't want to go to this place.* I've worked almost all my adult life. People can testify to this. I have papers—signed documents—that I have worked hard but *I do not want to go to this place.*

I get off the bus and go into the deli. I buy my cement bagel. I'm in a line with all the other robots. The guy says, "How you doing this morning, buddy?"

"Okay."

"Regular?"

"Yeah."

"You want a bagel toasted?"

"Yeah."

We're all standing patiently in line. Everybody always gets the same thing each morning. You recognize people after a few weeks. Up ahead is the cranberry muffin. Behind you is the cream cheese on rye. It reminds me of the mental hospital; people there had the habit of shuffling. You wore slippers and you shuffled around the ward. Three times a day at the nurses' station you lined up to get your medication. Shuffle, shuffle. "Thorazine on a bun to travel" (shuffle, shuffle). "Toasted Valium, regular coffee, no sugar. Here you go, buddy. Take it away. Next."

I go out the door of the deli. When you've worked in an office for a long time, you know times and distances exactly. You get off the bus and you know how many steps it is to the deli. You know unconsciously when you get out of the deli after standing in line with six people in front of you (shuffle, shuffle) exactly how many steps it is to the corner and that the light will be green and you can cross because it's that way every morning. And it will be that way every morning until Jesus wakes and the trumpets blow. I cross with the herd, and I pass by people giving out leaflets for health clubs and massage parlors, free sample packs of cigarettes, and brochures for a new vegetarian restaurant.

I walk exactly thirty-six paces to the lobby of my building. It is thirty-one stories high, all stone and metal. It looks like an evil tower in a frozen hell. I go into the lobby. At the newsstand everybody is buying chewing gum, cough drops, Rolaids, *People* magazine and *Wall Street Journals*. Whole starving populations in Africa could be fed by the money spent by Manhattan office workers on their morning junk.

The lobby of this building is all gray stone and polished steel. It is not meant for human beings. Everybody presses into the elevator. They're all in a rush.

I get out at the twenty-second floor—the reception desk. The young receptionist glares at me—she hates my guts because I'm unkempt and I come and go at any hour as I please. She wonders how I, who am *not* a lawyer, can get away with this behavior. It seems un-American. She's furious anyway because she's always on view and can't do even one little thing she wants except on her lunch hour and coffee breaks. She has to sit there all day welcoming people. She can't even do her nails or read Tom Selleck's autobiography.

The other receptionist, Florence, who's in her mid-thirties, thinks I'm very amusing with my crumpled pants and half-tied tie. She's been a receptionist/telephone operator with the firm for light-years. She thinks half the lawyers are pompous assholes. We have long chats about how life is one long raw deal. Florence checks me in 8:45 A.M. no matter when I show up. The reception area is crowded with horn-rims and monogrammed briefcases—all reading *US News and World Report* and the *Wall Street Journal.* I have an urge to buy a copy of *Gent* or *Cherry* in the lobby and stick it in the pile of stuff they keep for clients.

I climb a short stairway to the next floor to get to my little rodent hole. The rugs, the wallpaper, the ceilings are all gray. The place looks and feels like a morgue. On the wall are portraits of all the dead partners going back to the founder of the firm. They are all severe old men whose eyes seem to follow you down the hall saying, "Time is money, time is money." There's a group of portraits of recently retired and not-long-dead partners that were all obviously painted at the same time. The artist committed mass portraiture. Their faces all look the same and the oil is a little green and greasy-looking.

As soon as I walk down the hall, it starts.

"Good morning."

"How was your weekend?"

"Good morning."

If it's Monday morning they say, "Have a good one?" If it's Friday afternoon they say, "Have a good one!"

From the secretaries I meet with a mixed reaction, a combination of relief and hatred. They don't like me because I'm late all the time and they all have to be on time or they would get into trouble and of course they're not as self-destructive as I am, they want to keep their jobs.

All they really want to do is get home, see their families, or watch television. So they look at me, they're pissed off about my lateness but they also know *I don't care*, so I'm frequently a source of entertainment to them. I say, "How ya doin'?" and a secretary asks, "What am I gonna do with all these papers?" I say, "Shove 'em up the partner's ass." She laughs. So, they like me and they don't like me. There's a feeling of tension surrounding me, a kinetic energy as I walk along. My boss's secretary, Maryann, tells me, "I don't know what I'm gonna do, I'm having such a tough morning. I've got sixteen letters to send and I won't have time." I say, "Don't do 'em." She laughs—it helps her to get through the day. I arrive at my little windowless rodent hole of an office and sit down.

I spend most of my work hours daydreaming. But it's not good to daydream at your desk, so I have many hiding places where people can't find me. I go into the bathroom, for instance, into the cubicle, and sit down on the toilet. I'm smart though; I drop my pants so in case anybody is looking from the next stall it won't seem suspicious. I sit there for twenty or thirty minutes. Sometimes I take a nap, sometimes I daydream that I'm performing and Hal Prince is in the audience. He comes up to me after the show and says, "Can you do this kind of thing every night?" And I say, "Of course!" I'm on Broadway, I'm rich and famous. . . .

I feel awful because I'm hiding out. I'm humiliated because I'm almost thirty-nine and I'm too lazy and self-destructive to go out and look for a *real* job—something to do with radio and performing. I feel like I did at school when I hid out in the bathroom, or the school basement. It's a dirty feeling, not living up to the Judeo-Christian ethic. I am wasting time. I should be working. I should be at my desk. But I just can't go back. I don't want to face the portraits, the secretaries, the lawyers, the endless paper.

What do I hear when I sit there? A symphony of defecation and urination. I'm sitting in the middle stall. I always pick the middle one because that's where the light is on so I can read. The joke is on me, though, because I'm very squeamish, and that causes problems. The lawyers come in for their morning evacuations.

Let me tell you about lawyers. The main thing is you have to be *tough*. A lawyer who is kind or soft-spoken, or who knows his faults— that person is not a real lawyer. Real lawyers do *everything* the same.

They do not fool around. When you hear a lawyer in court say, "Your Honor I *demand* the death penalty," he's serious! And that is exactly how they piss and shit. They march into the bathroom, bang into the stall; the buckle is unbuckled; the pants slide down the legal thighs; then the heavy $200,000-a-year flesh plops onto the bowl. But a lawyer does not sit around. A lawyer does not waste time. Time is money. *Pluthhtpt!* It comes charging out of them.

They don't modify their voices just because they're in a bathroom.

"Well, John, took my boat out Sunday."

"Oh yes, Frank."

"Yup. Made of fiberglass you know. Stiff, fiberglass is stiff. In fact, John, I had the stiffest boat in the line."

"Decision come down yet?" *Pluthhtpt!*

"Nope!"

"Well buck up! There'll be one soon. Have a good one!" *Pluthhtpt!* They don't stop for a second, these guys. That's why they're successes and why I'm sitting on the toilet daydreaming.

I feel terrible, worse and worse, and it's only 9:45. I have seven hours to go. I get out and go back to my desk. On the way back to my office I'm struck by the first pang, my first heart-clutch of the day. As I walk past the partners and secretaries down the hallways, I'm seized with a vision of my little daughter. I feel an overwhelming surge of love and pain. I see her small round face which looks a little like mine. She's really beautiful, with blond hair cut short, a little smile. It's a sensation in my navel that radiates outward. Tears come to my eyes as I walk past the desks. Everybody's doing these petty meaningless things. Oh, they don't all think so, but it seems that way to me. Vanity, vanity of vanities, all around me and I feel a connection to my daughter as if a huge umbilical cord is stretching from Forty-third and Lexington Avenue, right up to the Seventies on the West Side. And I know that wherever she is, she's *connected* to me. She's in my blood, she's in my bones. This seizure lasts for a couple of seconds; then I'm back in the traffic again. I go to my desk, sit down, start working.

Now what is going on at this place? Mammoth Industries is suing Monumental Screw and Bolt. Serious stuff, you know, and my job is to file papers and stamp documents. I have a heavy metal stamper with a wooden handle and I have 18,000 documents to stamp, 1, 2, 3,

4 . . . infinity. The sound is awful. *Ka-chungh! 1, ka-chungk! 2*, my brain is vibrating already! So I've been stamping a batch of documents with a lot of pictures; brochures and annual reports of a California health ranch or something like that. There are 250 pages of guys with muscles and smiles relaxing on bicycle machines and beautiful women saying "I was a size 32 before I came here and now . . ." So I stamp all these beautiful men and women in their short leotards right smack across their genitals. *Ka-chunk! #1063*, "Since I started the Nautilus program, I . . ." *Ka-blam! #1064*, right across the balls.

I stamped the first 1000 or so last Friday. The lawyer I work for comes over to my hole, holding these documents. He says, "You know it would be a good idea when stamping documents to stamp them in the lower right corner. That way, when you're handling them you can see the numbers very clearly." He shows me the viciously defaced exercisers. He knows damn well what I'm doing, because the guy's twice as smart as I am and he knows that I'm stamping these people's privates because I detest everything the law firm stands for and I hate my job.

My boss. Everything is exactly in order on his desk. At the beginning of the day, his blotter is as stark as the Gobi Desert, not a speck of anything living in the middle of it. He comes in in the morning, hangs up his hat and coat, sits down, and starts to work. Doesn't say a word to anybody. If you say good morning to him, he's so intent on his work he hardly hears you.

So this is the man who's standing at my office door holding 250 pages of people's reproductive organs smeared by the mad stamper. But, God bless him, he must have taken a course in management techniques, or more likely he's just a very patient guy, because he will never raise his voice to me. And he has plenty of cause to, because I do some enormously destructive and stupid things. I'm trying in my very immature way to get out of the job, but far be it for me to just come out and say, "I can't stand this! I'm going to be a lumberjack!" No. I have to do something stupid like screwing up the documents. I set time bombs for myself.

After our discussion on correct paper stamping, I get a call. It's now 10:30 A.M.—I can't avoid knowing what time it is because there are clocks all over the place; we represent a huge clock company. "Hello, Joanne Accounting." Not Joanne in Accounting. *Joanne Accounting*. If you work in a big office your name is derived from your job like in olden days: Weaver, Parker, Carter. "Hello Joanne Accounting here." Marvin Maintenance. Florence Fileroom.

I'm wondering, what did I do now? "What's the story, Joanne?" I ask. Actually I'm glad to talk to anybody—it makes the time go faster. She says, "Uh, I wanna ask you a question. On the computer we're doing the charges. You know the billing?"

"Yeah," I say and tune her out.

There are three kinds of computer systems in our office. One is a Wang word-processing system. The second is a legal information computer called Lexis. And the third is what Joanne Accounting is calling about. In a law office everything you do is charged to the clients: stamping documents, photostating, blowing your nose. So they have a billing computer—each week you enter every minute of what you did and for whom. Everything you enter has complicated codes and procedures. Next to the machine is a legal pad where you record the same information in English. Now I'm the kind of person who, even though I have the exact change, goes to a toll booth with a person in it. I like to put my money in a human hand. In a building where there's an elevator sometimes I prefer to walk. Well, it's the same thing with this computer. I would rather write down all this information on the legal pad. Joanne is talking. "I don't understand these references on the computer to clients named *Goop, Wimple, Wigwam,* and *Omnigorge,* from August fourth."

"What do you mean?"

"Well, you know we're trying to—you have seven hundred and eighty dollars' worth of expenses to be charged to these clients and I don't know who *Goop, Wimple* is."

Shit. It turns out that the legal pad is just for my information, and I was writing all these nonsense words on the computer screen. That's the only record that they have of the last two months of my work. She tells me I'll have to spend at least three days in accounting straightening it out. For this I'm going to need morphine.

Gets to be about 11:00 A.M. I can look forward to lunch now. That's exciting. I can get out on the crowded street and get a Blimpie sandwich. But still an entire hour till lunch.

11:10 A.M., the phone rings, it's the office manager. "Feder," she says, "we have a new copier just installed on your floor. Training in twenty minutes."

This is *very* exciting. The old copy machine was leaking toner and like an old horse, it had to be shot.

11:30 A.M., we're all standing around the machine. The guy has come in from the copy machine company; he's very serious, dressed in a suit and tie. He's demonstrating the new copier, a state-of-the-art whatever. Everybody's excited, especially some of the secretaries. They're excited about anything new that happens at the place. A lot of them really take their jobs seriously. Secretaries to executives can get very team oriented, so if you insult their boss or even one of their clients they can be vicious. Maybe it's a part of the old patriarchal system. When I was there about two months, my secretary (whose services I shared with my boss) and another secretary got in a fight. The other woman had told me to turn off the lamp on my desk. "It's getting in my eyes," she said. "My" secretary whipped around like a mother lion and said, "You leave my paralegal alone!" I loved that.

So, there we are, all gathered around the new machine. The women are oohing and ahhing—touching it reverently like the obelisk in *2001*. The copy guy is saying it'll make six hundred copies in twenty seconds and cure leukemia. They're trained to deliver these monologues—a kind of a patter they've developed, like a comic or a magician. "You put the original in like this and press copy mode and presto! Now, my lovely assistant Roxanne will hand me that original document. Roxanne, thank you. Ah, here it is, nothing up my sleeves. And look, it's a copy!" After about fifteen minutes of watching him perform, I wander off.

Now it's almost noon but still not time for lunch. I have a daydream about a musical that I want to write about a law firm. This is the opening number: The partners come out, mostly beefy guys—the older they get and the higher they rise in the law firm, the more carnivorous they seem to get. They start to look like sides of beef. In the musical, twenty partners enter from the wings. They're all wearing suspenders because they like to think of themselves as kindly Jimmy Stewarts sitting around the potbelly stove when actually they're putting four thousand workers on unemployment by some agreement they just wrote. Like Cossacks, they'll all cross their arms and sing, "We are the partners. Watch out for us!" And then some heavy syncopated bass music plays and the "boys" in the mailroom, all Puerto Rican, come out and do a *West Side Story* type number—"I've got the package for you, boss." Now of course there's a love story in this musical. John Wellington Smythborn VI is a young associate rising to partnership. He's in love with a secretary, Joanne Delacaccio from Brooklyn. It's like Romeo and Juliet. How could two such families ever be united? They gaze at each other across the copy machine. It's heartbreaking. They can never consummate their passion because John Wellington Smythborn is not the kind of guy who goes to the Granada Hotel on Thirty-fifth Street—adult videotapes in all rooms—and Joanne's a good girl, too. They yearn terribly for each other. Then secretaries enter stage left, dressed like Carmen Miranda, and singing, "De Wang is down, my head is turning aroun', 'cause all de lawyers' briefs are fallin' down." There's also a strolling calypso band of paralegals that plays in the aisles.

12:00. Lunch! On the way to Blimpies I have another daydream—a man will have pulled a gun on Forty-second Street, held it to the heads of his baby daughter and wife and threatened to kill them. I walk over, break through the crowd, and talk to this man for six hours. All the TV, radio, and newspaper people are there. It's the most incredible virtuoso performance ever. The wife and daughter are saved! They have it on videotape. It becomes a famous movie. I become a cult figure. I'm hired by all the major police departments as a consultant. I become very wealthy. I write books.

Back from lunch. It's one o'clock. Another one of my innumerable land mines of self-destruction has detonated under my boss. I made five copies of something I shouldn't have copied, a secret document, and mailed it off to the other side in a major litigation. He calls me into his office. I'm very embarrassed. After all I'm thirty-eight; this guy's at least six years younger than I. He says, "You know we can't have this kind of behavior anymore."

"What did I do now?"

"You mailed off five copies of the rocket plans to Mammoth Industries." Oh Jesus.

"I called the other side," he says. "They agreed not to use it and they're mailing it back. Please be careful." I'm immediately drawn into the unwelcome and unwanted feeling of Truant.

The rebellious school kid. That's the emotional position. You see, all these men, even the young ones, are my father to me. Most of them are big guys, ex-athletes, ex-military guys—John Ramrod III, attorney at law. Sometimes, passing me in the hall, they say, "I hear you're an artist."

"Yeah."

"What do you do?"

"I tell stories."

"Oh."

They don't burst out laughing, or stare, or scowl with contempt or anything. A lawyer is trained to look you in the face and seem confident and happy to see you—thinking the whole time of course that you're a hopeless asshole.

"Hmm, that's interesting." He's thinking to himself, what kind of job is that for a thirty-eight-year-old man? "What do you tell stories about?"

"Autobiographical stories. In fact I'm probably gonna tell a story about all of you on the radio next week."

"Oh."

Suddenly it's as if Dracula has just seen a crucifix. He disappears down the hall. But the sad part is that I *very much* want all these men, whose jobs I detest, to love me. They represent people who build missiles and bombs. It's clear to me that these people are working very hard to protect and forward the interests of people who are truly destroying our planet. I don't like the way they dress or their political opinions or even their hobbies. But all of this makes very little difference. They're all my fathers. I want very much—more than I even admit to myself—to have their affection and approval. I'm not sticking it out in this place just for the paycheck. There are plenty of other miserable jobs I could get. But I don't even look. Every day I slouch to this place I say I hate. I make fun of them. I curse them, but actually I'm just another naughty schoolboy. If just once one of them would come over and say, "Good work on the Mammoth Industries case, Mike," and put his arm around my shoulder, I would turn to Jello-O. And what is yet more fatherly about these men for me is that they're very disciplined. I have no discernible discipline whatsoever. Ever see one of those organisms that has no skeleton? That's me. I can't ever seem to get anything *straight*. My mind is like a couple of dozen fireflies trapped in a jar.

I'm hoping just by hanging around them to learn the secret of their astonishing discipline. They will work twelve, fourteen hours a day, come in on weekends, eat at their desks. I'm in awe of this single-minded devotion to *work*. Of course the flip side of this behavior is that some of them don't seem to want to go home to their wives or kids. On rare occasions, they have affairs with secretaries. And that's not a musical.

Most of the lawyers are married. One guy, a senior partner, was due to go home to Long Island Friday night after twelve hours on the job. A case came in at the last second—another lawyer's case. A brief had to be written overnight. He took off his coat and said, "Let me get into this with you, boys." He is a decent guy, but work is the only place he could be happy.

Fathers. I once told a friend that if Adolf Hitler and Eva Braun said they would adopt me I would have rushed over to Germany. So much did I want to have a complete set of loving parents, especially a father. You have to learn how to be a man from your father. This senior partner I mentioned? I'm longing for him to come in one day and say, "You know, Mike, my son is a real son of a bitch. He's a hopeless juvenile delinquent. I have drawn up papers. If you just sign here you can come home with me tonight." I might leave my wife and kid in a flash if I heard this.

It's 2:45, my arm is half-broken from stamping documents, and I'm ready to start scratching the elapsed time on the wall of my office like the Count of Monte Cristo—what can I do to avoid work? The *Encyclopaedia Britannica*! They have a 1964 edition of the *Encyclopaedia Britannica* in the library. The library is very useful when you don't want to work. As long as you seem to be reading very seriously and you have a notepad next to you, you're cool. So I go down to the library, get a legal pad, choose volume 19, and begin reading all about Tasmania. Yesterday it was the life and work of Gandhi. The other day I read about frogs. I know all about the species of frogs, their mating habits, their skin temperature in winter. Now I read for twenty minutes and I know exactly how many people lived east of the desert region. I know how much grain they shipped each year. I know everything about Tasmania that I ever wanted to know.

All around me lawyers are feverishly researching and discussing cases. They are mostly associate attorneys, men and a couple of women working their way up. The associates are like young samurai. If you're an associate attorney and you don't become a partner at the end of eight years, a trapdoor opens and no one ever sees you again. These people talk behind each other's backs, compete with each other, stay up until four in the morning, and go two days without sleep if a partner tells them to. It's a relentless, sadistic life to make it up to partner. But to become a partner is to get the gold ring, the grail. Everything that is important in their world in embodied in that title.

So they're all around me reading, researching, taking notes, and what am I doing? Wasting time learning all about Tasmania.

I go up to the lunchroom, get a Hershey bar from the vending machine, go back to my office, and stare at the filing on my desk. As I sit there, I have another one of my spells. I think of my daughter and realize I'm a *terrible* father.

I once had a lot of money. I lost it all and had to go to work at this job. I'm bitter about this. I feel humiliated. I don't make as much money as these men all around me. I'm not able to buy the things for my kid that they can. But still, a little child will love you anyway if you're good to him or her. Your daughter will come up to you even though you might have blood on your hands and she'll kiss you and say, "Hi, Daddy." That love is rejuvenating. The one woman partner in the firm has a daughter who comes in to see her occasionally. She goes to ballet school and she demonstrates steps for everybody in the office. This engenders instant hatred in the partner's secretary, who works like a slave all day and gets pimples from all the makeup that *Glamour* says she's supposed to be wearing. Her husband is a garbageman who beats her sometimes. She's got nothing to look forward to except maybe having more babies and bills and maybe her husband leaving her or having affairs with other women. So she has to see this golden girl dance in, glowing with wealth. Wealth is the ultimate skin cream.

This kid is just so rosy and happy and good-hearted. She's like a puppy who's been fed steak all its life and never been yelled at. She has no sense that she's doing anything wrong showing off her ballet steps. She wears beautiful dresses that cost at least four hundred dollars, and she never feels the hatred coming out of the secretary's eyes. But I don't hate this girl; I have to take responsibility for myself.

I wish I could provide for my child the way these men do for theirs. I wish I could be like them although I really don't want to be a *lawyer*, please God. I would like to have their discipline, and the boundless self-confidence that seems left to them in their grandfathers' wills, maybe. Whereas I have to pretend, reinvent manliness every morning of my life.

5:00. I can leave but somehow I can't get out of my chair. I'm thinking how dismal my life is. Who knows, maybe I'm like the lawyers, maybe I don't want to go home either. I see Tom, the senior partner, wander out of his office. He's got a haunted look on his face that reminds me of *Citizen Kane*. How touching it was that a man who owned a great empire of newspapers, of whom everybody was afraid, yearned at the end of his life only for the sled he had when he was a poor kid playing in the snow outside the shack in the mountains.

Tom takes his glasses off. He's got a boyish face even though he's about fifty-five. He was born with five silver spoons in his mouth. He's Tom the Second. His father was a senior partner in another large firm. Tom has a perpetually preoccupied look. He is always gazing off in the distance. Always puzzled about something. One time he was going out to meet a client in the reception area and he suddenly smacked his head with his palm. "I better take one of my cards," he said, "or else I won't remember who I am." All the secretaries laughed. How could *he*, Tom the Second, not remember who he was? I was touched. I wanted to reach out and pat his shoulder and say, "Tom, *I* know who you are. It's you and me, Tom."

5:30. I got up to leave. All the secretaries are gone because they know there's more to life than work. I take the elevator down and wait for the bus. Everybody's pushing and shoving to get on. It's like a Charlie Chaplin film where all the action is speeded up. I finally get on and sit down. The bus takes the same route uptown that it took downtown a hundred years ago that morning. The porn theaters, the junkies and hookers and pimps. Forty-second to Fiftieth Street on Eighth Avenue is one of the sleaziest places in the whole galaxy. The corner of Forty-ninth and Eighth is the Macy's of drug sales in midtown Manhattan. Everybody on the bus is squashed. They stare out the window. Out on the street, lunatics with microphones are preaching how they're going to save the world. People are sitting on stoops two doors down from the Midtown North police station, shooting up. And it's hot and disgusting in the bus because although it's summer the air conditioning is broken and the heat is on. I get another flash suddenly, of my daughter's face.

I feel angry, suppressed, depleted. I'm hungry but it's a deeper hunger than food can fix. Like Dracula, I want blood, juice, something elemental to revive myself. There's no *blood* where I work. I look around the bus; there are no women to flirt with, they're all too angry or tired. I'm looking at some idiot with a Walkman stuck in his ears buzzing like a giant insect. I'm in the mood to fuck or kill; I just want to get my hands on somebody. I feel like I'm going to explode. I think about getting off the bus and having three sausage pizzas. Spicy red tomato sauce, warm soft cheese in my mouth, a huge tankard of ale. I close my eyes and daydream.

It's March 1945. I'm a major in the U.S. Army. Not only am I a major, I am the only Jewish major in the entire division. It's the First Division, the Fighting First, the Big Red One. Actually I am the most famous soldier in the world. I have more medals than anybody else. On D-day *I* broke it open. There, on Omaha Beach when everybody was being slaughtered and couldn't move, I charged a whole bank of machine guns and I blew them up with grenades, killed twenty-six enemy soldiers, received serious wounds. Franklin Roosevelt himself gave me the Congressional Medal of Honor with my proud parents looking on. He actually got up from his wheelchair to hang it around my neck. The Medal of Honor; I'm the bravest man that ever lived. I've been fighting for three straight years. I'm the kind of guy who, when they want to send me home to do bond drives or appear with the Andrews Sisters in the States, says, "Forget it, I'll throw my medal in the garbage if you make me do that." I want to be with my men. Now it's March 1945 and I'm standing on a cliff overlooking the Rhine. We have fought hard. I've got many scars. Reporters, writers, movie stars fly to the battlefront to meet me, I'm so famous. But I don't care about any of that. I just want to fight. I want to kill Germans and win the war for my country. But now the war is almost over. The army's about to cross the Rhine and everybody knows it's only a matter of months before the Germans are defeated. I'm standing at the top of the cliff. It's late afternoon and there's still a little danger for me; the occasional shell lands nearby. But that's all right. My life wouldn't be worthwhile if there was no danger at all. I'm standing straight up looking over a vast panorama: towns, forests, the beautiful Rhine River. It's a little cold. I have an overwhelming sense of regret that the war will be over soon; I don't know what I'll do. Me, the greatest hero of the whole war; I feel I don't know what I'm going to do with my life now that there's no war for me to fight. I look up at the sunlight coming through the yellow-leafed trees. They might be linden or beech, I'm not sure. On top of this cliff, everything is very still and the wind is blowing through the trees.

THE AFFAIR

Mike Feder. Age: forty. Profession: whining and jerking off. Hobbies: thumb sucking. Drink: warm milk. I had no job. I had no respect for myself. My wife was disgusted with me. My friends didn't talk to me because I had decided I was not even good enough to talk to them. Bad, bad times. Did I have anything at all in the fall of 1982? I had my radio show.

Starting three years before, in 1979, I did a two-hour radio show on WBAI every Thursday morning. It didn't pay anything, but thousands of people listened. I got calls and letters. Now, an interesting result of doing a live radio program on any station, and especially BAI, is that you will get very personal fan mail. I found to my shock (I'm somewhat puritanical) that after the first year or two of doing these shows I was getting letters from women saying that they would love to meet me, and more than just meet me. These letters were also very touching. Every once in a while I'd even get a nude picture too. You know, a home shot, the kind where you set the camera and jump back in front of it. But I didn't pay any serious attention to these letters. Why? I'd never thought about ever doing a thing like *that*. Well, I'd thought about it, but I never seriously considered being unfaithful.

Of course, I always told my wife everything about the letters. We have that kind of marriage. In fact, it scares other people sometimes. They don't even want to come and visit us because my wife will say, "Where the fuck is the broccoli? Didn't I tell you to get broccoli? You don't do anything else all day!" And I say, "Well, up yours! You get the fuckin' broccoli. You a woman, or what?" Or she'll say, "You don't care about me anymore! I'm going to go out and become a lesbian." "Be my guest," I say. But then we get along really well after that, you know. It's not as if we argue all the time but we always express our feelings pretty directly. I tell her everything, including a lot, I'm sure, she doesn't want to hear.

Now, I knew that *she* knew that I was not going to *do* anything with
the women who wrote in. But I used to leave these letters and pictures
on the kitchen table. In among the Cheerios, some writing I was doing
(the fourteenth play I'd started and never finished), my wife's psychology books—last but not least would be a nude picture of a woman
named Lulu who lived in Bayside and who desperately wanted to meet
me. Late in the afternoon I would lie in bed, hear my wife come in,
hear the door close, hear the keys, the pocketbook—all the sounds of
the reentering mate. Then she would come into the bedroom. "Hi,
how are you?"

"Fine," I would say.

"Any work today?" she would ask.

"I told you, I'm not looking for work! I don't have to work!"

"Why?"

"I don't know. I don't have to work. You work."

So she would say, "Well, look, what kind of day have you had?"

"Well, nothing much interesting happened," I would reply. "Did
we get any mail?"

"I don't know, you picked it up." Finally, about an hour later, I'd
hear, "Uh, what's this picture?"

"I don't know, it's one of these women—they just keep writing in.
You know, I don't encourage this. I don't know what they want from
me."

She'd say, "Hm. Hm. Okay. Why don't you throw it out? 'Cause if
you don't, I'll burn it."

Around the beginning of October 1982, with my prospects very dim,
I got a letter from a woman named Sandy. The envelope had stickers
of happy smiling faces on it. I opened it up. "Dear Mike: bla, bla,
bla . . ." Same old message. But no nude picture this time. The letter
said, "I am a media student at South Norwalk State Teachers College," someplace in Connecticut. "We have to have a year-end project
for our senior-year arts class. Mine will be an original radio production. I've been listening to you for years, I think you're really dyna-
mite, you're talented, and I want to star you in my production. I have
to check it out with my teacher, but first, we need to meet." I thought
to myself, well maybe I should respond to this letter—after all it *is* a
business proposition. I started to build a case in my mind. After all,
consider my position: I was just sitting at home doing nothing all day

long. Everybody I knew was working. My wife was working, she was a professional. I was just a shiftless asshole. Then I got this letter. Radio production! Of course. That would help my career!

So I wrote back: "Dear Sandy: Thank you very much for your comments on my show. I would like to get together with you because I think it's an interesting project." God, I was officious. About two weeks later she called me up. She had a very sexy voice but I didn't make any conscious connection to that. After all, this was a career matter!

So I arranged to meet her. Where? I told her, "Meet me at Muffin's Pub." This place had a big picture window, and was right across the street from where I lived. *And,* we would get together at exactly the same time that my wife usually came home from work, walking right past this window. I'll tell you something, the filthiest thing that a militant feminist thinks about a man is not bad enough. I'll tell you what men really act like and what they really think about women.

So, finally, the day came for my meeting with Sandy. On the phone the day before, it was already getting into high gear: "How will I recognize you?" she said to me. "Well," I said, "I'm not bad looking. . . ." Jesus. She vaguely described herself. We were all set. The night before I was fueling myself for the meeting by thinking of my wife saying to me: "You make me sick!" Mike would get revenge!

I told my wife that I would be meeting this woman. "Listen, I'm going to go ahead and see her. She's a media student, and I think it's good for my career."

"Your career? I thought your career was lying in bed."

"Listen, it will be an interesting experience. You could get a look at her. This must be psychologically fascinating, the fan mentality?" My wife just stared at me.

That day I arrived early and got a corner table where I could watch the door. After about eight women came in and passed by me to the back, a young woman came through the door. Tall, very thin, pretty, long red hair. She had a kind of trembly, childlike, hopeful look on her face which I didn't like because it didn't fit my suave, playboy daydream. I was sure this was her so I waved, very calm, very cool, though my heart was thumping like mad. This was my affair, after all. Also, in five minutes my wife would come walking into the place.

This woman came over to my table. As she was walking toward me with her big eyes, I could see instantly that she had the same kind of naive, sentimental idea about what this affair was going to be like as I did. She was trying to be slinky, and she was dressed in a nice tight sweater. And—bang!—she smacked right into a table and knocked over a guy's four-dollar scotch. He gave her a withering look.

Then she sat down opposite me and as she sat she fell slightly off the chair. "Are you all right?" I asked.

"Yes," she said. "Just a second." She reached into her pocketbook, took out the thickest glasses I ever saw in my life, and put them on. "Oh, hi!" she said. "Have you had a couple of drinks?"

"Yes I have," I said.

She lowered her eyelids. "Well, I'll just have to catch up with you, won't I?"

Oh boy! I was really excited but also very nervous about this; any minute my wife was going to be here, and I didn't want to get caught holding hands. I said, "Well, what's this project about? You know, I have to think of my career." My career. I was thinking of my career in the backseat of a Ford.

She told me she was going to produce a radio show and she thought it would be wonderful to star me. "Is anyone managing you?" she asked. She'd like to *manage* me. So we had a couple more drinks, and everything we said to each other was laden with sex. But not just sex. Television sex. It was a combination of real flirtation and imitation, miniseries romance.

Then my wife came in. She sat down. I said, very calmly, "This is my wife. Dear, this is, uh, Sandy." I was being so smug, and I was thinking to myself, that'll teach you. Turn your lip up at me. Be a professional. Work hard. Be a grown-up. I'll show you. There are women in the world besides you who appreciate me for what I am. Whatever that is.

This was my message to Sandy: You know, you may think you're in love with me, and you may think that it's easy just to come and get a "star" to sit with you, but I'm a happily married guy. I don't need you.

I was playing them off against each other. What a sterling character. My wife was being very correct, very proper. When my wife gets angry, she doesn't get wildly mad; she gets X-ray eyes, she just stares at you. She makes you want to crawl under a chair. And she was giving this poor woman the real treatment: "What did you say you do?"

"I'm a media student."

"Oh, that's interesting." There was another minute or two of meaningless talk and my wife said to her, "Well, it's been very pleasant to meet you." Then she got up and walked out. Sandy and I talked and flirted for another half-hour; we agreed to talk to each other in a couple of days about the "project." She left and I sat there for a while dreaming about what might happen.

About four weeks later, after submitting script ideas and talking to her on the phone, the payoff came. It was getting to be early November now, near Thanksgiving, the great family holiday. It was almost the time for the family to sit around and carve the turkey: me, my wife, my daughter. Meanwhile, I was having my "affair." I actually felt like I was having an affair, just talking to her on the phone. After I hung up, I would be shaking. I would check my pants. Then at last, what I'd been waiting for: "You've got to come out to my apartment. I think Monday would be a good time, because that way you won't be busy with your family. Come out Monday so we can discuss the script *in depth*." Whew! Okay, here was where I walk on stage.

So Monday came and I dressed for my affair. I made sure I was very clean, with clean socks, clean underwear, brushed teeth. I didn't know what I was supposed to do when I had an affair. After all, there's *Modern Gardening,* and *Rod & Gun* magazine, but there's no *Modern Affair* magazine, or *42 Tips for Your Affair*. Also, for years my friends have been making fun of me because they all had affairs and I didn't. "When you going to have an affair, jerkoff?" they'd ask. "When are you going to grow up?" My position was, "Well, no, I don't want to have an affair because I'm happily married and because I think once you've crossed a certain line that you ruin everything and it's a breaking of the contract of marriage." And they said, "You idiot." So now I called up one of my friends. "You know, I finally met a woman and I'm going to do it, I'm going to have the affair."

"Yeah, sure. You're going to have an affair like I'm going to be elected president."

So I said, "Well, fuck you, I'm going to do it and I'm not even going to tell you about it!"

By late morning Monday, my wife was at work, working hard, and my daughter was in preschool learning how to do sandbox things and draw pictures with crayons; their backs were turned. I was going to go out to Connecticut. It was raining, not hard, a sort of *A Man and a Woman* type of mist. I got in the car, my heart racing. She had given me directions; she lived in South Northport. I had to go on the Cross-Bronx Expressway and up the Connecticut Turnpike.

So I got on the West Side Highway on my way to my affair. I was on my way, I was actually doing it! As I was driving I felt at the same time scared to death and completely elated. A young, pretty woman was interested in me; I wasn't a total jerk, I didn't lie in bed all day, I was worth something even though I wasn't doing anything.

Suddenly I was aware of a huge van about two inches from my rear bumper. Actually I was in the middle lane, so I moved over to the right to let the van pass, but it didn't. It pulled up right in back of me. I was going forty-five miles an hour; we were inches apart. And so I did what I do when somebody tailgates me; I take the passive-aggressive approach—I just slow down to practically nothing. I'm one of those people, right. Usually what people do is get very angry, and pull around you. Well, what happened was that this guy got very angry, pulled around me, and then pulled in front of me, and *he* started to slow down. And leaning out, high up from this van, was the worst-looking, mean, vicious redneck I'd seen since I'd been down in the backwoods of Louisiana. I mean, this guy was a real son of a bitch with a red scarf around his neck, a red face, and a thin, droopy moustache, looking like a half-assed rock-and-roller from down South. He had a can of beer in his hand; he was screaming at me, gesticulating, spilling his beer: "Fuck you, mother fucker!" Unbelievable! I was on my way to my affair! So I had to slow down, he had me blocked, and it was wet and slippery and I didn't know what to do. And then, to my utter amazement, he stopped the van on the West Side Highway! That was against the law, right? I was stuck right behind him. I didn't know what to do. I was scared to death.

This guy got out of the van, and sure enough, he had cowboy boots complete with genuine clay and shit on them. He looked like "Rawhide" come alive. He was walking straight at me on the West Side Highway! I mean, how could this be, I went to college! When he was about ten feet away from me, he hoisted the can of beer and threw it at my windshield. My whole life was passing before me because that's how it is when you're about to die. And I was thinking, oh, good, I'll be stomped to death by a shit-kicker, a redneck, on the West Side Highway, I was out of work, my wife thought I was an asshole anyhow, and I was on the way to my affair. I had her address in my pocket: Sandy, South Northport.

I figured there was only one thing to do—I pointed the car right at him and stepped on the gas. Now, you have to know this about a New Yorker: If you drove right at a New Yorker, even if he acted cool, he would jump real fast right out of the way. Southerners, mean guys like this redneck, aren't like that. He tried to kick my car. I've seen these guys before. I was practically running the guy over, right, and as I drove past him—Bam! "Son of a bitch! You mother fucker!" I could feel the whole assembly shake when his boot hit it. I drove around, whoosh, I got rid of him, I looked in my rearview mirror and saw him run back to the van and start coming after me!

Zoom. I was going very fast up the West Side Highway—this couldn't really be happening! This was like all my daydreams when I was a spy or a detective and the bad guys were chasing me and I'd be driving along with one hand on the wheel of my Aston-Martin, the other hand reaching for my Beretta. Only this time I had an eight-year-old Mazda, and I was practically having diarrhea. He was driving faster, catching up, trying to get around me, just like in the movies. And I'm wondering what this guy was doing up North anyhow. He wasn't making a laundry delivery. He was obviously here to chase me. God had finally gotten me for the evil in my heart.

I got to the 125th Street exit but I couldn't pull off because the road was too slick. I looked in my mirror; he was screaming and yelling at me, pointing something at me. I realized now that my actual life, such as it was, was in danger. Suddenly, I found a certain increase in self-regard. Real trouble can do wonders for you. If some redneck is chasing you and wants to blow your brains out on the West Side Highway, you tend to get it together.

The next exit was the George Washington Bridge and the Cross-Bronx Expressway. By now I was doing at least eighty, in the rain, faster than I'd ever driven before. I screeched off the highway there, and the lunatic was still after me; I had hoped maybe he'd go over the bridge and go back down South and kill people down there. But no, he followed me off the fucking exit and all of a sudden there was all this traffic. All the daydreams went out of my head. I made a right turn; I had to get away to a local street. A couple more rights and lefts and I lost him! I pulled over to the curb. I looked up; I was right next to Columbia Presbyterian Hospital on 168th Street and Broadway. I was staring right at the floor of the obstetrics wing where my daughter had been born.

I was on my way to see Sandy to violate everything I held sacred; someone was trying to kill me; and God placed me like a checker right next to that hospital. Now, somebody, a psychologist, is going to tell me that I chose to get off at that exit, because I knew the hospital was there, knew to look up at the eighteenth floor . . . forget it, it's destiny.

I waited there for twenty minutes till my blood stopped beating like a tom-tom. I was outside the hospital where my daughter was born, flooded with guilt. I thought of my wife lying there all rosy with the little baby. What should I do? I got on the Cross-Bronx Expressway and headed for Connecticut.

I was really at the bottom. I had to *do* something. So I drove along and prepared myself for the next phase, which was to meet Sandy at her apartment. I put the killer out of my mind. About forty-five minutes later I arrived at South Northport, a really bleak, awful place. Sandy's part of town was near big refineries and next to a swamp.

So I found the street and parked in the underground garage. She lived in a modern, ugly apartment building. I went upstairs. I was into it again, Don Juan. I straightened my collar and pulled my hair down in front so it looked more naturally sexy. I knocked off some dandruff, checked my fly, and knocked on the door. The knock of fate. This was stepping into another world. I was ready for it and not ready for it.

The door opened and there she was, wearing blue eye shadow and no glasses. She was looking the part. A big picture window behind her looked over some woods, and the highway, and a huge shopping mall beyond. It seemed so instantly erotic. This was how I had always wanted it to be. She was wearing a little halter thing and very tight pants, and her midriff was bare! All she needed was a little jewel in her navel. She said, lowering her eyelids, "Hi."

"As the World Turns." "Hi," I said and strode into her living room. She closed the door behind me. "Would you like a drink?"

"Sure."

"Vodka and tonic, right?" She remembered what I had been drinking at the pub when we first met. Getting more excited by the second, I watched her walk into the kitchen. I sat on the couch and picked up the copy of a script I had sent her a week ago. There were notes on it, where music or sound effects would be added. She came back in holding two large glasses and set them down on the coffee table in front of the couch. "I'm going to put on a record, is that okay?"

I actually had a lump in my throat—it was hard to talk. "Yeah, uh . . . sure." The music came on, I couldn't even tell what it was, I was so carried away by my even being there with her—the danger, the possibilities. She came back over to the couch and sat down about two inches away from me. Her face was flushed. I cleared my throat and opened the script. "Um, maybe we should take a look at this, huh?"

"Well, all right," she said, "if you want to." She reached over, got her glasses from the coffee table, and moved a little closer. Now her knee, her unmarried knee, was actually touching mine! I took a big gulp of vodka.

Hardly knowing what I was saying, I discussed the script with her. She answered me, but I was having trouble making sense of anything she said as well. My heart was pounding. I could feel her face very close to mine. My throat was dry. I looked at her. "Listen, I . . ."

I grabbed my drink and walked over to the window. The sky was very gray and the rain was a little heavier now. Cars and trucks were moving steadily in both directions on the highway. The trees were just about bare. I felt her standing next to me. I thought, okay, this is how it will be: If she touches me now, it will be her doing, not mine. I gazed out at the scenery with what I knew was a sensitive, maybe even tortured, look in my eyes. I held my breath—everything was poised, utterly still—then I suddenly heard the music, the record she had put on several minutes ago. It was a black woman singing her heart out: "If loving you is wrong, I don't want to be right." It's about a woman in love with a married man. She tells him she doesn't care if he has a wife and two little children depending on him, she wants him so much.

She had taken off her glasses and was looking up at me. I felt as if I was going to explode. I wished she would say something but she didn't; she just looked at me with her mouth set in a thin line and tears forming in her eyes.

At that moment, in perfect collaboration with the movie quality of everything that was happening, the doorbell rang. She went over to open it and there was a man there. "Hello, Franklin," she said. He walked in, a guy about twenty-seven years old, in a button-down shirt and polished loafers.

"Hi, Sandy. I was just driving past and I remembered you said Mike was coming over sometime this week, so I thought . . ." He stood near the door, hesitated just for a moment, then walked right over to me with his hand extended. "You must be Mike Feder." He grabbed my hand hard and shook it.

In a choked voice Sandy said, "Mike, this is Franklin."

"Hi!" Franklin went over to Sandy, put his arm around her, and gave me an aggressive grin. "Sandy and I have listened to you for a long time. That was a really funny show you did last week."

A funny show. My show starts at seven on Thursday morning, and this guy is with her then? If I didn't get the point I'd have to be retarded. I wondered if she had invited him to drop in on us for some bizarre reason. Was she trying to get even for me having her meet my wife? By now Franklin had taken her by the hand over to the couch to look at the script. I wanted to leap over the coffee table and punch the guy. She was just sitting next to him with her head down. Over on the turntable the woman was shouting and crying now: "If loving you is wrong, I don't want to be right. . . ."

Suddenly, Sandy perked up and said, "Franklin, could you do me a favor? I need to move my car—it's parked in the wrong spot downstairs."

He glared at her for a second, then said with a shrug, "Okay, Sandy." She jumped up, ran into the bedroom, and came back with some keys. "It's in the visitors' section. Just move it to my spot."

He took the keys from her and looked at me. "I'll be *right back.*"

As soon as she closed the door behind him, Sandy came over and stood about an inch away from me at the window. The music was playing, "If loving you is wrong, I don't want to be right." I stood there, quivering, for what seemed like hours. Just as I turned to face her, there was a frantic pounding at the door.

Sandy opened it, and Franklin was standing there—a total mess. His button-down shirt was torn and hanging out of his pants. He was missing one of his loafers.

"Sandy, Sandy! There was this giant Doberman in the car. He practically killed me!"

"Oh," she said. "I forgot to tell you King was in the car."

Poor guy. His head swiveled back and forth between me and her. Finally he said, "I'm going," and he threw the keys, turned around, and walked out.

The door was closed and we were alone again. But as she stood next to me, the whole thing just cracked open. I couldn't stay there anymore.

I went over to the chair where my jacket was. "I've got to go now, Sandy."

"You have to leave right now?" she asked.

"Yeah. Good-bye, Sandy."

She came over to the door and opened it for me. "Good-bye, Mike."

I left her standing at the door looking at me, and got into my car and drove back to New York, feeling truly filthy and obscene for having let her down, and for having tried to have an affair in the first place. I was the worst half-ass of all the half-asses who ever lived. I got back to my apartment and lay in bed staring out the window.

It was all downhill after that. Weeks went by; it was getting toward Christmas. I actually did go to the school and do the radio show for Sandy. I was more distant; although I knew I was never going to do anything, I still knew that she thought I might. And that's where my nastiness came to the fore. Nastiness or, I guess, need for self-regard compelled me.

A listener to my show called and offered me a job. It was not a job I'd ever wanted to do, but at least it was a job and I would be earning money. I felt better. My wife had let up on me; it was Christmas time; I was being a good father. I went out and bought a Christmas tree with my little girl. I actually fixed something in the kitchen that was broken—a doorknob. I was beginning to rise in my own estimation. I didn't feel like the world was coming to an end.

But Sandy kept calling me and calling me. Finally she called me six days before Christmas and wouldn't leave me alone.

My wife picked up the phone. "It's your 'friend' from Connecticut."

"Thank you, dear, I'll take it in the bedroom." Wonderful.

I shut the door of the bedroom. "Listen, you've got to stop calling me, Sandy, it's for your own good."

"But I want you. I'm going to wait for you."

That's the kind of thing a lot of married men always dream of hearing, you know.

She went on to say I was so talented and so brilliant and handsome.

"Sandy," I said, "you really have got to stop this."

A week went by, it was Christmas Eve. I was in the living room, with all the lights on; my daughter was playing with some presents, which we always give her the night before Christmas because we have no discipline in our house. My wife was doing some home cooking, which she does about once a year. Everything was really *family*, and the phone rang.

It was a very ominous sort of ring. My wife got it and said to me, so full of Christmas cheer she didn't even mind, "It's her." She handed me the phone. Everybody loved everybody that night.

"I'll take it in the bedroom, dear."

I picked up the extension. "Sandy, I told you, you'll have to stop calling me because—"

She interrupted. "Don't worry. This is the last call you are ever going to get from me."

"Excuse me?"

"I'm not going to call you anymore because I was talking this over with my friend Allen and he says you're just being cruel and manipulating, so Allen and I are going to Bermuda for the holiday."

"Allen!" I said. "Who is Allen?"

"Allen is a friend and he and I have become very close, he is in stocks, and he says you are being very cruel to me. He has opened my eyes. So this is really the last time that you will be hearing from me. I hope you enjoy your life." And she hung up on me.

I stood there, stunned, thinking to myself, Allen? I smashed the phone down on the floor. It has a crack in it to this day.

I opened the door to the living room, completely dazed. Allen? Bermuda?

I went into the living room and my wife said to me, "That was a big noise. What happened? Was there any trouble?"

"Trouble?" I said. "No, there was no trouble. No trouble at all."

MARILYN

I had the most tremendous crush on Marilyn when I was a kid. In fact, it was much more than just a crush. I'm sure I was in love with her, and probably still am a bit to this day. Marilyn was short and just a little thin, with soft brown eyes and long black hair. What was really special about her was her smile; it started with a quick pixie grin, then relaxed into a sweet smile with just a touch of sadness at the edges. To me she was beautiful.

In the fifties and sixties in my neighborhood in Queens, which was part Jewish and part Baptist, there were always a couple of Jewish girls who went out exclusively with black or Italian guys from nearby neighborhoods. Marilyn was one of them. They abandoned without question or quarrel all Jewish boys; why they did it we never understood, although we had our definite suspicions. Most of us had a double attitude toward these girls. They were held in contempt because they were lowering themselves by mixing with "goys" and "shvartzers." On the other hand, they set us burning with desire and jealousy. Marilyn was one of those girls who said, "Screw it." She and the others got fed up with our trembling hands, the corsages we gave, and the pecks on the cheek. She wanted more and she just went ahead and got it.

Marilyn had been in my class in junior high school for months but I was far too shy to speak to any girl, let alone one so good-looking. One afternoon I was riding my bike over to a friend's house and I saw her walking up the block where she lived. She was holding hands with a black kid named Cecil who was in our class. I nearly fell off my bike in astonishment when I saw her stop and kiss him! To do what she was doing in our all-white neighborhood could actually be dangerous. She waved to me and giggled. "Hi, Michael."

"Hi. Hi, Cecil."

I could feel every eye on the block burning through the venetian blinds. I was thinking, Holy Shit! She's right outside her house! Sure enough, her mother opened the door and said in a furious voice, "Marilyn, I want you in here right now!"

"Yes, Mommy," said Marilyn. She gave Cecil a peck on the cheek and ran inside. The door slammed shut behind her. Cecil and I stared at each other for a couple of seconds. Then he walked off.

We were in a special class at school, something called the SP, for high-IQ kids. I was a world-class underachiever, a real sullen punk, and I always sat in the last row of all my classes, slumped way down in my seat—never speaking a word to the teachers. Yet, defiant as I tried to be, I was always scared enough to do at least some homework and just pass my tests. Marilyn sat two seats away from me, also in the back row. She didn't even *pretend* to do any work. The teacher would say, sarcastically, "And when may we expect to see your homework Miss Stein?" Marilyn would just smile and say, "Never." Fantastic.

She and I had a friend in common, Stuie, who lived right across the street from her. They had known each other since they were babies. Stuie was the kid in the neighborhood who did everything before everybody else. He was the first to smoke, to drink, to drive. He even knew how to mambo when he was seventeen. He was always bragging about exotic people he knew outside the neighborhood, jazz musicians, drug dealers, and the like. I used to see him and Marilyn driving around in his father's car.

After I got to know Marilyn better, we spent a lot of time together, mostly just walking and talking. She used to laugh all the time—she loved jokes and funny stories. I told the jokes and the stories and she laughed.

After I had known her about three years, when I was eighteen, I went to a New Year's Eve party at Stuie's house. His parents were away in Florida so he invited all his wild pals from Manhattan. I was sitting on his living-room couch feeling really miserable. First of all, I never drank, so I was already an alien. And some people were smoking grass. It was the first time I had ever seen it; I was worried the police would break in and arrest us all. But the worst thing was Marilyn. All night long I had been watching her go up the stairs with different guys to Stuie's bedroom. I thought I could hear the bedsprings squeaking. Stuie came over, really drunk, and suddenly he was talking to me about Marilyn. He looked over at the stairs. "Why don't you take a turn?" He was grinning at me. I was so angry I couldn't speak. "We been doing it for years," he said. "She gives great blow-jobs." He knew how I felt about her. I just stared back at him till he got up and lurched up the stairs.

I was truly astonished. I thought we were all just pals, hanging around, joking pals. I had never dreamed they were doing IT. I was boiling with anger. I wanted to kill the two of them. I climbed the stairs to his room. The door was open a little and I heard both of them laughing. I stood absolutely still listening to the sounds they made. I had difficulty believing it was actually happening. Finally, I went downstairs, got my coat, and went home. I lay in my attic bedroom and wanted to be dead.

I stayed away from both Marilyn and Stuie for a couple of months. I couldn't bear even to look at her knowing that she had defiled herself in such a manner. Once she came over to my house. I watched her from the upstairs window. My mother told her I wasn't home.

When we got out of high school we went to different colleges, I to Hofstra out on Long Island and she to City College in Manhattan. We had new circles of friends, so we didn't see each other for a couple of years. In my junior year I started hanging around with Stuie again. He took me on nighttime tours of Greenwich Village and the Lower East Side. Sometimes Marilyn came along, and little by little we got to be friends again. She and I would sit in her basement watching TV and talking. It felt so natural to be with her.

My first summer out of college, June 1966, I moved to a beach house my family owned out in Far Rockaway, Queens. This is not to be confused with beach houses or cottages on Fire Island or Cape Cod. These were tiny three-room places no more than three feet from each other, with no phones and only outside showers. I lived out there by myself, alternating between a kind of blissful Spartan solitude and plain hopeless loneliness.

I was taking a course in summer school because I had failed art and couldn't officially graduate till I completed another course. How did I fail art? Simple—I had to do sixteen drawings or paintings representing the history of art from cave drawings to Campbell soup cans and I only did twelve, leaving me stranded somewhere in the eighteenth century. I quit because I was angry at the teacher for not paying attention to me. I was the only male in the class and not a bad artist, but the instructor spent the entire class time *carefully* helping the girls with their great masterpieces. Good reason not to graduate, right? I probably didn't want to leave school.

I had a part-time job as a Pinkerton guard. This fulfilled, partially at least, my childhood fantasies of being a cop, although in truth I'd never dream of actually hurting someone. Nevertheless I had a uniform, a hat and a badge, and, greatest treasure of all, a nightstick. All I ever did was guard private beaches and parking lots but I considered myself at least a lieutenant colonel.

I ran at least five miles each morning on the boardwalk, took cold showers, and read Russian novels for the nineteenth-century literature course I was taking to complete my BA. I never finished these books because I couldn't keep anybody's name straight; Piotor Ivanovich Petrov entered the salon of Countess D. "Grushka," she called to him. Grushka?

At the beginning of July, Stuie and I helped Marilyn move into her first apartment, in Manhattan on the Lower East Side. It was a third-floor walk-up in a tenement building—a real mess. Plaster was falling all over the place, giant waterbugs skittered across the slanted floor, and all the faucets dripped constantly. But we tried to fix it up as best we could.

This was the time of flowers and drugs and Marilyn was constantly stoned. She was the first of the many people I knew who were high every waking moment. She was so stoned that when I crossed the street with her, I had to hold on to her shirt, as if she were a little kid or a leashed puppy; otherwise she would just wander right into traffic. "Oh wow," she'd say, "that red light is so beautiful," and she'd start to walk. "Hold it," I'd tell her. "Green is even more beautiful." I was forced to take on the role of protector all the time, which irritated me. It wasn't the same kind of palship we had before. When I told her about something funny that I had seen, her usual bright smile had a tinge of sadness and preoccupation about it.

We used to walk together near the lake in Central Park. She was silent for long stretches, and then she would burst into some meaningless paranoid chatter. "Michael," she whispered, "I think that man over there is following us. He's probably a narc." I looked around but I couldn't see anybody.

"Where do you want to go now?" I said.

"I don't know," she said. "Maybe back to the apartment?"

When I thought about it, it occurred to me that maybe she was stoned all the time because she was trying to avoid something. She used to have terrible arguments with her mother on the phone. If I tried to talk to her after one of these conversations she'd say, "Michael, I have to take a nap," and she'd go into her bedroom and take a handful of pills or light up.

Her apartment was a crash pad and picnic ground for an incredible assortment of characters: dope addicts, drifters, pimps, and lost kids who floated in off the streets. In the sixties, people were always coming and going at all hours, and you never even knew their names. Locks and privacy were considered oppressive and old-fashioned.

I used to drive in to visit Marilyn after a day of Russian novels and guard duty. You could get high just by standing on the stairwell outside her apartment. One night Stuie was there. He had gotten into law school and was giving me a hard time.

"Hey it's General Pinkerton. Here, General, have a toke."

"No thanks, where's Marilyn?"

"In the bedroom, but she's got company."

I sat down on the mangy couch in her front room. It was about ten thirty, late for me but early for the people who hung out in her place. A guy with a black eye patch and a bearskin vest (this was July) walked over to me. "Hey, man, got any bread?" I gave him a dollar. He told me he knew a place where you could buy day-old boxes of Ritz crackers for ten cents but he needed more money 'cause the place was in Woodstock.

"Sorry," I said, "that's all I can spare."

"Hey, man," he said, "that's cool."

From everywhere in the apartment I heard and dimly saw, if I looked, various groupings of people having sex. I tried to ignore it and stared at the Day-Glo stars painted on the purple ceiling.

Maybe an hour later, Marilyn drifted in from the back and sat next to me on the couch. "Hi." She had a dreamy smile on her face. We talked and, as always, I was so drawn to her that I was soon able to remove her from this place and be with her in a private world of our own. I told her about my course and the foolish jobs they assigned me to at Pinkerton's.

"So, I pick up the phone at the command post and say 'Dick Tracy here.' "

"Michael, you'll get fired!"

But she laughed. She seemed to think everything I did was interesting and funny. But as we talked I was painfully aware of all the sex going on around us and even more aware of my aching desire for her. She had shorts on, and her knee was almost touching mine. But for some reason, I couldn't touch her. I was frustrated; it got worse as the hours passed, and the more frustrated I got the more I talked. Inevitably, sometime in the middle of the night, some guy with an earring or a motorcycle jacket came over and took her into the bedroom. She smiled at me over her shoulder and waved. "Bye, Michael." I wanted to shout, "Wait!" but I didn't. After a minute I got off the couch and drove home to my monk's cell out at the beach.

Near the end of August, Marilyn moved back home to Queens. She'd only been gone about eight weeks. Her parents had never approved of her new life style, of course, but it was more than that. I think she just got tired of the endless routine of sex, drugs, and aimless wandering. She never really lost her sense of humor, no matter how far gone she was, and she could never avoid seeing how absurd and sad all her new friends were.

So, she was moving back temporarily and maybe longer to her parents' home, although she hated them. Stuie and I helped her. After everything was U-Hauled back to Queens, she turned to me at her parents' front door. "Oh, Michael, I forgot a whole box of papers and letters. They're still at the apartment. Could you get them?" I couldn't tell her no, so I drove all the way back into the city.

I stepped over broken pipes and ripped-up floorboards to get to her bedroom in the back. Everything had been removed or destroyed; all the Day-Glo posters were ripped off the walls, all the hanging bead curtains were gone, and even the stars painted on the ceiling had been cut out. I went into the bedroom, which was just a pile of stained mattresses. In the corner was a cardboard box full of papers and on top were three school notebooks—you know the kind, black with a white marbled pattern. They were diaries.

It took about two seconds for me to give in to the urge to open one up. It was the one for July. She used code letters like a nineteenth-century novelist: "Went to M's today—heard L was at the Duke's ball." Naturally, I started putting names to the initials. It was pretty easy to figure out. I came to a section for the middle of July. There was a heartfelt yearning entry: "M is so nice, I like him so much. . . . I wish he would just fuck me." I tried not to be M but it was impossible. I kept reading. She wrote, "S and I have been doing it for a long time. I hardly even like him. M and I have such nice talks. I like him so much and I know he likes me. Why doesn't he ever do anything?"

I was devastated. It was a tragic waste of affection, a terrible throwing away of time. I was disgusted and ashamed. It was as if someone just handed me the documents and said "Here's the proof, you really are a pathetic asshole. Sign here, please." Nevertheless, always the good boy, I carefully placed the diary back in the box and brought it all back out to her house.

I gave her a meaningful look as I handed her the box, thinking maybe she sent me there to read the diary—to make me face it, so I would make a move finally—but she just gave me the usual vague grin as she took the box from me. As I drove off, I could see her staring at me from behind the screen door.

Out at my lonely beach house, I reached a point where my self-enforced isolation and abstinence were almost causing me to hallucinate. I spent every night, hour after endless hour, lying in my bed sweating, jerking off, and dozing. Eventually I'd take a couple of antihistamines to put me to sleep. I had terrible dreams: "M" won't do it. "M" can't do it.

Somewhere, finally, I found the courage to invite Marilyn out to the beach. We lay near each other on the couch in the front room and smoked some hashish that she had brought out—my first serious drug. Time stretched out, then disappeared entirely. We curled up back to back like two babies, listening to flamenco on the record player and dreaming out loud. I was finally touching her! I was filled with love and a terrible ache. We held hands behind our backs and then . . . nothing. I couldn't roll over and put my arms around her, couldn't kiss her. And she wouldn't. Where is the moment, that point hovering in the air between two people? Where is the precise location of the proof that you are wanted? Well, the green light was shining

right in my face but I couldn't cross the street. The moment passed.
The feeling receded, the ache throbbed for a while, then disappeared
behind a wave of hashish. Negligence. Criminal violation of need.
Loneliness.

There was a loud knock at the door. I stumbled to open it and there
were the cops. The neighbors had called them because it was late and
the flamenco record had been stuck in a groove for an hour playing
full blast. I sobered up quick, said some words, and Officer Muldoon
left. I drove Marilyn back to her mother's house. Then in the bleakest
part of the night I returned to my den.

It was the last weekend in August, a week after Marilyn had come
out, and most of the summer residents were moving back to their
regular houses in Brooklyn and Queens. It was the beginning of
hurricane season—nasty weather coming in.

Stuie drove out to visit. He told me Marilyn was getting married.
Bam, just like that, she's getting married. I was shocked. There she
was, a hippie, taking drugs, walking around in traffic with dirty
sneakers without laces, living in a stinking crash pad, and she was
getting married?

Unbelievably, it turned out to be a guy from the neighborhood
named Herb. He lived in the slightly poorer section of Laurelton.
Herb was the squarest guy I ever met; he had a crew cut, and he
looked like a Mormon although he was Jewish. He wore dark suits all
the time and always carried a briefcase. Most of the people in the
neighborhood paid no attention to him. Herb worked real hard and
had just graduated from business school. He had been visiting Marilyn
in her hippie apartment and we all knew he had a crush on her but we
treated it as a joke. He'd walk in, see some guy with a needle sticking
out of his arm and say, "Hi there, I'm Herb!" He was a major source
of entertainment all summer long, following Marilyn around with his
tongue hanging out. And who laughed hardest of all? Marilyn.

Well, if Stuie's news wasn't astounding enough, Herb, who had met
me only a couple of times, but knew I was Marilyn's close friend,
came out to see me a week later. He knocked on the door and
introduced himself in his formal Dudley-Do-Right business-school
manner as if I'd never met him before. "Hi, I'm Herb Stern." He acted
as if he wanted to sell me something but, of course, he couldn't sell me
what I really wanted. "I'd, uh, really like to talk to you," he said.

We walked along on the boardwalk saying nothing. The wind was blowing hard; the beach was cold, rainy, and deserted, and I was thinking, Maybe I'll just throttle him, kill him, and throw his body into the ocean. But, as usual, I was trying to be nice. Don't touch a girl you burn for, by all means be nice.

Herb was trying to speak. "I, uh, don't know how to say this, but . . ." This was Herb's problem: He was getting married to Marilyn but he was afraid of her because of her vast sexual experience. Well now, wasn't that proof that God enjoys a really good laugh? Herb went on with his tale of woe. He told me he was impotent with Marilyn. The situation was absurd but I couldn't even crack a smile. After all, he was going to marry her. What would be the good of telling him about my deep burning impotent love for his future wife? So I just walked along next to him and kept quiet.

When he was through, I told him how good-hearted and sympathetic she was, which she was indeed, very sympathetic. "Don't worry," I told him, "everything'll turn out all right." He was very grateful, thanked me over and over, and shook my hand till it hurt. He left me standing on the boardwalk, watching the waves smashing into the rocks.

About a year later, I was working as a caseworker for the welfare department on the Lower East Side, my first grown-up job—and in walked Marilyn. I actually dropped my files. She was dressed in a tartan skirt and a white blouse, and she was carrying a white pocketbook. She looked like she was about forty-two even though she was only twenty-three, but more important, she had lost that special cute look. She had a worn, set, almost frozen aura about her.

And I thought, Good. Good for her. She abandoned me, her only true love, to go off to Westchester with that jerk. She deserves whatever happens to her. Let her live up there and water her lawn. Let her go find chicken bargains in the supermarket.

"Could we go some place and talk?" she asked.

I deliberately took her to the sleaziest place I knew, the kind of place where your lunch could just as well be scuttling across the counter as lying on your plate. But she didn't blink an eye, just sat there nibbling on her greasy sandwich. "So," I said, "how's Westchester?"

She giggled. "I learned to drive, isn't that great?"

I was never sure she meant anything she said. "Nice clothes," I told her. "You even got a pocketbook."

"Yeah, isn't it funny-looking?"

She told me she had a big new house and that her parents came up to visit her sometimes. Her parents? This I found almost unbelievable.

"Your mother comes to visit you?"

"Uh-huh, she got me a set of towels."

I turned sideways on the stool to look at her. She just sipped her coffee and smiled. I was seized with a perverse desire to jerk her out of her frozen Birdseye existence. I decided to take her on my rounds, to visit the welfare clients. This was certainly immoral and probably illegal too, but I didn't care, I was too angry at her. I dragged her up and down a half-dozen tenements and at every stop I left her standing in the unheated, garbage-strewn hallway. I explained to her, in great detail, the kind of awful lives these people led: rats, slumlords, violence. I wanted to make her miserable, to startle her out of her apparent numbness. But she just listened to all this, sighed, and said, "Michael, it's so sad. How can you stand it?"

Two hours later, we were standing on the corner of Houston and Second Avenue. Marilyn looked frozen and forlorn in her silly suburban coat. I felt sorry for what I did and I wanted to put my arm around her but I didn't. "Where are you going now?" she asked.

"Home."

"Well, I guess I will too."

I watched her disappear into the subway and I stood for a long time on that corner thinking. I was trying to figure out why she had gone to the trouble of coming all the way in from where she lived to see me just for one afternoon. Not a word for a year and then this. Was she trying to remember something she left behind when she started her new life? Was she verifying that she had made the right choice? And what, in the end, did I really mean to her? I recalled the entry in her diary: "If only M would fuck me." Well, M still hadn't done anything. He was standing on a corner of Houston Street, a monument to inertia and indecision.

Ten years went by. In the fall of 1976, I was sitting, cynical and disgusted, in a health food restaurant in Park Slope, Brooklyn. In the past ten years, I'd lived with someone, split up, gone crazy, and been locked in a mental hospital; I'd been a probation officer, spending years prowling slums and jails all over the city. In the past year and a half, both my parents had died violently and left me a lot of money. I lived in a brownstone I bought with their money and ran a used book store. Six months before, a woman I had been living with for a year left me to go to Manhattan and find, she said, "a mature man." So there I was, loaded with money, with not one but three girlfriends and, as usual, lonely.

Let me tell you about Park Slope in 1976. It had a variety of residents but one kind was predominant—the confused single, the separated, the lost and lonely therapy cripple. All of us gathered there, perched in the health food stores and crafts cooperatives, flapping our wings and squawking. In short, Park Slope was a sinkhole of marriage—even people whose second marriages had broken up moved there. Sex, drugs, and rock-and-roll were left behind. People wanted to get a fresh start. You know, eat granola, wear Mexican sandals, and center themselves through pottery and analysis. It was a hiding place, a safe house, where we licked our emotional wounds and hoped to meet someone new.

I was in a men's consciousness-raising group. There were three of us: me, a married guy named Sydney, and Charley, who was confused about his sexual orientation. We initially met in each other's apartments but Sydney's wife and my girlfriend were always walking into the meetings and telling us we were too noisy or that they had work to do. So we moved the meetings to my store. It seemed as if all our monologues began with, "She won't let me . . ." or, "I can't . . ."

I remember our last meeting. I was going on and on about how "We, as men, have to get in touch with our feminine natures because only—"

Charley interrupted. "How much you weigh?" he asked.

"One-seventy-five."

I continued. "Because only by truly knowing our inner female selves—"

"You know," said Charley, "with your muscles, you could be a good light heavyweight."

There was also a large gay community, including one group of very militant lesbians who were renovating a brownstone that had been almost totally destroyed in a fire. They were really roughing it, living in the building and fixing it at the same time. The group used to march up and down Seventh Avenue, the main street of the neighborhood, dressed in blue work overalls with tools sticking out of their pockets. Their leader was a very large woman with short dark curly hair and intense black eyes. She and I had spirited discussions about my allegedly inadequate women's book section. Actually I think there was a lot of sex between us, unexpressed of course.

So, I was sitting in the health food restaurant one day, choking over my brown rice and listening to my friend tell me how seaweed would solve 90 percent of my mental problems. I was nodding my head at him, thinking of steak and banana cream pie, when I saw Marilyn walk into the restaurant. Ten years! I half rose out of my seat. "What's wrong?" asked my friend. "It's an old girlfriend," I told him. "I haven't seen her in years."

I stood up to greet her as she walked down the aisle. "Hi," I said, and she walked right past me! Just like she was hypnotized. She didn't even seem to know I was there; her eyes were fixed on the back section of the restaurant. There was a sort of balcony there that the lesbians had appropriated as their territory. She walked up, pushed the little gate open, and went in. I sank back in my chair, bewildered and angry. I had to wonder for a second if it was really her.

It was, but no more suburban togs. She was dressed again in sloppy clothes, except more expensive sloppy—Pendelton work boots, new Levi's coveralls—après-sixties attire. One change was remarkable. Her beautiful long black hair was chopped off, frizzed and short, a sort of Jewish Afro. In fact she looked almost plain.

On the balcony, she walked right over to a large circular table where the head lesbian was, gave her a kiss on the cheek, and sat down.

What's happened to her husband, Herb? I wondered. What about life in the boondocks, matched towels and all? Well, what the fuck, now she's a militant lesbian—maybe in two years she'll be a stunt woman or a fashion designer. What goes on inside that head of hers?

This was all too much for me to sit passively and wonder about. I stood up to go confront her. My friend put his hand on my arm. "You can't go back *there*," he said.

"I don't care," I told him. "I've got to talk to her."

I went up, opened the gate, walked over to the table, and said, "Excuse me, can I talk to you, Marilyn?"

She looked at me, turned pale, and said, "No, Michael, I can't, I'm busy."

I was furious. I leaned forward to say something to her and just like in a John Wayne western, the head woman, Sally, said to me menacingly, "I don't think she wants to talk to you." At first I considered a big showdown but then I could see it was hopeless, so I retreated back down to my table and sat there with my chin in my hand, muttering. "Have some seaweed," said my friend.

About three weeks later, I was stopped at a light, still glooming about Marilyn's betrayal. There she was walking right past my car. I honked. She jumped, saw it was me, and started to hurry along. I followed her. "Hey," I yelled. "Marilyn, what are you doing? What do you have, amnesia?"

"I'm sorry, Michael, I just don't want to talk to you."

She turned up a one-way street so I couldn't follow her. I felt like driving up there anyway and running her over. It was as if someone were surgically removing part of my past with no anesthetic.

Later I moved from Park Slope because I entered a new life style myself. By 1983, I was married and living on the Upper West Side of Manhattan. I had a three-year-old daughter, a radio show, and a new set of friends.

One spring afternoon I was walking aimlessly on Broadway, something I did frequently. I had just come out of a used book store and I was feeling melancholy and nostalgic about my past. Not more than ten feet in front of me was Marilyn.

Her hair was long again, and she was wearing jeans and running shoes, the absolute requirement for most residents of my neighborhood. And she was hand in hand . . . with a man.

He looked just like her, thin, with dark hair. In fact, they almost looked like twins—the same jeans, same running shoes. I could tell immediately they were happy with each other. Happy in a matched-set way. I followed them down Broadway, about half a block behind them, like an amateur Sam Spade. I hid in doorways or behind people when they stopped for a light. I followed them all the way downtown, about forty blocks.

They stopped outside a theater, I forget what show it was, and he went inside, I guess to buy tickets. She waited on the sidewalk out front. I hid behind a newsstand across the street, staring at her. After a couple of minutes she turned to go into the theater, then abruptly turned and looked in my direction as if she knew someone was looking at her. She smiled, that old sad sweet smile, then went inside.

After a long time, I roused myself. I went into a bar on the corner and gobbled three straight scotches. I was in there a long time because when I got out, the sun had set and it was a lot colder. I walked back up Broadway to my apartment.

More than two years passed. One Sunday, in February 1986, I was sitting in a restaurant having brunch with a friend—he's forty-five and divorced. We were both grumbling into our Bloody Marys about wives and kids, what a drain they are; they ruin your life, put you in debt, blah blah blah. It was a kind of men's consciousness-lowering group. I looked up, and at a corner table, Marilyn was eating and reading the Sunday *Times*.

I immediately read the cultural signs. People don't sit at brunch in Manhattan on Sunday reading the *Times* by themselves if they're living with somebody. Her life had probably changed again. This time I was cautious; I got up and walked quietly out of the restaurant, leaving my friend to his monologue about alimony and shrinks. I went home and tuned in some sports event so I could take a nap, but I couldn't get her out of my mind. I was angry again.

Marilyn Stein. There she was in the phone book, no more than six blocks from where I lived. I copied her address and wrote her a letter. I was angry and self-righteous: "How dare you not speak to me after all these years? How can you deliberately throw away our growing up and everything we've been to each other?" I demanded that she get in touch with me.

Two days later, the phone rang and it was Marilyn. "Hi, Michael," she said cheerfully, as if we were still kids and nothing else had ever happened. I arranged to meet her a couple of nights later for dinner at the pub across the street from my apartment.

The night arrived. Before going across the street to meet her, I told my wife where I was going; I told her the whole story. "Just remember you have a present as well as a past," she said.

I got there early and found a table in the back where it was quieter. Marilyn arrived a little late, practically hidden in a huge down coat. It was snowing very heavily outside. She sat down and we looked at each other—a very nervous moment. She didn't seem to have changed much. Although I could see she was a little heavier and there was some gray in her hair, she was, to me, not much different from the giggly Marilyn I had known when I was fifteen.

There were about two minutes of stupid conversation—how cold it was, whatever—and then we were talking about our lives, all the things we'd gone through in the twenty years we'd been apart.

This is what happened to her. It took her roughly seven years, she said, to get loose of Herb, seven years of business dinners and shopping malls. Since seven years is a long time, practically a record for a modern relationship, I had to ask, "Wasn't there something good about it? I mean, seven years is too long for something completely awful."

"No. He was a prick, he used to hit me."

"So why did you stay with him?"

"Because my parents wanted me to."

She said they convinced her (as did Herb) that she was too loony to be wandering around in the world by herself. That she needed Herb as an anchor. The rare times she complained to them about him, or about the life she was living, they told her she was lucky to have him. Nevertheless, she finally broke free of him, drifted for a while, then landed in Park Slope. "I remember that," I said. "I thought you were in love with Sally."

"I thought I was too, but those women used to take advantage of me. They made me do all the shit jobs. Sally too."

So she left the commune and moved to Manhattan. She got involved with some sadistic therapy group in Pennsylvania. She stopped that, then came under the sway of a crazy vitamin therapist who practically killed her. On and on—it was an unrelenting tale of masochism and passivity. As she sat there telling me all this with her sad smile, I realized something I should have known a long time ago—that despite all her crazy adventures, all her scandalous behavior, she was just scared; most of her life, except for some brave teenage spurts, she was always doing what everybody and anybody told her to do.

The present. Now she was a social worker in the Bronx, working with retarded kids. And she lived alone. "I'm forty-one now, Michael," she said, as if reminding both of us. She always wanted kids but now she realized it was not very likely.

Finally, I got to what I considered to be the real point of our meeting. I told her how hurt I was that she had ignored me that time years ago in Park Slope. "Why did you do it?" I asked her.

She looked pained and amused. "Do you really want to know?"

"Yes."

"Do you remember that summer, when I moved out of my house and you were living out at the beach?"

"Yes, I remember."

"Well, I was waiting for you. I was waiting for you to do something. If you had come to my house and told me not to marry Herb, I wouldn't have. You were my best friend, Michael. I waited for you to come and get me . . . but you never did."

Here I was going on about my bruised feelings, how she hurt me, and she tells me about the chance I missed so long ago. Perfect.

There wasn't much to say after that. I helped her on with her coat. Outside, the snow was really coming down. I said something lame like, "Um, maybe I can bring the kids over to visit sometime?"

"That would be nice," she said. Then I hugged her and kissed her for the first and only time. She faded off into the snow.

Back in my apartment, I stood in the dark kitchen with a drink in my hand, looking out the window at the funeral parlor across the street. I had tears in my eyes. My wife came in. "How'd it go?" she asked in her practical, professional way. (She is a psychologist.) I told her the whole story—if only so long ago, for that one moment in time, if only I had acted, *done something*, my life and Marilyn's would be completely different. What a tragedy.

My wife listened to the whole story very patiently, then said, "That is the biggest load of neurotic O. Henry crap I have ever heard."

I looked at her, thinking, What a vulgar, insensitive peasant she is. "Go away," I told her. She went out shaking her head. Hamlet resumed staring out the kitchen window.

A month later I was sitting in the playground around the corner watching my kids on the monkey bars. I saw Marilyn standing outside the fence looking in and I waved to her. We sat next to each other talking about how really warm it was for March and whether or not the schools in Westchester were better than those in our neighborhood. Emily ran over. "Dad, can you tell Sam not to throw mud at me?"

"Sam, no mud! Emily, this is my friend Marilyn."

Marilyn talked to her for a minute, then Emily ran back to the monkey bars. "Cute kids," she said. "Your daughter looks like you."

"Yeah, she does, doesn't she?"

We sat there for a while, and as I watched her watching the kids, it was hard for me to imagine that I had known her for twenty-five years, that she was a grown woman with a job and a studio apartment on Columbus Avenue. If you had seen us that March afternoon in 1986, sitting three feet away from each other, you would have thought we were just two strangers who had strayed together onto the same playground bench.

HOLLYWOOD
AND BUST

My grandmother was in the kitchen prophesying: "One day," she told me, "your mouth is going to get you in a lot of trouble." Thirty-three years later I was sitting in a very fancy hotel suite in Hollywood, eating a thirty-five-dollar room-service steak and sweating over the final version of a TV pilot. I was sick to my stomach and constantly dizzy. There was a huge color TV set on and I couldn't seem to figure out how to turn it off. I was calling my wife in New York every few hours. How did I get from that kitchen to that hotel suite? My mouth, of course.

Growing up in my house, I was constantly engaged in a kind of world finals talking competition. Between my mother, my sister, and me, there was hardly ever a silent moment. If you were quiet for five minutes you were out of the competition. I was always surprised when I was taken on rare visits to my father's side of the family. As a group they never really said anything unless they had something to say. Amazing.

Throughout my life I have gone through periods of constant talk and periods of prolonged silence, but always on an amateur basis. This story really starts in 1978 when I was thirty-three years old, and still trying to figure out what to do in the world. I was bored with the bookstore I had been running for three years in Brooklyn. I had vague notions of writing and, in fact, managed to get a short story published in a local Brooklyn paper. I was sitting down to begin another story one day when my constant companion, WBAI radio, announced they were looking to hire an assistant program director. That sounded interesting. I'd always loved WBAI, and the idea of working at a radio station appealed to me. I sent in my application and two weeks later I was on the job.

It was exciting: people running around with news copy in their hands, On-the-Air lights flashing, the broadcasters mouthing behind the glass booths of the studios like fish in an aquarium. My job was just minor and bureaucratic but it was electrifying to be in a place of such urgent activity. Everything was *Very Important* and had to be done *Immediately!* After six months on the job they asked me if I wanted to be assistant manager. "Sure, why not?" I told them. Bad mistake. I turned out to be a front-line commander in a relentless three-front war: The listeners were always threatening to sue or withdraw their financial support because of some offensive program, the creditors were constantly on the verge of shutting the place down, and the staff who worked fourteen hours a day routinely threatened to quit because they never got paid on time or because of racism, sexism, ageism, you name it.

I never had the slightest interest in going on the air. Since the beginning that one part of it didn't appeal to me at all. In fact, I secretly believed you had to be somewhat manic and childish to want to expose yourself like that to thousands of strangers. So, every time they asked me to come on during the frequent fund-raising drives, I refused. There I was, paying, or rather not paying, bills, ordering tape, arguing with the staff, all about thirty feet down the hall from master control.

Fate. One day I came to work and no one was there. The transmitter had broken down and the announcer on duty was sleeping in an upstairs office. I managed to locate the chief engineer, who came in and kicked some piece of machinery and put us back on the air. Then he left. So who was supposed to go on the radio? For personal, chemical reasons known only to himself, I couldn't seem to rouse the announcer. The next live show wasn't for about two hours. So I went into master control and turned up the dial that somebody had once shown me when I first started at the place. "Um, er, this is WBAI. We, um, apologize for the interruption. We're now back on the air." Then I put on a record. I had sounded like one of those late-night local radio or TV spots where the president of some discount carpet warehouse does his own commercial. But as the record began to play and I sat there waiting to say something, I felt some kind of mysterious power rush through me. At home, later, I ate a pound of steak practically rare. When my wife got home from work I wanted to grab her and carry her into the bedroom. I told her how great it felt being on the air.

About a week later I asked the program director if she had any fill-in spots available here and there. I did a show or two and then I was given a regular Thursday-morning spot as a tryout. By this time, too, I was fed up with my administrative job. A perfect coincidence, right? So, in September of 1979, I quit the assistant manager job and went on the air with a regular show.

Actually, I grew up listening to the radio. I'd listen to anything but usually I was tuned to WOR. John Gambling, Arlene Francis, Carlton Fredericks, Jean Shepherd. Occasionally I tuned into Barry Gray on WMCA. Now, except for Shepherd, who was unique and personal, these people did essentially the same show over and over again for years. They did interviews, reviewed books, gave little discourses on health, theater, and manners, and occasionally took calls. Naturally, they announced some news and gave some weather. So, what did I do when I finally got a radio show? The same thing. I read the *New York Times*, had guests on, and took calls. I even was telling people the weather. The weather? I mean, if you want to know what the weather is, you hold your hand out the window. Yet, that's what I did, and every ten minutes I'd tell people what time it was. Give me twenty-two minutes and I'll tell you the time.

This went on for about a year and a half until one night—it was January 30, 1981, the eve of the anniversary of my father's death—I got the notion that I'd like to get on the radio and talk about my father. The show was the next day, Thursday morning. That night I had an awful nightmare. The radio station was surrounded by barbed wire as I approached it to do my show, and my father was standing in front of the entrance wielding a butcher knife and saying, "You're not going to talk about me on the radio." I woke up in a sweat. I went straight down to the station, told the listeners about my dream, then described my father, how I grew up, my whole relationship to him.

The last person who had allowed himself to be this personal on the air was Jean Shepherd, and he was somewhat less intense. I got dozens of letters from people telling me about their fathers; some people called me on the air, elated, in tears, or both. And they liked it because it *was* so personal. To me it was extremely liberating. I felt as if I had received fifty analytic sessions in one shot, that I had lifted a tremendous burden off myself. I started off the next week talking about my mother, my stormy relationship with her, and the terrible way she had ended her life. After that I talked about my jobs, marriages, kids, sex, yearnings, art, death. As long as it was personal I thought other people might feel it too. That's all I needed.

After I'd been talking on the radio weekly for about two years, a director friend talked me into going to SoHo to see someone named Spalding Gray perform.

Onto a bare stage walked this guy looking very nervous. He sat down behind a plain wooden table. In front of him he had a glass of water and a notebook. Then he started to talk and performed a brilliant monologue about himself, dry, weird, yet urgently personal. Seeing him inspired me; if he could speak so well in front of all those people, well maybe I could too. Why I wanted to attempt a live performance was not clear to me. After all, I was, relatively speaking, safe, encased in the womblike privacy of my radio studio. Why take the chance? I don't know but I wanted to. I wasn't thinking of making money at it although I knew he did make a living from it. About four months later, June 1983, I appeared at a theater in midtown. I had a pretty large crowd, based, I think, on sheer curiosity. People wanted to see what face went with the voice they had been listening to for three years. It was strange to talk to actual, present people, and to make matters worse, since I had no theater training, I left the house lights on the whole time, so I could see every face in the crowd. Nevertheless, it was exhilarating—with even more of the same kind of risky excitement of radio plus the added attraction of immediate response. Laughter, applause.

I didn't do another show till three months later, September. But I followed soon after that with a regular series of performances at the Seventy-eighth Street Theatre Lab (now a comedy club called Stand-up New York). By this time I was confident enough to let my wife come see me. After the performance, we had dinner at the pub across the street from our apartment. "It was strange to see you up there, everybody applauding. . . ." She looked at me as if she hadn't really seen me before. Yet she was proud of me, and I basked in the feeling. Working to a live audience was a whole new world and I soon hooked up with my director friend. It took her a while, but she smoothed out a lot of kinks and physical tics, and taught me how to use my voice more effectively. Slowly but surely I was getting better at it, and even starting to earn a little money. Now this was important because at WBAI, naturally, they didn't pay anything, and by the end of 1983, I had used up the money left to me by my parents in the mid-seventies. My bookstore and some property I owned had all disappeared, mostly through some monumentally self-destructive business deals I entered into. For about a year I had been working as paralegal to pay the bills. I complained constantly to my wife about it. "They make me use computers!"

"I know," she said, "but we have to pay rent and we need the health insurance."

Somehow I decided it was *her* fault I had to toil away at this law firm like Bartleby the Scrivener. I guess I wished she would support me while I lived the life of an artist—whatever that was. Nobody there was especially interested in my stories. "Feder, file this brief," a senior partner would say.

"Hey," I told him, "you know your office reminds me of my father's office in Istanbul when—"

"Just file the brief."

"Right."

As I got better at performing and drew bigger crowds, I began to get the notion that I should be able to make a living at it. After all, Spalding did; why not me? But it was quite a leap from my daydreams to the reality of rent and health insurance payments, so I toiled away in noisy desperation at the office. In July 1986, a friend and listener, Kathleen O'Reilly, who was managing editor of the *Village Voice*, brought a friend of hers down to see me at the West Bank Cafe Theatre. Her friend, Samuel G. Freedman, was a very well-known arts and cultural writer for the *New York Times*. He came up after the show and asked me, "Do you mind if I write about you for the *Times*?" He was being polite of course, but I sure as hell wasn't going to say no. The *New York Times*! I went home and told my wife about it. She is a religious follower of the *Times*, reads it every day, and thinks of the Sunday *Times* as a combination *Encyclopaedia Britannica* and Delphic oracle. Like thousands of other people she saves various sections of it for months. When she heard I was going to be in the *Times*, she was overwhelmed. This was truly arriving.

Samuel Freedman called me two days later. "They've agreed to do it. It will most likely be in the September seventh Arts and Leisure section." That was the *Times*'s yearly preview of the arts, what to look for in the year ahead! That very afternoon at the law firm I submitted my resignation, effective in two weeks, August 31. About a week later Freedman came to interview me, and that same day, a friend promised to lend me about four months' living expenses. I decided to launch myself into the world of show business as a free-lance artist.

On September 6, Saturday night, the night before the article was scheduled to run, I was sitting on a brownstone stoop about four doors down from my apartment building. I sat there whenever I was feeling pensive or mellow. I was thinking, Tomorrow is Sunday, the paper will be out; I know my whole life will change the very next day. I didn't rush off and buy an advance copy of the paper. I was cool. After all, this wasn't all there was to life, right? Ten o'clock, a nice warm night, people walking past me alone or in couples. As I watched them I felt as I imagined God felt, benevolent and protective, the possessor of great power and secrets. The poor mortals didn't even know who they were passing on that stoop.

The next day I got up real early and bought ten copies of the Sunday *Times*. I staggered home and dropped them smack in the middle of the living room floor. My wife and I sat looking at each other. She reached for a copy, leafed through it. "It's here," she said, and held out the paper to me.

"Wait a minute," I said. I wanted to hold the moment. Finally I opened the Arts and Leisure section. There it was on page 11, a full-page article with a picture and continued on another page! Continued! This was it, the Klondike, the Gusher, the Hope Diamond.

We were down on our knees on the floor, reading it. "Look at this," she said. "He compares you to Woody Allen!" Every once in a while she glanced up at me in awe, a look I'd never seen from her before. At that moment, a neighbor brought my daughter home from the Y, where she'd had her gymnastics class. "What are you doing on the floor with all the newspapers?" my daughter asked.

"Dad's famous," said my wife, holding up the paper with my picture.

"So am I," my daughter said. "Look, I can do two cartwheels!" And she did, right into her room, where she immediately concerned herself very loudly with Barbie and Ken. That woke up my one-and-a-half-year-old son, Sam, who came waddling into the living room crying. "Mommy, Mommy."

"Look," said my wife, "Dad's picture."

Well, he was a very neat little boy; my wife and his baby sitter had trained him to pick up any junk from the floor and throw it into the trash. He looked at my picture for a second. "Yuckie," he said. He ripped it out and threw it into the garbage. Children. What do they know?

I knew the calls would be coming in from my friends and relatives. But I was learning something new about the world. By nine that night I had gotten calls only from my best friend and my mother's cousin in Cleveland, who said, "Well, dear, if you feel that you can become famous by telling awful stories about your poor mother, you go right ahead."

The next morning I went down to the office of one of my managers, near Times Square. By this point I had acquired two managers. A month before I had five keys on my key ring and a couple of dollars in my wallet. Now I had two business managers. One of them I knew from years ago. When I once had some money, he had represented a friend of mine and was looking to raise money for a rock-and-roll demo tape. He brought in another manager who handled the careers of movie stars. The idea was to sell my stories to the movies and TV. After my meeting I was going back uptown on the 104 bus, and I was thinking to myself, When they write about me years later, you know, like in *Elvis—Ten Years After,* when they write my biography, they'll say that this was the one thing that best indicated the man's true character: After he was famous, he *still* took the bus.

I was playing blocks with Sam when the phone rang, and a woman said, "I'm calling from the Coast, will you hold for Sandy Goldstein?" "Sure," I said, "why not?" This was no strain for me. I felt like I had been holding for Sandy Goldstein from the Coast since the day I was born. Finally, Sandy herself came on the line. "Hi, this is Sandy Goldstein. I'm the vice-president of American Pacific Television. I've just read your article in the *Times*."

"Good."

"Well," she said, "I'm very excited but I don't know what to do." I felt like saying, "Sandy, let me tell you what I do when I get excited." But I had been warned: Do not talk business to anybody. "Sandy, you have to talk to my manager," I told her. "Okay, I will, right now." She hung up, but of course I was really excited now. The vice-president of American Pacific Television—I was definitely on my way! I received at least a dozen calls the next couple of days, all from New York and Los Angeles, movie and television companies interested in the stories as screenplays, pilots, situation comedies. Visions of world cruises danced in my head.

The weekend following the article, I had three shows scheduled at the West Bank. The place was jammed. I was the hottest ticket in town. There were VIPs everywhere, including representatives of ICM, the world's largest talent agency. They seemed to feel that they had discovered me like Columbus discovered America. It didn't exist before he laid eyes on it. But I was learning that that was the way of things in public life. You're nobody and then instantly you're somebody. The ICM people were very excited. They said I had to meet with Sam. Who's Sam? Sam Cohn. If you're in show business and you don't know who Sam Cohn is, then you're not really in show business. He is the most powerful talent agent on the planet. We set up a meeting for the next Tuesday.

I walked into the conference room flanked by my two managers. They'd been around money and talent all their lives but even they seemed nervous, like little kids on their first day of school. We sat down at one end of a long oval table. Everybody was there, the heads of all the departments: literary, movies, television, bookings, T-shirts, mugs . . . These were expensive-looking people, people who made at least a hundred thousand a year. We were all waiting for Sam. There was only hushed whispering. After a minute went by, a woman said, "Maybe we should start without Sam?" Everybody glared at her. "Start without Sam!" Finally, Sam Cohn strolled in, a rumpled-looking guy with an amused-cynical smile. He reminded me of my grandmother. He sat down, leaned back, and put his feet up. Nobody said a word. If he leaned forward, they leaned forward; if he leaned back, so did they. He looked at me. "Mike, what do you expect to get out of this business?"

"Well, Sam, I expected you to bring a check in here for one million." I was cute.

He smiled. "Well, I had the check with me but I must have dropped it in the hallway." Everybody was laughing now. After some random conversation among the smaller fish, Sam leaned forward and said, "This is what I'd like to do, Mike. We'll send you out of town to a regional theater, Philadelphia or Boston. You polish up your show and then we'll bring you back to a small Broadway house like Whoopi. . . . What do you think?"

What did I think? All my dreams were coming true, even some dreams I never had before. But I was cool. "Sure," I told him, "that sounds good."

"I understand you're with that radio station, WBAI," he said.

People never refer to WBAI as simply WBAI; it's always "that" radio station WBAI. "Yes, I am with them," I told him.

He leaned in, they all leaned in. I had the feeling this was a question that had been rehearsed. "What's your allegiance to that station, Mike?"

I thought for a split second and I said, "None . . . that is, nothing special." God, I tried to sell the place out in a second. Misery, oppression, racism, free speech, bye bye. Broadway here I come.

My managers and I walked over to the New York Deli on Fifty-seventh Street to celebrate my imminent fame and fortune. Salamis were hanging in the window. Salamis were sitting at the tables. Immediately my agent Dave ran into a guy at another table who had just flown in from the Coast for the day. He was a short, powerful-looking young guy, with a gold belt buckle and French sneakers. It turned out he had almost completed writing a TV show for Transcon, on the NBC network, and the only part not done was . . . the part of a performance artist—a monologist. All my planets must have been lined up in the right place. We immediately struck a deal. In about two months' time, they would fly me out to Hollywood to write the part of the monologist; there was the promise that I might get to do the part for the finished episode as well. Me on national TV! Television is an obscenely rich medium. Just for having the title creative consultant next to your name as the credits roll by at the end you get twelve hundred dollars. The agreement was to put me up in a hotel and pay me five thousand dollars for what would amount to about three days' work. Five thousand dollars was more than I made in three months as a paralegal.

I had offers from several publishers to write a book of stories. I chose Crown Publishers, because I liked the editors best and because they brought a publicity person to their meeting with me. They were serious about selling books. The publicity woman was very sophisticated, with pearl earrings and swept-back blond hair. She asked me, "How are you at parties, Mike?"

"Parties? Why?" I asked her.

"Because, you know, there'll be a lot of book parties after the book comes out. So how are you at parties?"

How am I at parties? Well, probably like a cross between a mass murderer and a catatonic schizophrenic. But I tried to reassure her that although I wasn't a party type, I'd come through in the clutch. The deal was made, with only the contractual details to work out. I had a publisher. Amazing.

Galaxy Pictures was interested in the story of my honeymoon trip, a very sweet-and-sour adventure. They liked it but told me the ending needed to be less ambiguous, much more upbeat. I promised to change the ending and write a treatment for them. UA and Columbia were very excited about two of my other stories and they told me they'd try to get John Sayles or somebody of his caliber to co-write with me. Finally, Sandy Goldstein of American Pacific TV, who was still "very excited," told me that when I flew out to LA next month to write for Transcon, she and some CBS network executives wanted to have breakfast with me to discuss a TV pilot based on my eight years in the welfare and probation departments in New York City. They'd give me three thousand for an option. Although I was still occasionally bowled over by big names and big figures, I had started to take it for granted. I felt like a star and that it was just my due.

But, strangely enough, accompanying all this promised fame and fortune, all the options and excitement, I was starting to have some pretty serious mental/physical problems. I felt tired and slightly dizzy all the time. I felt the need for a great deal of bed rest although I was not actually doing any work. These symptoms of fatigue and fogginess continued and got so bad that in November I finally went to an internist, who gave me about eight hundred dollars' worth of tests. He couldn't seem to find anything wrong except a too-high level of Valium in my blood. He was really puzzled. He looked at the test results. "Did you say you were in show business?" That it was all psychological was no surprise to me. I've never been good at allowing myself pleasures, and that's probably putting it mildly. All this rich attention was literally making me sick.

Worse than my disorientation was what was happening to my wife. She, whom I always depended on to be stable and practical—that was one of the main reasons I married her—became giddy about all the glamour and big promises. Suddenly she had several credit cards and was buying furniture and clothes, a couple of thousand dollars' worth. Although she made good money on her own, I was alarmed by this. "What are you doing?" I asked. "We can't afford all this." She said, "Well, you're going to be rich, aren't you?" I only had about six weeks' left of the money I had borrowed back in September and none of the money promised from the book or TV companies. "Don't budget these promises," I told her. But she didn't really listen. She was swept away by all the glittering predictions—especially from my managers, who were always assuring me that within a year or two I'd be a rich man. This behavior of hers upset me more than anything else. I depended on her to keep her feet on the ground.

I increased my visits to the therapist to twice a week. I was much more anxious than usual. I was running up a large back bill but it was okay. I told him about the book, movie, and TV deals; I'd pay him when all that came through. A few days before Thanksgiving I was flown out to Hollywood.

They sent a car to take me to Kennedy Airport. In the back was a color TV. They put me in first class and handed me a champagne cocktail for breakfast and a leather-bound menu with my name on it. "Do you want lobster or filet mignon for your in-flight meal?" the stewardess asked me. I arrived in LA and was met by an even larger car with a larger color television in it. By now I was becoming very disoriented and had the worst headache I'd had in years.

I was driven to a very expensive hotel on Sunset Boulevard, Le Mondrian. They put me into a suite big enough to house my entire family. I had a view of all of Los Angeles from my huge picture window. Everything in the hotel, from the marble in the lobby to the architecture, the wallpaper, and the bedspreads, looked like a Mondrian painting. When I ordered breakfast the next morning, they brought me two fried eggs and bacon, laid out on the plate just like a Mondrian painting. Breakfast was sixteen dollars, coffee was three dollars extra. Transcon told me not to worry about expenses, everything was on them. In the evening I stood at the picture window. I missed my wife and children. I felt like I had been sent into deep space and that my life in New York was a dream.

They rented me a car, a brand new four-door something-or-other. As I drove over to Transcon's offices the first morning, I noticed that the people in the streets, the few I saw, and in the cars were all beautiful, or so it seemed to me. They were young, tan, very smooth and healthy-looking. I missed the sour, twisted faces of New Yorkers. The streets out there were spotless and the buildings looked new and clean. There was no sense of the misery, decay, and violence that you feel in New York; but also no sense of the electricity, or passion, the juice that oozes right out of the air in Manhattan. It was almost Christmas and there were decorations set up across the boulevards. Palm trees were hung with fake snow and Santa and his reindeer. It was about seventy-five degrees and sunny.

I pulled up behind four identical blond kids in a blue convertible Cadillac. They had a vanity plate that read "Hey dude, it's casual." Here I am, the kind of man who wakes up and almost see bats coming in the windows every morning. "Hey dude, it's casual." I guess for them it was. I saw no poverty whatsoever, although I knew it existed. I drove about thirty blocks. Everybody I saw was white, about thirty years old, and looked rich. This was not the city for me.

When I arrived at Transcon, I was introduced to the president of the company. His name was Bob. He and the writer for the pilot puzzled over which office I should use to write. "Hey, what about Rob's office?" said the president. "Rob's on location right now."

They put me in Rob's office. That was a very famous TV and movie star's office, complete with leather easy chairs, a huge aquarium, plaques all over the walls, and autographed pictures of presidents. My head was swimming.

Right away we got to work. My job, according to the head writer, was to "lay out in sixteen tight paragraphs no more than four or five sentences long" an original story of mine, one that fit the already finished show. For this I would get five thousand dollars. I thought about my grandmother who came from Poland at the age of nine in 1897. She used to tell me what is was like on the Lower East Side. Her father was a tailor who worked twelve hours a day, six days a week, and made $2.50 a day. Jesus. At first I had some trouble. I did the first paragraph of a story we agreed on and gave it to the writer. As soon as I got back to Rob's office, Stan, the writer, was on the intercom. "Mike, you say here, 'The woman was in despair.' That's a little heavy for the network. Can we say 'upset'?"

This was the pattern. It took me about two hours to get it, then I was able to give them the formula style they needed. The whole point of writing for TV seemed to be, Under No Circumstances show or say anything that would really Worry Anybody. Once I got that straight, I was all right. Stan told me I was a quick learner and "really terrific to work with." "I'm very excited about this episode, Mike," he said. Outside my window the entire three days I worked there, there was a man parked at the corner in a blue convertible Mercedes. He was blond, tan, in his late twenties or early thirties. He spent the whole day calling people on a cordless telephone and writing in a small notebook with a gold pen. What was he doing? What was the writer of this TV show doing? What was anybody in California doing?

Back at the hotel in the evenings, I watched the color TV. Dave, my agent, told me to familiarize myself with sitcoms so I'd get the feel of television writing. I tried to make sense of them and chewed my thirty-dollar breast of chicken with avocado. At bedtime I looked out over the city and wondered for the hundredth time what on earth I was doing there. The only thing that felt real was talking to my wife on the phone. "Don't worry," she said. "It'll be over in two more days. We miss you."

Now in the midst of all this, there was a patch of reality. A guy who was writing and producing a documentary on the resurgence of story-telling in America had contacted me two months earlier. There is, by the way, a great resurgence of this art form. Thousands of people every year go to festivals to hear live people, not electronic images, tell them stories: stories about themselves, stories from the hills, from the farms, from the Old West. There's a great movement in America of people actually talking *to each other*.

I was to be their Northeast Urban storyteller. The man who came to pick me up for my story and interview was *not* blond and beautiful, and he had brought his wife, who was nursing a baby, along. He was driving an old car with real dents in it.

We went out to a college campus where they had set up a mock radio studio for me. These people were obviously engaged in a labor of love. They were animated and intelligent. I could feel my personality returning. They asked me to tell a three-minute story about sitting on the stoop and talking to my daughter about the people passing by. After the story they interviewed me on camera. "Tell us," said the director, "why do you think there's such a great revival of storytelling in America?"

"I think it's because people are poisoned, sick to death of television and the movies. They are tired of having their brains and hearts electronically manipulated. Jerzy Kosinski said once that this is the only country in the world where masses of people come home from work at the end of the day and sit next to each other listening and watching someone else speak to them. I think television is the great cancer of America." We all shook hands and promised to keep in touch. Then they drove me back over to Transcom where I resumed writing the TV pilot.

The next morning was my three-thousand-dollar breakfast with American Pacific and the CBS network. It was at the Beverly Hills Hotel, palm and orange trees everywhere, fountains, and silk on the walls. We sat in a sunlit atrium. On the table were gold-rimmed plates and crystal juice glasses. I looked at the menu. The prices were amazing, but no matter, American Pacific was picking up the tab. Dave was sitting next to me and on the other side was Sandy Goldstein, who told me how excited she still was. A couple of minutes later, the vice-president of CBS arrived. God, he was cool. He might have come out of his mother's womb wearing a Rolex. He was extremely polished. "Tell us what it's like on the streets, Mike," he said. I imagined people like him in California are carried by litter bearers from their mansions to their limousines and from there into hotel lobbies. Maybe he hadn't ever actually walked on a street. So I told him about the "street": about the eight grueling years I spent in the welfare and probation departments in New York, the violence and poverty and despair.

When I finished, he and Sandy looked at each other and it was as if little light bulbs lit simultaneously over their heads. They paused a second and said, "Half-hour sitcom!"

Well, this was too much for me. I was ready to tell them I thought they were a pair of insane greedy assholes and I wished they would choke on their twenty-dollar french toast. As I opened my mouth, I got the most incredible kick in the shin from Dave. I still have a scar. Outside the hotel Dave looked me right in the eye. "What do you think you're here for, Mike?" he asked. "Are you here to make money or what?"

"You're right, I'm sorry," I said.

"Just remember that. You can always be a paralegal again if you want."

I finished up at Transcon the next morning and caught the plane back to New York, arriving in the early hours of Thanksgiving Day. By this time my disorientation was overwhelming. I felt as though I was losing my mind; I had the same awful symptoms as the time years before when I had been in the mental hospital. I felt suicidal. My poor wife. She didn't know what to do. I could hardly talk to the kids, they were a blur to me. My wife and I took a ride out to the beach. "I think this new life is too much for me," I told her.

I could tell she was disappointed. She had her heart set on the better life all the money was going to buy, a house, a back yard for the kids. "Well," she said, "I guess you have to decide if you can do it or not."

That Monday I asked my shrink if I could see him three times a week. I was desperate. My back bill was now almost three thousand dollars but he agreed since it was obviously an emergency and, as always, there was the solid promise of all the money to come in soon.

Every day I struggled just to stay alive, and in the midst of this I still had meetings with various executives and producers who were interested in developing my stories. In January I had a meeting with the head of Tri-Continental Pictures about the possibility of turning my story "The Fishing Trip" into a movie. The office had a beautiful view of Central Park. I sat away from the picture window because I was full of phobias. The president of Tri-Continental had stopped in New York just to see me. He was enroute to LA from London. He was an extremely tall, thin man, at least six foot five, with dark red hair slicked back on his head and pale white skin. He was wearing a lizard-skin tie and lizard-skin shoes. His eyes were black and utterly without expression. When he shook hands his skin was cold. "Let's hear the story, Mike," he said.

Of course he interrupted me at least three times to take calls from the Coast. "I'm sorry, Mike, this is very important. You understand, don't you?"

When I got to the climax of the story, where my father and I felt a personal bond for the first time in our lives, I paused. He sat there, absolutely still, like a lizard. That did it.

"Frank—you don't mind if I call you Frank, do you?" I was very angry. "Frank, at this point in the story most regular people have some kind of reaction."

Poor Dave, he was too far away to kick me.

After the meeting, Dave said, "You better watch yourself. I think you blew that."

"I don't care anymore. I'm tired of being a performing monkey."

By March, I was piling up debts. The movie and TV companies had put all my stories on the back burner because they implied they weren't "high concept" enough and were maybe a bit too grim and raw. I hadn't been paid for my work at Transcom and had to get ICM and the Writer's Guild to threaten them before they honored their contract. When I asked ICM about Sam Cohn's original plan to get me a theater run out of town, I was told Sam was away in Europe talking to Meryl Streep. Now, my wife had a couple of huge credit card bills and was worried about paying them. She was becoming very frustrated and bitter. "Well, what *is* happening with the movies and TV?" I didn't know what to tell her. She was disgusted with my agents and their big predictions of fame and fortune. We started to argue a lot. It was as if I were to blame for all these mysterious failures. "You need a new agent," she said.

"Don't tell me what to do!"

We had applied to private school for my daughter. She was accepted but the tuition was incredible, five or six thousand a year—for the *second grade*. My wife had expected one of the movie or TV deals to cover it.

Things got worse and worse between us. My wife and I were increasingly cold and nasty to each other and the kids were a huge cross I had to bear every day. I spent a lot of nights up at a studio on Riverside Drive that a friend had loaned me a few months back to write my book. There was talk of my moving out permanently.

The final blow came in mid-March. My therapist informed me he'd have to cut my visits back to once a week immediately.

"But you can't do that! I'm practically crazy," I told him.

"I'm sorry," he said, "but the back bill is too large. I suppose I was taken in also by all the promises of money you've been telling me about these past months."

I was humiliated. There was no more money left to borrow. I looked at the *Times*'s Help Wanted section. It made me bleed inside to think it, but I might have to go back to being a paralegal. When I called my old law firm to see if they had any work, the personnel manager asked me, "What happened to all your movie deals, Mike?" They didn't have any work for me right then in any case. Of course, there was the advance check for the book, but after paying off back debts, it still left me only six weeks or so of living expenses.

In the beginning of April, coming back from failing a proofreading test at a big law firm, I ran into a friend of mine on the street. This guy did voice-overs. You know what a voice-over is? On TV or radio, when the smooth friendly announcer comes on and tells you to drive a Buick because Dave Winfield does, or buy a Du Pont product because "they care," that's a voice-over. The money made in that business is obscene. I knew one man who spent a half-hour in a studio one day, said five words on a national TV commercial, and made nine thousand dollars in royalties that year from that one commercial. It was America at its most putrid. "How can I get into voice-overs?" I asked him.

"Call your agent," he said.

Sure enough, ICM had a voice-over agent. She was very nice and sent me out immediately on several auditions. The first one was for Friendly Ice Cream. Now you understand, at this point, I was bitter, angry, and half-mad, especially as I'd just been practically banished by my shrink. My marriage was really in jeopardy. Everything was a mess.

At the casting agency for the Friendly Ice Cream audition, the producer gave me the copy and I cleared my throat and read, "Friendly, the kind of ice cream you want your children to have." It sounded more like I was selling nuclear weapons than ice cream. The casting director asked, "Could you be a bit more friendly?"

"No," I said.

"Okay," she said, "I guess that's all for now."

I went straight from there to an audition for Miller Beer. "How do you want this to sound?" I asked the casting director.

"Fierce and manly," he said.

Good, I thought, that's the mood I'm in anyway. I read, "Miller Beer, I drink it. You drink it!"

He jumped back a little. "Could you be a little less fierce and manly?"

But it was hopeless. All I really could do was tell stories to people. After a few more auditions, I told my agent to tell ICM not to send me out anymore. He called me two or three days later. "I've got one more for you to go on," he said.

I said, "No!"

"C'mon, just try this last one, it's perfect for you."

"What is it?"

"A commercial for Chiquita Banana. You're supposed to be a giant banana."

Oh God. But I agreed to try it. I had to. My financial situation was desperate. The audition was for eleven the next morning. All night I rehearsed being a banana. I was getting into the part. I imagined myself big, yellow, and curvy, with a firm skin on the outside but all sweet and mushy on the inside. I could be a banana. It didn't seem too far from my actual self.

I called up my wife from the studio. "Hello," I said. "How are you and all the little bananas?"

"Oh no," said my wife. "What is it now?" At this point she was completely fed up with anything concerning show business. I told her I was to be a banana tomorrow. "If I get it there's big money involved."

There was a pause. "Maybe," she said, "you shouldn't do it." This made me angry.

"What about the private-school bill?" I asked.

"Well, you have to consider your integrity," she said.

"Fuck integrity. I owe nine thousand dollars!"

"All right," she said, "do what you want," and she hung up.

The next morning, all the way down on the subway, I was a banana, I was yellow and mellow, really getting into the role. I walked into the casting agency's office. At least a dozen men, most of them in their fifties, were walking around pretending to be giant fruits. The commercial for Chiquita was called "Big Fruit." It was a new frozen dessert. There were oranges, strawberries, and bananas all over the place, rehearsing their lines.

My turn. The casting agent said, "Okay, read your line."

I read, "Excuse me, where's the freezer?"

He frowned. "What are you reading?"

"The banana," I said.

"You're not the banana," he told me.

"Yes, I am."

"No, you're not."

Now I was getting mad. "Listen," I said, "I was the banana all last night in my studio. I was the banana all the way down here on the subway. I *am* the banana!"

"No, you're not," he said. "You're the lobster."

It turns out that the tag line, the joke of the commercial, is that a lobster asks for the freezer near the end. We argued for a minute or so. Then he said, "Look, you're a lobster now. Take it or leave it." So I gave him a few lobster renditions, but it was a mess. My humiliation was complete.

In April I got some performing work at a midtown cabaret. I got good reviews but the crowds dropped off and I did my last show in mid-June.

By midsummer, I spent most of my time alone in my studio brooding and watching the boats go up and down the Hudson. The excitement, the acclaim, the movies, TV, my trip to Hollywood—it all seemed like a bad dream, a mirage that I never wanted in the first place. What remained was the radio show, the book of stories, and my live shows. I realized that all I ever really wanted to do was to talk to people, tell them about my life, what I saw and heard, in the hopes that my telling would reach them, even help them, as it helped me.

Over the past couple of months, things have improved between me and my wife. Hard times seem to have brought out a little more sympathy and understanding. The children seem more valuable to me than ever, sort of a key to what is real and enduring in such a crazy world. I spend a lot of time at home now and plan to move back quite soon. At bedtime I kiss my daughter and read my little son, Sam, his favorite book, *Goodnight Moon*. Goodnight room, goodnight stars, goodnight noises everywhere. Goodnight. Goodnight.